"I CAN BE READY
TO LEAVE WITHIN THE HOUR."

Trent was surprised by her announcement. "You don't understand—"

"What don't I understand?" She looked up at him in irritation.

As he met Faith's challenging green-eyed glare, Trent realized again what a good-looking woman she was, and he grew even more annoyed. The last thing he needed was her kind of distraction while he was trying to work.

"I work alone," Trent stated firmly.

"What are you talking about?" Faith's regard turned into a cold-eyed glare across the desk. In the years since she'd taken over running the ranch, she'd dealt with all kinds of men. She hadn't backed down from any of them, no matter how arrogant or demanding they were, and she wasn't about to start now—not when her sister's life was hanging in the balance.

"You've hired me to do a job, and I'm going to do it—my way. I work alone. It's better like that."

"No, you don't understand," she countered in a tone that brooked no argument. "Like you just said—I hired you to do a job, and that means I'm your boss." She paused for effect. "You work for me. When you head out, you won't be going alone. I'll be riding with you."

HIRED GUN

BOBBI SMITH

LEISURE BOOKS NEW YORK CITY

A LEISURE BOOK®

November 2006

Published by

Dorchester Publishing Co., Inc.
200 Madison Avenue
New York, NY 10016

ISBN 0-8439-5665-8

The name "Leisure Books" and the stylized "L" with design are trademarks of Dorchester Publishing Co., Inc.

Printed in the United States of America.

Visit us on the web at www.dorchesterpub.com.

This book is dedicated to the memory
of my cousin, Harry Lee, and to Bob Tackett.
They were true heroes and will be missed by all.

"Hi" to the whole gang at the Northeast Texas
Writer's Organization. You're wonderful!

"Hi" especially to the real Cathie Fleenor,
Bill Fike and Alnette Scribner.

PROLOGUE

Dry Gulch, Texas
Late 1860s

It was early afternoon. Brett Marshall, the sheriff of Dry Gulch, was sitting at the desk in his office when Gary Jones, one of the men from town, came hurrying in.

"Sheriff! We got trouble down at the Stampede Saloon!"

"What kind of trouble, Gary?"

"There's a mean drunk looking for a fight."

"Who is it this time?" He'd grown accustomed to the rowdiness at the end of the month when it was payday.

"Some stranger. I ain't seen him before, but he's a rough one."

Brett got up to follow Gary from the office. Dealing with mean drunks was usually ugly work, so he drew his gun as they made their way down the street to the Stampede.

As they neared the saloon, a thrown chair came crashing through the swinging doors, and they could hear the ruckus going on inside.

"What are ya? A bunch of cowards?" the unknown troublemaker was shouting. "C'mon! I'll take you all on at once!"

"Wait out here," Brett ordered Gary.

Gary didn't need to be told twice. He took off, glad to distance himself from what was to come.

Brett made his way to the swinging doors and looked in. The place was in chaos, so he didn't waste any time. He stepped inside the saloon and fired his gun at the ceiling.

At the sound of the gunshot, a sudden, tense silence fell over the place.

"What's going on in here?" Brett demanded. He glared at the drunken troublemakers, his expression deadly serious.

"He's the one who started it, Sheriff! That man over there!" The barkeep pointed him out.

Brett looked over at the man and thought he recognized him as Will Anderson, a deadly gunfighter he'd seen on a recent wanted poster.

"Hold it right there!" he ordered.

Anderson ignored him and made a run for the back door.

Brett didn't want to take a shot at the man there in the crowded saloon, so he went after him, following him out into the alley, where he could see the man running away as fast as he could. He gave chase, but he didn't get far.

A shot rang out from behind him, hitting him in the back.

Brett fell and lay unmoving in the dirt.

Some of the men in the saloon looked out to see what had happened. They'd thought it was the sheriff doing the shooting and expected to see him hauling the drunk back in. They were shocked at the sight of their lawman lying dead in the alley. They were even more shocked when an armed man they hadn't seen before stepped out from his hiding place to confront them.

"Get out of here now!" the killer ordered.

The drunks fled back inside, terrified by the sheriff's cold-blooded murder.

The gunman hurried off to meet up with his partner.

Will Anderson had gone to get their horses and was waiting for him at the edge of town.

"Taking out that sheriff was easier than I thought it would be," the black-hearted Anderson said with a smile as he handed his partner in crime, Charlie Hunt, the reins to his horse.

"It always is when you back-shoot 'em. You suckered him into it real good," Charlie complimented as he mounted up.

"I knew he'd fall for it, after hearing all the talk about how hard he was working to clean up the town."

"He ain't going to be cleaning anything up anymore," Charlie said as they hightailed it out of Dry Gulch.

"Thanks to your straight shooting."

They were wanted men, and they knew the crime they'd just committed would make them even more notorious. They liked the idea of having a deadly reputation. They figured from now on they would have free rein in Dry Gulch whenever they showed up, and that was the way they wanted it. The towns-folk there were a real cowardly bunch. The outlaws knew none of the townspeople would try to track them down.

Life was good—real good.

The Diamondback Ranch

Fifteen-year-old Trent Marshall picked himself up off the dirt and knocked the dust from his clothes. He grabbed up his hat, jammed it back on his head, then stalked across the corral to where Old Jim was holding the new bronc's reins. Trent was deter-mined to break the stallion, but so far in the contest of wills, the stallion was winning.

Old Jim watched the youth walk his way. Tall and lean, Trent was growing into a fine young man. Having worked on the Marshall ranch for years, Old Jim knew how tough Trent was. Once the boy set his mind on doing something, he did it—no matter how long it took. But this bronc was a stubborn one, and Old Jim was beginning to believe it was going to be a long afternoon.

"You ready to try it again?" he asked, trying hard not to smile at the boy's frustration.

"Oh, yeah. I'm ready." Trent was feeling a little battered as he came to stand with Old Jim and the stallion. He could tell the ranch hand was enjoying himself. "You think this is funny, don't you?"

"No, I just think you and Big Boy, here, might be two of a kind." Old Jim looked up at the spirited stallion with admiration.

"I think you're right." Trent smiled at his friend. He had learned a lot from him through the years. Old Jim was a half-breed, and he had taught Trent how to track and shoot with the best of them. Now, if only his lessons on breaking horses held up . . .

Trent was just getting ready to mount up again when he happened to notice a rider in the distance.

"Someone's coming," Trent said.

It was unusual for them to have unexpected visitors, so Old Jim let Big Boy go and went with Trent to see who the man was. As the rider drew closer, they were able to make out that it was Reverend Johnson, the minister of the church in town, and they were both puzzled.

"I wonder if there's been some kind of trouble," Trent said, concern in his voice.

His older brother, Brett, had taken a job as the sheriff in town, because money was so tight on the Diamondback that they'd feared they might lose the ranch. The small spread was all they had after their parents had died several years before; it was up to the two of them to keep it going. Life had been rough, but Trent and Brett always believed things would get better.

"Afternoon, Reverend," Trent called out when the minister reined in near where they were standing. "What brings you out to the Diamondback?"

Reverend Johnson didn't smile. He couldn't, knowing what he had to do. He dismounted and went to Trent. "I need to speak with you."

Trent heard the edge in the man's tone and knew something was wrong—very wrong. "What's happened?"

"We'd better go up to the house. . . ." The minister wanted to tell Trent the bad news in a more private place.

Trent went still. "You can tell me whatever it is you've got to say right here."

Reverend Johnson was troubled, but didn't want to make things worse than they already were. "All right, Trent. The news I bring isn't good. It's about your brother. . . ."

"What about him?"

"I'm sorry, Trent—Brett was killed today. He was ambushed in town."

"What . . . ?" That was all he could manage to say as he stared at the preacher in disbelief.

"From what I've been able to find out, Will Anderson called him out, and then Charlie Hunt shot him in the back."

"They set him up," Trent agonized, realizing immediately what had happened, and it sickened him.

Brett had told him about the wild gunfighters who were always causing trouble. He had even mentioned Anderson and Hunt by name. Brett had suspected they were the deadliest of the troublemakers, and now Trent knew he'd been right.

"It looks that way," the reverend admitted.

"Have Anderson and Hunt been arrested?"

Reverend Johnson was mortified as he told him, "No. When Deputy Lawton found out your brother was dead, he quit."

The deputy's cowardice inflamed Trent. "What about the gunmen? Where are they?"

"They left town."

Trent was silent for a moment, his emotions in turmoil. He looked over at Old Jim, a fire burning in his soul. "Will you ride with me?"

The ranch hand nodded. "I'll get the horses."

He hurried off, leaving Trent alone with the preacher.

"What are you planning to do?" Reverend Johnson asked worriedly. He knew this tragedy was a heavy burden for someone as young as Trent.

Trent looked at the man of God. "I'm planning to put my brother to rest—and then I'm going to track down the men who killed him."

Two Weeks Later

Leaving their horses tied up some distance away, Trent and Old Jim made their way on foot across the night-shrouded, rock-strewn landscape toward the campsite. They could see the light of the outlaws' campfire and knew their search was finally at an end. The killers' trail had been hard to follow, so the going had been slow. Hunt and Anderson had proven elusive, but no more. Thanks to Old Jim's tracking ability, they had finally caught up with them.

Trent had learned a lot about following a difficult trail from Old Jim on this trek, and he would forever be grateful for his help and guidance.

"You ready?" Old Jim asked in a low voice, not wanting to alert Hunt and Anderson to their presence.

Trent nodded.

They drew their guns.

It was time.

Silently, they moved ever closer until they could see the two men sitting by the fire.

Trent could easily have gunned them down where they sat, but he controlled the urge. He wasn't a cold-blooded killer like they were. He was going to take them in and let the law deal with them—and when their judgment day came, he'd be there to watch them hang for murdering his brother.

Trent and Old Jim positioned themselves a distance apart so they could cover the men in case they tried to make a run for it. Old Jim signaled Trent, and Trent knew what to do.

"Hold it right there, Hunt, Anderson," Trent shouted out. "Don't even think about going for your guns! We've got you covered, and we're taking you in!"

"What the . . ."

Both outlaws looked around in a panic, trying to figure out where the speaker was hiding.

"Put your hands up where we can see them," Trent ordered.

Hunt looked over at Anderson, guessing it was a posse from Dry Gulch that had them trapped. He had no idea how they'd managed to sneak up so close without being seen or heard, but that didn't matter now. All that mattered was finding a way to escape. Hunt knew what he had to do, and he hoped his partner was smart enough to take advantage of the distraction he was going to cause.

"All right!" Hunt called back, lifting his hands.

Anderson followed his lead, as he always did.

"Now, stand up—real slow!" Trent directed.

It was then that Hunt made his move. Acting as though he were getting up, he leaned forward, but instead of getting to his feet, he scooped up two handfuls of the sandy soil and threw them directly on the fire. Hunt hoped the dirt would kill the flames and give him and Anderson the cover of darkness they needed to make a run for it. He grabbed up his gun and began firing in the direction of the man's voice as his partner did the same thing.

His ploy almost worked, but Trent and Old Jim had been expecting trouble. They returned fire, and their shots found their marks. They took down both of the outlaws before they could flee into the night.

Trent moved cautiously into the campsite to

check on the gunmen. He had never killed a man before, and he was tense and uneasy as he made certain they were dead.

Old Jim had been staying back to cover Trent, but he joined him then. "You all right?"

"I am now," he answered.

Trent felt no joy at the outlaws' deaths, only a deep satisfaction that his brother had been avenged and the two deadly gunmen would never hurt anyone again.

"Let's take them in."

CHAPTER ONE

Silver Mesa, Arizona Territory
Ten Years Later

Sheriff Ben Wallace looked up from his desk as the door to his office opened and a stranger walked in. Ben eyed the man warily. Tall, lean, and dressed in black, he wore his gun as if he knew how to use it, and moved with a confidence that would set him apart in any crowd. The lawman realized immediately that the man had a dangerous, hard edge about him, and he wondered who he was and what he was doing in Silver Mesa. Things had been reasonably quiet in town lately, and he wanted it to stay that way.

"Afternoon," Sheriff Wallace greeted the stranger, pushing his chair back from his desk and getting to his feet. "What can I do for you?"

"My name's Trent Marshall," Trent answered, stepping up to the desk.

Sheriff Wallace frowned slightly. The name

sounded vaguely familiar to him, and he struggled to place it. "Nice to meet you. What brings you to Silver Mesa?"

"I'm here on business."

"What kind of business?"

Trent reached into his pocket and drew out a business card. He handed it over to the sheriff as he explained, "The Central Stage Line hired me to bring in the outlaw Matt Sykes."

Sheriff Wallace stared down at the business card that read, MARSHALL'S LAW—TRENT MARSHALL, GUN FOR HIRE, and he suddenly understood why the name had sounded familiar to him. He'd heard talk from other lawmen about how successful this man was at tracking down killers.

Trent went on, "Sykes and his partner robbed a stage and killed the driver and the man riding shotgun. His partner's already been arrested, but Sykes is still on the run, and I have reason to believe he might be in the area."

"Do you need any help?"

"No. I work alone."

"Good luck to you." Sheriff Wallace eyed him with renewed respect. "If you need anything, let me know."

The two men shook hands and parted ways.

The lawman watched the hired gun leave his office. He hadn't heard that Sykes was in town, but if the killer was anywhere around, he felt certain Trent Marshall would find him.

* * *

Later that night, Matt Sykes entered the noisy, crowded Sundown Saloon in Silver Mesa. It was a rowdy bar that catered to a rough crowd, and he'd been frequenting it ever since he'd arrived in town several days before. Sykes had money to spend, and he enjoyed spending it on the hard liquor served in the saloon and the pretty girls who worked there.

Harry, the bartender, saw him coming and wasted no time pouring him a glass of whiskey. He shoved it across the bar to Sykes when he stopped before him.

"That's what I like about your place here, Harry," Sykes told the bartender as he picked up the glass and took a deep drink of the potent liquor. "Fast service and good whiskey."

"We aim to please," he answered.

"Yes, we do," added a very buxom bar girl wearing a very low-cut gown as she came to stand close beside Sykes. Missie pressed enticingly up against him, affording him a good view of her bosom. She remembered him well from the night before. He was far from being the best-looking man in the place, with his scraggly hair and several days' growth of beard, but she knew his pockets were well lined, and she had a special fondness for big spenders.

Sykes put an arm around Missie and pulled her closer as he took another drink. His gaze dropped hungrily to the bodice of her gown.

"There was a stranger in here looking for you earlier," Harry told him.

13

Sykes stiffened at the news and quickly turned a cold-eyed look on the barkeep. "Did you get his name?"

"No. He didn't say."

"What did he want?"

"He wanted to know if you were in town."

"And what did you tell him?" He tensed.

"I told him I didn't know you." Harry had learned over the years to keep his mouth shut.

"Where is he now? Is he still here?" Sykes glanced around the saloon, looking for any new faces among the crowd.

"No. He left, and I ain't seen him since."

"How long ago did he leave?"

"A couple of hours."

Sykes finished off his drink. He'd been keeping a low profile ever since he'd pulled off a stagecoach robbery a few weeks back with his partner, Billy Winter. He hadn't thought anyone would be able to catch up with him after they'd split up, but it looked like he'd been wrong. "What did he look like?"

"He's tall and got dark hair. Had a mean look about him. He could be trouble," Harry warned.

Sykes frowned. The description he'd just been given could match any of a hundred men he knew. "I'll keep a look out for him. Thanks."

Sykes handed his glass back to Harry for a refill and turned his attention back to the beauty beside him. He'd come to Silver Mesa to lie low for a while and enjoy living large with his share of the money from the robbery. Tonight he was going to do just that. He had Missie to entertain him, and he planned to join a big, high-stakes poker game going on in the back room. He'd find out more about the stranger in the morning.

Trent lingered in his hotel room, trying to figure out what to do next. Earlier that evening he had made the rounds of the saloons in Silver Mesa and had made no headway in his search for Matt Sykes. Even so, he wasn't about to give up. He had a feeling he was close, and he'd learned over the years to trust his instincts, thanks to Old Jim. Old Jim had died a few years before, and, though he had taught him well, there were still times when Trent missed his wisdom and insight.

Picking up the wanted poster, Trent studied the likeness of the outlaw again. It wasn't a skillful drawing, but it was a clear enough rendition that Trent knew he'd recognize the killer if he saw him. He folded up the poster and put it in his pocket, strapped on his gun belt, and left the hotel room. He wanted to check around town one last time before calling it a night. He particularly wanted to pay another visit to the Sundown Saloon. The bartender there had seemed a little edgy when he'd asked about Sykes earlier, and it made him wonder if the man had something to hide.

Trent made his way to the Sundown and went in. He stood just inside the swinging doors to take a quick look around the crowded saloon. He saw no sign of Sykes, so he made his way to the bar to have a drink.

"What'll it be?" Harry asked.

"Whiskey," Trent answered, turning to lean back against the bar so he was facing the room. "You're busy tonight."

"The boys know there's always a good time to be had here," Harry answered as he gave Trent his drink. Then he asked, "Did you have any luck finding the man you were looking for?"

"Not yet."

"Maybe he's moved on."

"Maybe."

Harry saw the determined look in the stranger's eyes and turned away to wait on someone else. He knew Sykes was in the back room playing poker, and he hoped the man stayed there. Harry was considering finding a way to send someone back to warn him that the stranger had shown up again, but before he could take any action, the door to the back room flew open and Sykes came out, with Missie clinging to his arm, gazing up at him adoringly.

"Drinks are on me!" Sykes shouted, waving a fistful of dollars triumphantly as he crossed the room.

At the prospect of free drinks, all the drunks in the saloon erupted in cheers and hurried up to the bar to get their liquor.

Harry quickly began pouring the rounds as Sykes sat down at a nearby table and pulled Missie onto his lap. He kissed her hotly as he stuffed a large wad of dollars down her bodice, openly groping her in the process. In his drunken excitement over winning the big pot in the poker game, he'd forgotten Harry's earlier warning about the stranger who was in town looking for him. This was his lucky night.

Trent recognized Sykes the minute he came out of the back room, but knew this wasn't the time to confront the killer. He didn't want to risk anyone else getting hurt in a possible shoot-out. Taking advantage of the chaos the free drink offer had created, Trent walked out of the saloon unnoticed. He found a quiet, secluded spot a short distance down the street with a clear view of the main doors and waited there. Sooner or later, Sykes would have to come out of the Sundown Saloon, and when he did, Trent would be ready for him.

Once things had calmed down at the bar, Harry went over to the table where Missie was entertaining Sykes.

"That fella who was looking for you came in again while you were in back playing poker."

"Why the hell didn't you tell me he was here?" Sykes demanded angrily, feeling uneasy.

"I couldn't. Not with him standing right there at the bar. If I'd gone running off to tell you, he would have followed me. He's gone now, but I wanted to let you know he's still in town."

Sykes managed to unlink Missie's arms from

around his neck and shoved her from him as he got to his feet.

Missie sensed the change in his mood and hurried to get away from him. She didn't want to risk becoming a victim of his drunken temper.

"Did you see him leave?"

"No."

Sykes swore under his breath as he started toward the swinging doors. "Well, let's go. You're coming with me. We're going to go find him and see what it is he's after."

"I can't leave the Sundown right now," Harry argued, sensing that there might be trouble ahead. "I have to tend bar."

"You're the only one who knows what this man looks like," Sykes said. "Missie can take care of things for you while we're gone. Ain't that right, Missie?"

"Sure. I can do it, Harry."

Leaving Missie to tend bar and keep all the boys happy, Harry reluctantly accompanied Sykes from the saloon.

Trent had kept a careful watch, and when Sykes emerged from the saloon, he was ready. He was surprised to see that the bartender was with him, but the other man's presence wasn't going to stop him. He'd come a long way looking for Sykes, and now that he'd found him, he wasn't going to let him get away. Trent drew his gun and stepped out of the shadows to confront the outlaw.

"Hold it right there, Sykes!" Trent ordered.

Harry recognized him instantly and told Sykes, "That's him! That's the man I was telling you about!"

When Harry saw that the stranger had his gun drawn, he turned tail and ran back inside, leaving Sykes to face the man alone.

Sykes went still. He warily watched the man, who was walking slowly toward him with his gun in hand. "Who are you? What do you want?"

"My name's Trent Marshall. Unbuckle your gun belt and let it drop," Trent directed. "I'm here to take you in."

Sykes recognized the name and panicked.

"Like hell you are!" he shouted as he went for his gun. He fired wildly and ran for cover.

Trent had expected that the outlaw wouldn't be taken in without a fight, and he'd been right. He, too, dove for cover as he fired at the fleeing killer.

His aim was true.

Sykes's gun flew from his hand as Trent's bullet found its mark. The outlaw collapsed and lay unmoving in the night-shrouded street.

Gun in hand, Trent got up and cautiously moved toward Sykes. He picked up the outlaw's gun, then went to check on him.

As soon as the gunfire had stopped, Harry and the patrons of the saloon had crowded up to the swinging doors to find out what had happened. They saw Sykes lying in the street with the stranger standing over him holding a gun on him, and they weren't sure what to do. A few of the men thought about confronting the man who'd just shot Sykes, but they held back when they saw Sheriff Wallace come running up to the scene, gun in hand. They would let the law handle it.

"So the killer was right here in town . . ." the lawman remarked as he came to stand beside Trent.

"Yes, he was," Trent said. Once he was certain Sykes was dead, he slowly holstered his gun. He glanced at the sheriff. "And he won't be causing anyone any more trouble."

"You're right. He won't," Sheriff Wallace agreed. He looked over at the hired gun with even greater respect as he holstered his own sidearm. The man had just proven that all the talk he'd heard about him was true. When it came to tracking down killers who were on the run and bringing them to justice, Trent Marshall was the best.

CHAPTER TWO

Coyote Canyon

It was getting late as Trent concluded his meeting at the stage office with Cal Harris, the representative of the stage line. They stood up from where they'd been sitting at the desk and shook hands.

"Fine job, Trent," Cal praised him. He fully appreciated the danger Trent had faced apprehending Sykes over in Silver Mesa. "What are you going to do next?"

"I'm going to take it easy for a while," Trent answered. The weeks he'd spent tracking down Sykes had taken their toll on him. He needed some rest.

"That sounds like a good idea. You deserve it. Why don't you stop by the social that's going on in town tonight? It's one of the highlights of the year for the folks here in Coyote Canyon. People come from miles around to enjoy the food and dancing."

"I just may do that," he replied as he started toward the door. First and foremost in his mind was his plan to head to the nearest saloon and have a drink. After that, he could always stop by the social before heading back to the room he'd taken at the small hotel in town. He'd stopped there only long enough to get cleaned up before his meeting with Cal, but when he went back, he planned on getting his first good night's sleep in a long time.

"Trent," Cal called to him.

Trent turned back.

"Thanks again." Cal was grateful for the man's hard work and expertise.

Trent nodded and let himself out of the office, closing the door behind him. He stood on the sidewalk for a moment, enjoying the peace of the night. He could hear the music coming from the social, but he was more in the mood for a drink. He remembered the saloon he'd passed on his ride into town, and he headed that way.

Faith Ryan stood at the side of the dance floor with her brother, Mason, watching their younger sister, eighteen-year-old Abbie, dance with Rick Taylor, the man who owned the livery stable in Coyote Canyon.

"Doesn't your sister look pretty tonight?" Faith said, thinking that the new gown Abbie had had made for this occasion looked wonderful on her.

"Why are you always looking for compliments?" Mason grinned at her.

"Oh, you . . ." She laughed. "You know I was talking about Abbie."

"I know, and, yes, she does, but then so do you. You both clean up real good," he teased. The fancy dresses they were wearing were a far cry from the working clothes they wore on the ranch.

"You should talk," she countered. "You could almost pass for a city slicker tonight."

"Do you feel like dancing with a city slicker?" Mason invited.

"Why not?"

They were laughing as he took her out to join the other dancers.

"This reminds me of when we were little," he told her, remembering the dancing lessons their mother had given them.

"Just don't go stepping on my toes like you used to," Faith cautioned.

"I'll do my best."

"You'd better." There was a threatening note in her voice.

"I'm not scared of you anymore," Mason countered. "I'm bigger than you are now."

"Yeah, but I'm still meaner," she shot back at him.

"I won't argue that point with you."

"Smart man."

They relaxed and enjoyed the dance.

Faith looked up at her younger brother, studying his handsome, chiseled features. At nineteen, he bore little resemblance to the pesky, towheaded boy who used to torment her so much when they were young. He had grown into a fine young man who wasn't a bad dancer.

"What are you thinking about?" Mason asked, noticing that she was staring at him.

"I was thinking that you remember your dance lessons pretty well."

He grinned again. "So far, so good, but the dance isn't over yet."

They both fell silent, relishing the moment. It wasn't often that they got to come into town to have fun this way. After their parents' deaths some years before, Faith had had to take over not only raising her brother and sister, but running the family's ranch, the Lazy R, as well. It hadn't been easy for her. She'd been only seventeen at the time, but somehow she'd managed to keep the ranch going. Faith had always been a strong-willed, smart woman, and she'd proven that to anyone who'd doubted her over the last few years. Mason and Abbie were older now, but Faith, at twenty-three, was still considered to be the one in charge.

When the song ended, Faith and Mason returned to the side of the dance floor and watched as Rick escorted Abbie over to join them.

"Thanks, Rick," Abbie said flirtatiously.

"Thank you," Rick returned before moving off.

"There should be a social every weekend!" Abbie sighed happily.

"You'd love it, wouldn't you?" Faith smiled,

knowing her sister was in her element here at the dance.

"Oh, yes. It's so much fun to get dressed up."

"Well, you know you could wear that gown at home, if you wanted to," Faith joked.

"I don't think I'd do a very good job riding stock dressed like this."

"You'd get a lot of attention if you tried it; that's for sure." Faith laughed.

"Tried what?" neighboring rancher Jake McCullough asked as he came up to join them.

Faith quickly explained to the tall, good-looking rancher what they'd been discussing.

"That's right. You would," Jake agreed, smiling. His dark-eyed gaze was fixed appreciatively upon Abbie. He thought both the Ryan girls were pretty, with their blond good-looks, but he especially cared about Abbie. "If the word got out that you were dressing like that to check on your herd, you'd probably have some ranch hands from my place riding over just to help you."

Abbie smiled at the thought.

"Let me know when you're planning to wear it, and I'll tell the boys," he went on.

"What about you, Jake McCullough? You mean you wouldn't come and help me yourself?" Abbie challenged. She'd been secretly in love with Jake for what seemed like forever, but no matter how much she flirted with him, he always kept his distance.

"You know that if you ever need me, all you have to do is ask," Jake told her seriously.

Abbie realized she was pushing the limits by being so daringly straightforward with him, but she didn't care. "All right, I'm asking—let's dance."

"And it's not even ladies' choice," he said with a grin.

"I know," Abbie said, a twinkle of delight shining in her eyes.

He didn't have to be asked twice. Jake took her hand and led her out onto the dance floor.

Mason looked at Faith. "I guess we don't have to worry about Abbie being able to take care of herself."

"She's one capable woman," Faith agreed.

"Faith, would you like to dance?"

Faith looked up to see Rick standing there. "I'd love to."

Mason didn't waste any time. He spotted one of the single girls on the far side of the dance floor and headed her way.

Trent drained the last of the whiskey from his glass and set it back on the bar in front of him.

"You ready for a refill?" asked Max, the barkeep at the Ace High Saloon.

"No. I'm done for the night."

"Why? You heading over to the social?" he asked.

"I heard it was a good time."

"You heard right. That's why business is so slow tonight. Most of the boys are over there, but they'll be in later when the dancing's over."

"I may just check it out."

Trent left the bar, but stood there in front of the

saloon, feeling relaxed and at ease for the first time in weeks. He could hear the music coming from the social and decided to take Cal's and the barkeep's advice and go see what was going on. He headed down the street and reached the site of the social, to find the outdoor dance floor crowded with couples. Brightly colored lanterns had been strung about, and a small group of musicians was playing a rousing tune that all the couples were enjoying. Trent joined those looking on as the music came to an end.

"All right, ladies!" a member of the band called out. "It's the moment you've been waiting for!"

Trent had no idea what he was talking about, and he was even more surprised when a loud cheer went up from the women.

"Go grab your men, girls! It's the ladies' choice dance!"

All the women acted on his order immediately, racing off to select the men of their dreams.

Trent had just started to walk away when someone took his arm.

"Not so fast, young man. You're not going anywhere just yet," a woman ordered sternly.

He turned, puzzled, to find that he'd been claimed for the dance by an elderly, well-dressed, very proper-looking lady. "Yes, ma'am."

"Like Johnny just said, it's the ladies' choice dance, and I'm choosing you." She had no idea who he was, but she had seen him when he first walked up and thought he was a strikingly handsome man.

Tonight was all about having fun, so she intended to do just that. Besides, who would dare to criticize her for being so bold at her age? Dottie realized there were some benefits to aging, and dancing with this good-looking man was one of them.

"I'm honored," he answered as the music began, realizing there was no way out of dancing.

"My name's Dottie, by the way," she offered.

"And I'm Trent."

"It's nice to meet you, Trent. Let's dance."

Trent took her arm and escorted her out onto the floor.

"You're a good dancer, young man," Dottie complimented him as they circled the dance floor together.

"Why, thank you. So are you."

"You're new in town, aren't you?"

"I'm just passing through." He didn't offer any more.

"Well, I'm glad you were passing through tonight."

Trent squired her around until he heard the next announcement.

"Ladies! Change partners!"

Since it had been ladies' choice, Faith had looked around and claimed Zach Martin for her partner. Zach owned the dry-goods store in town, and she knew he was a fine dancer. They'd been enjoying their dance together when the time came to switch. She and Zach parted, and she turned around to seek a new partner and found herself face-to-face with a complete stranger—a stranger who happened to be the best-looking man she'd ever seen, tall, lean, and darkly handsome. Her heartbeat quickened as she gazed up at him, and her reaction surprised her. Faith almost felt like a young schoolgirl. The music never stopped, though, so she had no choice. She knew she was going to be forced to dance with him. She smiled at the thought.

"Let's dance," she said.

"Let's," Trent agreed.

Faith realized Dottie had been his previous partner, and she wondered at their connection.

Trent said no more; he just took the green-eyed, curvaceous blond beauty into his arms. He'd enjoyed his dance with Dottie. Women like Dottie were rare, but this one made the whole trek to Coyote Canyon worth it. He didn't know what he'd done to merit such luck, and he wasn't going to question it. He was just going to enjoy his good fortune.

They began to move gracefully about the dance floor.

Excitement tingled through Faith at his touch. She gazed up at him, studying the lean, hard line of his jaw as he whirled her around. "Are you and Dottie friends?"

"You could say that," he answered, thinking now that he was quite grateful Dottie had claimed him for the dance.

"My name's Faith."

"I'm Trent."

"You're new in town, aren't you?"

"Yes, I just rode in today."

"Will you be staying long?"

"No, I'll be moving on soon." He looked down at her, thinking how tempting she was, and how he might just stay around for a while if Coyote Canyon proved to be this entertaining. "I take it you live here?"

"Yes, my family has a ranch nearby." She was sorry to hear he would be leaving, and was about to ask him more about himself when the announcement came again.

"Ladies! Change partners!"

Faith wanted to stay right there in his arms, but she knew she had no choice but to switch partners. Already, Cathie Fleenor had appeared out of nowhere and was all but throwing herself into Trent's arms. Faith was shocked by the unexpected sense of jealousy that filled her as she watched Cathie flirting with the newcomer.

Faith turned away to find that Mike Stevens, one of Jake's hands, was available, so she hurried to claim him as her next partner. As they danced, she kept trying, without being too obvious, to catch another glimpse of the man named Trent.

Trent made it through the dance with his new partner, who introduced herself as Cathie and didn't stop talking the entire time they were dancing. She asked him question after question, and he tried not to look too excited when the call came to switch again.

Abbie saw that the handsome stranger her sister

had danced with was free, and quickly claimed him for her own.

Trent was coming to understand why this was quite the social event in Coyote Canyon. Here he was, dancing with another pretty blonde. It wasn't often a man got that pleasure. This one didn't say much, so he never learned her name. He just enjoyed the moment.

Trent didn't have much of a chance when the change came. Cathie had planned her strategy well. She had made sure her dance partner kept her close by the new man in town so she could grab him up again once he was through dancing with Abbie. Trent knew there was no way to escape, so he squired Cathie around, biding his time as he circled the floor with her. He thought the music was going on far too long.

CHAPTER THREE

Trent was glad when the music finally came to an end and he could take his leave from Cathie. She'd made it clear in no uncertain terms that she was interested in him, even though he hadn't encouraged her in any way. If he'd been interested in getting to know any woman better that night, it would have been the one named Faith. Something about her had touched him. Not that he had time for any involvement with anyone, though. With the dangerous life he led, he couldn't afford any personal commitments.

"Are you sure you don't want to get some refreshments?" Cathie repeated one last time in hopes that he would change his mind and stay with her for a little longer.

"No. I have to go, but thanks for the dance."

"I hope to see you again," she called out, watching in disappointment as he walked off. When she caught sight of Mason Ryan, she put the stranger out of her thoughts and went after him.

Trent was about to leave when he glanced back one last time, wondering what had happened to Faith. He caught sight of her across the dance floor, standing with another man, smiling up at him. He let his gaze linger on her for a moment, thinking once again how lovely she was, and then he moved off and disappeared into the crowd. He was looking forward to returning to his room and getting some sleep.

"That was a pleasure," Paul Davis told Faith.

"Yes, it was. I always like the ladies' choice dance."

Paul moved away, leaving Faith alone. She was smiling as she turned to look around. She hoped to see the man named Trent again, but there was no sign of him in the crowd. She thought it was strange that he'd seemed to appear out of nowhere and then vanished again the same way. She decided that she would seek Dottie out later and ask her just who he was.

During the ladies' choice dance, Abbie had been thrilled to claim Jake again for her partner. They'd stayed together talking after the dance, and now as the music started up once more, he didn't say a word, but simply led her back out to the dance floor.

Abbie was in heaven. She gave herself over to

Jake's lead, closing her eyes to lose herself in the joy of the moment as they moved about the floor as one.

Jake was considering just how lucky he was. He'd been thinking seriously about telling Abbie how much he cared for her, but he wasn't quite sure of her feelings for him yet. He decided that maybe to-night was the night to take a chance with her. He danced them over toward the side of the floor, and when they got close, he stopped dancing and took her by the hand to lead her off.

"Jake? Where are we going?" Abbie was surprised by his move—and intrigued. She didn't want to make a scene, so she didn't resist as he drew her away.

He didn't respond. He just led her outside to a dark, secluded corner in an alleyway nearby.

Abbie was thrilled. He was being daring and ro-mantic. "Oh, Jake . . ."

"Don't say a word, Abbie," he said in a low voice as he loomed over her.

He backed her up against a wall and then took her in his arms and kissed her, his lips claiming hers in a hungry, passionate exchange. He wanted to tell her that he loved her, but until he was more certain of her feelings for him, he kept his own to himself.

Abbie responded eagerly to his kiss, excited by the forbidden quality of their embrace. She'd been kissed before by other boys, but she'd never known excitement like this. Abbie realized as she gloried in his embrace that this was no boy she was kissing—Jake was definitely a man. She lifted her arms to link them around his neck and pull him down even closer.

Her unspoken invitation evoked a low, sensuous groan from Jake, and he reacted instinctively. He crushed her even more tightly against him, loving the feel of her soft breasts against his chest. His lips left hers to explore the sweetness of her throat, and then he kissed her again, hungrily, passionately.

Feelings Abbie had never experienced before ignited within her. She arched to him in an unspoken offering, loving his kiss, wanting his closeness, wanting—

The sound of voices nearby jarred them both back to reality and forced them to break apart.

Abbie stood there in the shadows of the night, gazing up at him, stunned by what had just passed between them. It had been heavenly—pure ecstasy being in his arms.

"We'd better get back," she breathed reluctantly.

"I know." Jake realized she was right, but, in truth, he wanted to stay right there and keep her in his arms for the rest of the night. He couldn't take the risk, though, for he didn't want to endanger her reputation.

They emerged from their heated, passionate tryst, breathless and totally aware of each other's nearness.

"I know Mason's here somewhere," Larissa Murray told her friend Katie.

"The way the girls are always after him, they've probably dragged him off somewhere."

"That's exactly what I'm afraid of," Larissa

moaned. She'd been waiting for this night for ages. Mason worked so hard out at his family's ranch that she didn't get to see him very often. Now that he was in town, she wanted to be with him as much as she could—but then, it seemed as if every other girl in town felt the same way.

"You'll get to dance with him again; I'm sure of it." Katie tried to cheer her up.

"But the ladies' choice dance is over."

"He's going to ask you. I'm sure he will. You just wait and see."

"I hope you're right." She sighed.

"Look! There he is!" Katie pointed him out to her friend. He had just moved into view with Cathie clinging possessively to his arm.

They both groaned at the sight. They knew how man-crazy Cathie was, and the way she was hanging on him, Mason would be lucky if he could get away from her at all.

"Maybe you should go help him out," Katie suggested daringly.

"You think a man like Mason needs help? Maybe he's enjoying himself with Cathie."

Her friend gave her an exaggeratedly pained look. "With a girl like her? What do you think?"

"You're right." Larissa rethought her position. She had always considered herself a woman of action. When she wanted something, she went after it. She suddenly realized that Mason Ryan should be no different. She wanted him for herself, and she couldn't let the poor man suffer at the hands of the notorious Cathie Fleenor. "You're right, Katie. He does need me to rescue him."

Just as Larissa started to go to them, a new song started up. She watched as Cathie continued to hold Mason's arm so that he had to dance with her again or cause a scene. Now was the time. Cathie had had him long enough. It was time she learned how to share.

"I'm cutting in," Larissa announced, tapping Cathie on the shoulder in an outrageous move that, had her mother seen it, would have gotten her in trouble.

"But . . ." Cathie started to protest. She never got the chance to finish her sentence.

Mason quickly let her go and turned to his new partner.

In a huff, Cathie glared at Larissa for a minute and then stalked off.

Larissa knew she'd drawn a few stares with her blatant ploy, but she didn't care. She was with Mason—at last.

"I didn't know this was another ladies' choice dance," Mason said, giving her a quizzical smile.

"It wasn't," she responded as she looked up at him, careful to keep her expression innocent. "It was the 'Larissa's choice' dance."

Mason laughed out loud as they continued to dance. There weren't many men in Coyote Canyon who could say they'd had women almost fighting over them. He was definitely enjoying himself this night.

Trent wasted no time getting back to his room. He was more than ready to stretch out in a real bed and get a good night's sleep. As he settled in, he could still hear the music in the distance, and a vision of the woman named Faith lingered in his thoughts. She was a beautiful woman, and the man who ended up with her would be very lucky.

There were occasions when Trent regretted that he didn't have a family, but mostly he kept too busy to have much time to dwell on such thoughts. Trent knew that what he did was important, and he found himself wondering what his next job would be. He finally put the thought from him and just allowed himself to relax. As he'd told Cal, he was going to take some time off.

Faith's curiosity finally got the best of her, and the first chance she got, she went looking for Dottie. She found the older woman sitting with some other ladies, watching the younger couples dance.

"Why, Faith, dear, how are you tonight?" Dottie asked when Faith sought her out and sat down with her.

"I'm wonderful. The social is always such fun."

"Yes, it is. How are things out at the Lazy R?" Dottie had known the Ryan family for many years, and she knew the hardships Faith had had to deal with. She also knew Faith had been very successful running the ranching operation.

"Same as always. We're working hard to keep the Lazy R going."

"Well, I'm glad you made it into town tonight."

"So am I. Dottie . . ." Faith paused, not quite sure how to ask about the man named Trent. "I was wondering . . ."

"Wondering about what, dear?" She was puzzled by Faith's hesitancy. This wasn't like her at all.

"Who is that man you were dancing with during the ladies' choice? The one named Trent," she finally blurted out. "He said he was a friend of yours when I danced with him, but I don't remember ever seeing him around town before."

Dottie found herself smiling brightly at Faith. Obviously they had the same taste in good-looking men. "Trent was my knight in shining armor tonight."

Faith frowned. "I don't understand."

"I needed a partner for the ladies' choice and there he was, so I grabbed him. He was perfect, don't you think?"

"So you don't know him?"

"No, and that's too bad, because he was a real good dancer." Dottie got a devilish gleam in her eyes as she said, "If I were forty years younger, I'd be looking for him right now so I could dance with him again. Why don't you go find him?"

"I think he left already."

"I'm sorry, dear. If I see him again, I'll let you know."

"Thanks, Dottie."

Faith gave Dottie a quick kiss on the cheek and moved away.

Several of the other ladies sitting with Dottie were curious after listening in on their conversation.

"You say you don't know who he was?"

"No, I'd never seen him before tonight."

"And you asked him to dance?" Alnette Scribner gasped, shocked by Dottie's brazen actions. "What were you thinking?"

"I was thinking I wanted to dance with a young, good-looking man!" she countered, accustomed to such comments from the gossipy Widow Scribner.

The other ladies laughed aloud at her quip. It wasn't the first time Dottie had done something wild, and they knew it wouldn't be the last.

It was almost midnight when Faith, Abbie, and Mason returned to the ranch. There was no doubt they would all have preferred to stay in town overnight, but they couldn't. They had a ranch to run.

Abbie had been particularly quiet on the ride back in the buggy, and Faith was a bit concerned. She knew her sister loved having a social life, and it was unusual for her not to be chattering on all the way home about the fun she'd had in town. As they were about to go to bed, Faith sought her out to talk to her and make sure everything was all right.

"Did you have a good time tonight?" Faith asked.

"Yes, why?"

"It's just that you've been so quiet. I was afraid something was wrong."

Abbie sighed. "No, I'm just tired—and tomorrow we're back to work."

Faith understood then, and, wanting to brighten her spirits, she asked teasingly, "Well, are you going to wear your fancy dress again tomorrow? You know Jake said some of his boys would come over to help if you did, and we can always use the extra hands."

Abbie did manage a smile at the memory of the conversation—and the memory of her special time alone in the dark with Jake. "Believe me, if it would get Jake over here, I'd be tempted. I'll see you in the morning."

Faith watched as Abbie went into her room and closed the door. Then she retired to her own room.

It would be dawn soon enough, and as Abbie had said, it was back to work in the morning.

CHAPTER FOUR

Mason and Abbie were hot, tired, and hungry as they rode for home late the next afternoon. They'd been working stock since just after sunup and were more than ready to call it a day.

"You know, if you'd worn that dress like you said you might last night, we would have had some help from Jake's boys, and we would have been done a lot sooner," Mason teased her.

"I know. I thought about it, but I just didn't want to get it dirty," she answered him primly.

He laughed at her comeback.

"How many more weeks until the next social?" Abbie asked, smiling as she thought of all the fun they'd had the night before, and wishing there were a dance every week.

"Too many," Mason replied.

"You had a good time last night, too, didn't you?"

"Yes, I did," he agreed.

"I figured as much when I saw all of those girls

43

throwing themselves at you." She cast him a mischievous sidelong glance. There were times, like now, when she still found it amazing that the bothersome brother she'd tolerated all these years had grown into such a handsome young man.

"Yeah, I had a real rough time fighting them off all night, but then, I wasn't the only one." Mason gave her a knowing look.

Abbie looked uncomfortable as she tried to play the innocent. "What do you mean?"

"Why, you and Jake. I saw you two sneak off the dance floor." He grinned when he saw that she was actually blushing. It wasn't often he got the upper hand on one of his sisters, and he was going to enjoy every minute of this.

"You knew?" Abbie had had no idea anyone had seen them.

"I'm the man of the family. It's my job to watch over you and protect you. I was just about ready to go after you when you came back."

"Well, I'm glad you didn't come after me."

"Why? Did you enjoy your time with Jake?"

"That is none of your business, Mason," she answered in her most dignified tone; then she put her heels to her horse's sides and raced away from him.

He only laughed at her attempt to avoid him. He urged his own mount to a quicker pace to stay right with her.

* * *

From their hiding place among the craggy boulders on the rocky hillside, the Apache warriors watched the two unsuspecting riders draw near.

"One is a woman!" Lone Eagle said in surprise when he saw that she had long hair the color of the sun.

Crooked Snake, the leader of the raiding party, was pleased by the discovery. "Kill only the man. We will take the woman with us."

Lone Eagle and the other two warriors with them, Little Dog and Black Cloud, knew he was right. White women were valuable. There were many men who would pay a high price for one.

The warriors remained patient, waiting until they were certain of victory before attacking.

When Mason caught up with her, Abbie reined in and slowed their pace.

"Is Jake seriously courting you now? He sure was acting like it."

"I don't know how serious he is, but he is special."

They fell silent, thinking about everything that had happened at the social. Without any warning at all, the first shot rang out.

Mason and Abbie were caught totally off guard by the attack. They looked around and were filled with terror when they saw the warriors charging their way.

It was their worst nightmare come true.

"Ride for the canyon!" Mason shouted.

They were still miles from the ranch house, and there was no one around to come to their rescue. They both knew that seeking cover in the narrow, rock-strewn canyon a mile or so ahead would be their only hope—if they were lucky enough to make it that far.

Mason and Abbie both drew their guns and began returning fire. They spurred their horses to a breakneck speed in their desperation to escape what they were sure would be certain death.

When Mason ran out of ammunition, he cast one last glance back over his shoulder to find that the warriors were closing on them. He was glad Abbie was keeping up with him. He leaned low over his horse's neck and prayed for a miracle as he raced on.

A moment later he heard Abbie scream.

He looked over to see that her horse had stumbled and fallen. Abbie lost her seat and was thrown violently to the rocky ground. Determined to save her, he reined in to try to get back to his sister in time.

But he never made it.

The moment Mason slowed down, a bullet slammed into his chest. He was knocked from his horse and lay unmoving in the dirt.

Crooked Snake, Lone Eagle, and the other warriors rode quickly to the woman. They reined in and dismounted to check on her. They had seen her violent fall, and all feared the woman with hair the color of the sun had been killed.

"Is she alive?" Lone Eagle asked, watching as

Crooked Snake reached down to turn the female over.

Abbie had been stunned and battered by her fall, but at the sound of the Apache warrior's voice so close by and then the touch of his hands upon her, she didn't think. She only reacted. She hit out at the renegade with all the force she could muster.

"*No!*" she screamed, frantically praying that Mason would be coming to her rescue.

The white woman's attack surprised Crooked Snake, but even so, he easily overpowered her. He looked up at the other warriors as he stood, holding her trapped against him, her back to his chest, her arms pinned to her sides.

"Yes, she is still alive," Crooked Snake said, speaking in his native tongue and smiling slightly at her show of spirit. He ordered the others, "One of you go get her horse."

Abbie had no idea what they were saying, and she didn't care. She only cared about getting away from the warrior who held her. She continued to struggle against his domination. She twisted sideways as hard as she could, trying to break free, and it was then that she caught sight of her brother lying unmoving in the distance, his shirt soaked with blood.

"Mason!" she screamed.

Fury unlike anything she'd ever known possessed her. Desperate to help her brother, she stomped her booted foot down as hard as she could on her captor's foot and at the same time jabbed her elbow violently into his side. The warrior holding her gave a grunt of surprise and loosened his grip on her for just an instant. That instant was all Abbie needed. Tearing herself free, she ran to Mason.

"Mason, please . . ." Her heart was breaking as she dropped to her knees beside him.

He had been coming back to save her when he'd been shot.

It was all her fault.

She took his hand in hers and was relieved for an instant when she saw the slight rise and fall of his chest. Her relief was short-lived.

Outraged by her defiance, Crooked Snake had gone after her. He grabbed her by the arm and jerked her violently up to him.

Abbie screamed and tried to fight him off. She battled as hard as she could against his superior strength, not only to try to get away, but to distract him from Mason. She didn't want the warriors to suspect her brother was still alive. Her ploy worked, but she paid the price. Her captor finally overpowered her and hit her harshly, bloodying her lip. He dragged her back toward his horse.

Physical pain radiated through Abbie, but the pain in her heart was worse. She wanted to help Mason, but there was nothing she could do. Mason was grievously wounded, possibly dying—and now, as the prisoner of this raiding party, she knew she was as good as dead, too.

Abbie glared up at her captor as he bound her wrists before her. All the hatred she was feeling for him was reflected in her eyes. When another warrior returned with her horse, she tried to resist her captor's effort to lead her there, but he hauled her bodily to the horse and lifted her up into the saddle. He kept control of the reins, giving her no chance to escape.

The warriors mounted up and they rode off, leading her horse.

Abbie was hysterical in her grief. The horror of what had just happened was too great. Over and over again she prayed that her brother would somehow survive, but she feared the worst for him. The emotional pain finally overwhelmed her, and she retreated deep within herself. She stared straight ahead with unseeing eyes.

It wasn't like Abbie and Mason to be late, and Faith was getting worried as she watched the sun sink ever lower in the western sky. She left the house and was on her way out to the bunkhouse when she saw a saddled, riderless horse in the distance running toward her. She recognized the mount immediately as Mason's Lightning, and shouted to the hands for help as she ran to try to grab the horse's reins.

The ranch hands heard her frantic call and knew the boss lady didn't yell like that for nothing. They came running out of the bunkhouse, wondering what was wrong. They caught sight of Faith going after Lightning, and they knew there had to be trouble—bad trouble.

"Easy, boy. Easy, Lightning," Faith said in a low, calming tone as she approached the frightened horse.

Lightning was pacing skittishly before her, but

she was finally able to get hold of the reins. Faith stroked his neck as she looked him over. True horror struck her when she saw blood on the saddle blanket.

"Mason must have been hurt," she told Tom, her foreman, as he came running up to her side.

"Where's Abbie?" Tom asked, looking off in the direction Lightning had just come from for some sign of her.

"I don't know—she must have stayed with Mason," Faith responded. She hoped there had just been an accident and that they would be able to find her brother and sister quickly. She didn't even want to consider any other possibility. "Tom, you and Hank saddle up, and get my horse ready, too. As soon as I tell Rose what's happened and get my guns, we'll ride out."

There wasn't much time before dark, but none of the hands tried to dissuade Faith. She was a tough, hardheaded woman, and they respected her decisions. They hurried off to get ready.

"What do you want us to do, Faith?" another of the ranch hands asked.

"Take care of Lightning, Will." Faith paused to look at them, her expression grave. "And pray."

Will's gaze met hers as he took the reins from her. He promised her, "We will."

Will watched her walk away, impressed not for the first time by her inner strength. He wasn't alone in his admiration for her. All the men who worked on the ranch appreciated her intelligence and her determination. Will knew she would do everything in her power to find her brother and sister and bring them back.

Faith went into the house to speak with Rose, the cook and housekeeper. She explained to her what had happened, and then got ready to leave. Faith strapped on her gun belt and got her rifle, along with some medical supplies that she hoped she wouldn't need. After stowing the supplies in her saddlebags, she was ready to ride out.

Time was of the essence. Faith, Tom, and Hank followed Lightning's trail, hoping to find Mason and Abbie before night fully claimed the land. They rode hard and didn't rein in until they topped a low rise.

"I don't see any sign of them anywhere," Faith said as she stared out across the landscape, heavily shadowed now in the fading daylight. She'd been hanging onto the hope that they would find her brother and sister riding double on Abbie's horse, but it looked like that wasn't to be.

"There! I see something," Tom shouted, pointing off in the distance. He kneed his horse to action and led the way.

Faith and Hank rushed to follow.

At first Faith wasn't sure what it was Tom had spotted, but as they rode closer, her heart sank.

It looked like a body. . . .

It looked like Mason.

CHAPTER FIVE

Tom reached Mason first and quickly dismounted to go to him. "It's Mason! He's been shot!"

"Oh, my God." Faith all but threw herself from her horse's back. "Is he . . . ?"

Tom knelt down beside Mason. He'd obviously lost a lot of blood, and Tom thought for sure the man was dead. He was shocked when Mason let out a low groan.

"He's alive!" Tom shouted in relief.

"Hank, get my saddlebags," Faith ordered as she dropped to her knees beside her wounded brother. "Mason!"

"Faith?" he muttered, and slowly opened his eyes to see his sister and Tom hovering over him. He frowned and tried to focus as a myriad of wild, conflicting visions tormented him.

"Mason, where's Abbie?" Faith asked frantically.

"Abbie . . . ?" Mason's voice was hoarse and rasping as he struggled to think. And then the memory of the attack returned. "Apache! They were after us, and her horse fell. . . . They must have taken her captive! We have to save her! We have to go after her!"

He fought to get up, but the effort cost him too much. He fell back, weak and exhausted.

Faith and Tom shared a horrified look as they realized the full truth of what had happened.

"The only place you're going is back to the ranch," Faith said, taking the saddlebags from Hank as he came up to her.

"But Abbie's in trouble," Mason groaned. The thought of his sister in the hands of the renegades sickened him.

"We'll find her," Faith promised him as she began to treat his wound. The gunshot was an ugly one, and she knew her brother was lucky to be alive.

"We have to," Mason insisted.

"Hank, you and Tom ride out a ways and look around. See if you can find anything," Faith directed.

The two ranch hands did as they were told, while Faith turned her attention back to Mason's wound.

"The bullet's in too deep. The doc's going to have to get it out. I'll get you wrapped up and we'll start back. Are you strong enough to sit a horse?"

Mason was pain-ravaged and weak from loss of blood, but determined to survive. "I'll make it," he said fiercely.

Faith finished binding his wound, and it wasn't long before Tom and Hank returned.

"Any luck?" Faith asked hopefully.

"Their trail headed south. We'll be able to tell more in the morning."

Relief flooded through her that they hadn't found Abbie dead, but the thought of her sister being taken captive by the renegades terrified her. "All right, let's get Mason back to the house."

Tom and Hank carefully lifted him up and half carried him to Tom's horse. It wasn't easy, but they finally managed to get him in the saddle. Tom climbed up behind Mason and kept a grip on him so he wouldn't fall off.

Hank and Faith mounted up, too, and they started home. The going was slow. Mason was in and out of consciousness as they covered the long miles.

Inwardly, Faith was frantic, but she managed to control her emotions. She silently cursed the fact that there was no way they could begin the search for Abbie until first light. Her sister was in danger, but for the moment she was helpless to do anything to rescue her—and Faith didn't like feeling helpless.

"As soon as we get back, I'll send one of the boys to town for the doc, and I'll make sure he tells the sheriff, too. Then at dawn we'll ride out again."

"I'll be riding with you," Hank said fiercely.

"Me, too," Tom added.

Faith was never so glad to see the ranch house as she was that night. Rose and the ranch hands who'd stayed behind had kept the lights burning and were watching for them. They ran out to help as soon as they heard the search party riding in. Several of the men carried Mason to his bedroom, while one of the other hands rode for town. Faith and Rose made Mason as comfortable as they could while they waited for the doctor to arrive.

It was late when Faith finally heard riders coming in. She'd been sitting by Mason's side keeping watch over him, and she went out on the porch to see the ranch hand returning with Dr. Murray and Jake McCullough. She was surprised to see Jake, then realized he must have still been in town following the social. She had watched him with Abbie and had begun to suspect that he had feelings for her sister. Faith hurried forth to speak with them.

"Mason's in his bedroom, Doc," Faith told him. "It's in the back."

The doctor quickly related that the sheriff had said he would be out at first light to help search for Abbie. Then he went into the house to examine Mason.

"Jake . . ." She faced him for the first time, seeing his concern etched in his features.

"Is what the ranch hand told me true? Has Abbie been taken by a raiding party?" Jake began worriedly.

"Yes—Mason managed to tell us what happened. They were attacked by a group of renegades and the Apache took her." She told him what little they knew and added, "We're going to ride out again in the morning."

"I'm going with you," he stated fiercely.

"Good. We can use your help."

"How's your brother?" Jake looked past her into the house, where the doctor had gone.

"It's serious." Her mood was grim. "Let's go inside."

They went into the parlor to bide their time while the physician tended to Mason's wound.

Several times while they were waiting, they heard Mason cry out in pain. Agony ate at Faith. She wanted to help her brother, to ease his torment, but she knew there was nothing she could do. The doctor had to remove the bullet, and there was no easy way to dig it out.

Jake was tense as he waited with Faith. He got up and began to pace the parlor, worrying about Abbie and Mason. Mason's pain-ravaged cries haunted him, too, and Jake wondered if Abbie's brother was going to survive.

Nearly an hour passed before Dr. Murray finally sought Faith out.

"Faith?"

She'd been sitting on the sofa and came to her feet the moment he appeared in the doorway. "How is he?"

"He's resting quietly now. I did manage to get the bullet out, but he's lost a lot of blood."

"Is he going to make it?" she asked, in torment as she awaited the doctor's answer.

"Your brother is a strong young man. If no infection sets in, I believe he'll be able to pull through."

"Thank heaven."

"He's going to need a lot of bed rest, though. Make sure he stays quiet. I don't want him up and moving around too soon."

"Don't worry. I will."

"I'll come back to check on him in a day or two. If anything happens in the meantime and you need me, just send word." He went on to tell her how to tend to Mason's wound, before getting ready to leave.

"I'll make sure Rose knows everything you've told me."

"Rose?" He wondered why the housekeeper would be the one nursing him instead of his sister.

"I'll be riding out in the morning to try to track down Abbie," Faith told him.

"Do you think that's wise?" He knew what a capable woman Faith was, but he believed a job as dangerous as tracking Apache warriors was best left to the men.

"She's my sister. I'm going."

"I hope you find her," he said sympathetically.

"So do we," Jake put in. He was glad to learn that Mason was going to survive, but he was anxious to go after Abbie.

"Be careful," the doctor added.

"We will."

Once Dr. Murray had gone, Faith went out to the bunkhouse to tell the ranch hands about Mason's condition. Jake went with her, so he could bed down there for the night and be ready to ride out at dawn.

Faith returned to the house to stay by her

brother's bedside in case he woke up and needed something during the night. As she kept watch, her gaze went over him. With his clean-cut features and dark hair, her little brother had grown into a handsome young man. Although he was pale and his breathing was shallow, she knew how strong he really was.

Mason was a Ryan.

He would make it.

He had to.

A tear traced a path down Faith's cheek as she realized she'd almost lost him. She loved her brother and sister, and the agony of thinking about what Abbie might be suffering at the hands of her Indian captors haunted and sickened her.

Morning couldn't come soon enough.

She had to save her sister.

Jake lay in the bunk, unable to sleep. Images of Abbie helpless at the hands of her Apache captors haunted him. Tension and a terrible anger and fear gripped him. He cared about Abbie—deeply.

Thoughts of how it had felt holding her in his arms when he'd danced with her at the social returned, along with the memory of the sweet, stolen kiss they'd shared that night. Abbie was beautiful and all woman, and he loved her. Regret filled him that he'd never told her of his feelings for her.

Jake knew he needed to be alone for a while, so without disturbing the other ranch hands, he got up and dressed. Silently he left the bunkhouse.

The night was as dark as his mood. No silver moon brightened the sky. Had Abbie been with him, he would have thought the stars were beautiful as they twinkled in the heavens above, but knowing she was in danger, he only wanted the night to come to an end.

He wanted to be on the trail.

They had to find Abbie and bring her home.

Every minute that passed took her farther and farther away and made the tracking more difficult.

Jake stared off into the darkness of the night, wondering where Abbie was and hoping no harm had come to her.

CHAPTER SIX

Abbie had slowly managed to gather her wits about her as they'd ridden over the endless miles that took her farther and farther away from her home. She'd clung to the one hope that she might find a way to escape that night when they made camp, but that slim hope had disappeared when they'd finally stopped for the night. Her captor had forced her to sit on the ground near the campfire and then had bound her feet. She had stayed emotionally numb until then, but tied up as she was and anticipating the night to come, she was overwhelmed by the terror she'd fought so hard to control.

Abbie could only imagine the horrors that awaited her at the warriors' hands. Her face was sore and aching from where her captor had hit her earlier, and she dreaded what would happen next. Abbie would not submit to their abuse without a fight. She had heard the stories of the torture other captives had suffered, and believed she was facing the same fate.

As she sat there bound before the fire, one of the other warriors came to stand over her. She kept her gaze downcast, playing the submissive role until he spoke to her.

"Eat," the warrior ordered, and he held out a piece of dried meat to her.

Abbie looked up at him in shock. "You know how to speak English? Talk to me! Tell me, why are you doing this to me?"

Lone Eagle just looked down at her and repeated, "Eat."

When she still didn't take the meat from him, he dropped it in front of her, then turned his back on her and walked away.

Abbie stared after him, wondering how he'd come to know English, wondering if he was different from the other warriors—if he would help her. But he didn't look back at her. He just returned to where he'd been sitting and sat down to eat his own meat.

Abbie's brief moment of hope was gone. She was aware of the other warriors watching her from where they sat opposite her, so she looked away. She hated them all with every fiber of her being. They had shot and possibly killed her brother. Somehow, she vowed to find a way to avenge Mason.

When her captor returned and sat down beside her, she tensed, expecting the worst. She was shocked when he made no move to touch her. Momentary relief swept through her, but she knew better than to allow herself to relax.

"She is not so wild now, is she, Crooked Snake?" Little Dog said, eyeing the beautiful blond captive sitting so quietly beside the other warrior.

"No. The Golden One has learned her place," Crooked Snake answered as he glanced over at her. He hadn't been quite sure what to expect out of her after the fight she'd put up when he'd first taken her, and he was glad she had become submissive. She would be worth more to the man buying her if she were unmarked. He knew the bruise on her face from where he'd hit her earlier would fade before they reached the meeting place.

"That she has." Little Dog's thoughts were dark and erotic as he wondered how submissive she really would be—to him.

"Do you think anyone will come after her?" Black Cloud asked.

"It does not matter if her people try to track us. They will never catch us." Crooked Snake was confident the whites would be unable to follow their trail over the harsh, rocky terrain.

Little Dog's gaze lingered hot and hungry upon the woman with hair the color of the sun. He wanted to rape her, to take her right then and there, but he knew better than to challenge Crooked Snake's possession of her. No one dared to defy Crooked Snake. He was too fierce and too deadly. Little Dog fought to control his desire for the woman, but it wasn't easy.

Abbie had no idea what the two men were saying, speaking as they were in their native tongue, but she understood full well the look in the other warrior's eyes as he kept staring at her from across the campfire. She shuddered, and her flesh crawled at the thought of him touching her. She struggled to stay in control emotionally.

Abbie turned her thoughts back to her home—and to Mason. Guilt filled her at her brother's fate, and she offered up a silent prayer for him. If her horse hadn't stumbled, they might have made it to the canyon safely and been able to hold off the raiding party. She was certain Mason had been on his way back to help her when he'd been shot, and she would carry that terrible knowledge with her forever.

She thought of her sister and wondered what Faith was doing. Abbie was certain Faith would have gone out looking for them when they didn't return on time. She knew once her strong-willed sister found out what had happened, she would do everything possible to find Abbie and bring her back home. That was the only glimmer of hope Abbie had left to cling to in the total darkness of her captivity.

Jake slipped into her thoughts then, and Abbie's heart ached. Just a day before, she'd been with him at the social and they'd shared a kiss. And now . . . now she wondered if she would ever see him again.

Abbie bit back a sob and tried to be strong. The

days ahead were going to be pure hell, but she told herself that she would survive. Knowing she had to maintain her strength, she picked up the piece of meat and took a bite. It tasted terrible to her, but she had no choice. She ate it.

Her captor got up and moved away from her again, and Abbie breathed a quick sigh of relief. Her reprieve didn't last long, though. He quickly returned, and she tensed, expecting him to assault her. She was surprised when he simply tossed a blanket to her.

Abbie grabbed the blanket and wrapped it around herself as best she could with her hands bound as they were. She huddled beneath the blanket's protection. The night wasn't cold, but the cover gave her at least a small feeling of having a shield from the harsh reality that surrounded her.

Abbie wasn't sure what to expect next. She waited, prepared for the worst, and was surprised when the warriors left her alone. They all went ahead and bedded down for the night. Abbie did not know why she was being spared further abuse, but she was thankful. Trembling with relief, she curled up on her side. She closed her eyes and prayed to be saved from this terrible, horrible, unending nightmare her existence had become.

Faith had stayed awake all night, sitting in the chair beside Mason's bed. She'd kept watch over her injured brother as he'd slept. Mason was pale, but she knew that was to be expected, considering what he'd been through. His wound was serious, and he'd lost a lot of blood. He was lucky he was still alive. Dr. Murray had said he should make a full recovery, and she prayed the doctor was right.

When Faith glanced out the window and saw that the eastern horizon was starting to lighten, determination gripped her. She quietly got up to leave the bedroom.

"Faith," Mason managed to call out to her in a rasping whisper.

She hadn't realized he was awake, and she quickly went to him to see what he wanted. "I'm right here."

With what little strength he could muster, Mason reached out and grabbed her arm. He looked up at her, his gaze revealing the torment that filled him, physically and mentally. "Find Abbie."

"We will," she promised him.

At her words, Mason's hand fell weakly away. In his heart he wanted to be riding out with the search party. He wanted to help find his sister, but the pain and weakness that filled him were overwhelming.

"We'll bring her home, Mason," Faith said.

He nodded, then closed his eyes.

Faith left his room to get ready to start their search.

She changed clothes, donning pants for the long days of riding ahead. Then she packed what she needed for the trek, including a small tintype of Abbie she wanted to carry with her for luck. She made her way to the kitchen, where she found Rose already up and working.

"How was Mason overnight?" the housekeeper asked.

"He stirred only a couple of times."

"That's good. The more rest he gets, the better." Rose was relieved. Her husband, Tom, had been the foreman on the Lazy R for many years, and she served as the housekeeper. She'd watched the Ryan children grow up, and she cared deeply about them. "What about you? Did you get any sleep?"

"No. There was no way I could rest—not with what we have to do today," Faith answered.

"I understand. I was awake most of the night, too, worrying about Mason and Abbie," the housekeeper said sympathetically. "Tom's already down at the stable waiting for you. He's ready to ride, and so are Jake and Hank."

"Good. I don't know when we'll be back. Take care of Mason for me." She glanced back toward his room for a moment.

"I will." Rose gave her a quick, encouraging hug. "Now, you go find Abbie and hurry back home."

Their gazes met in understanding as Faith took the supplies Rose had put together for them.

The housekeeper's heart was heavy as she walked outside with Faith. She hoped they found Abbie quickly. The thought of the young woman being taken by the raiding party was horrifying. She had heard the stories of what happened to captives, and sometimes she believed the women who were rescued would have been better off dead than returned to their families. The thought disturbed Rose, and she put it from her. She went back in the house to check on Mason.

Faith found Tom, Hank, and Jake waiting for her at the stable, just as Rose had said.

"Last night, Dr. Murray told me that Sheriff Fike planned to ride along with us."

"I guess we'd better wait for him," Tom said.

"I hope he gets here soon." Faith wasn't pleased with the idea of having to wait. She was anxious to get going. Every minute counted, but she knew the lawman was a decent tracker and, even though her men were good, they might need his help.

She was relieved and grateful when she saw Sheriff Fike riding in a short time later, along with several other men from town.

"Thanks for coming," Faith greeted them when they reined in before her.

"How's your brother doing?"

"He was awake and talking when I left him this morning."

The lawman was glad to hear Mason was doing so well.

Faith went on to tell him everything they knew about the attack as she mounted up. They didn't bother with any small talk. Time was of the essence. They had a lot of ground to cover.

By the time the sun had cleared the eastern horizon, they were riding away from the Lazy R, intent on their search.

CHAPTER SEVEN

Four Days Later

Mason lay in bed, awake and miserable. The days since Faith and the others had ridden out in search of Abbie had seemed like an eternity. His physical pain was bad, but the emotional pain of not knowing what was going on was agonizing for him. Abbie was on his mind every waking moment, and he could only pray that she would be found and brought home safely.

He turned his head to stare out the bedroom window. The sun was shining brightly in the cloudless sky, but it did nothing to ease the darkness of his mood. Only a slight knock at the door distracted him from his thoughts.

"Yeah?"

"I've got your lunch," Rose said, opening the door and starting into his room. She hoped he would start eating better than he had been. She knew he would never get his strength back if he didn't take care of himself.

Mason said nothing as she marched inside, carrying the tray of food. He hadn't had much of an appetite, but he knew the housekeeper well enough to know she'd start spoon-feeding him, if she had to.

Rose set the tray on the bedside table. "Are you strong enough to sit up?"

"Let's try it," he agreed, weary of lying flat on his back.

Rose slipped an arm beneath his shoulders and helped lever him into a sitting position. It wasn't easy, but finally she got him up.

Mason let out a muffled groan, then drew a ragged breath as he straightened and leaned back against the headboard. "There."

"Is that better?" she asked, hoping the change in position would help.

"Yes. Thanks."

Rose picked up his tray, ready to put it on his lap, when they both heard the sound of riders coming in.

Mason tensed, unsure of what to expect. If it was Faith returning after only four days, the news could be good—or bad.

"Go see if it's them," he urged. He was uneasy, torn between excitement and dread.

Rose didn't hesitate. She put the tray back on the table and hurried from his room at the back of the house.

Mason waited, and it wasn't long before he had his answer. He heard footsteps coming down the hall and saw Faith appear in the doorway. The ordeal had taken its toll on his sister. Her face was sunburned and dirt-streaked, and her clothes were filthy from the long, hard days on the trail. Across the width of the room their gazes met, and he knew immediately by her tormented expression that the news she had for him was not good.

"What did you find?"

"Nothing," Faith answered flatly.

"Nothing at all?"

She came into the room to stand at his bedside, so she could tell him what had happened. "We lost the trail after the first day out and then spent the next two trying to find it again. We never did. It was almost as if they just vanished."

"Jake and Sheriff Fike couldn't find anything?" Mason was surprised, for he knew they were good trackers.

"Not after that first day. It was horrible." Faith pulled the chair up and sat down, tears burning in her eyes. She'd been strong through all the adversity, but suddenly she felt hopeless. "I don't know what more we can do."

Mason heard the sound of defeat in her voice, and it startled him. Faith was a fighter. She never gave up on anything. After their parents had died, she'd taken over the ranch and made it successful. She'd never backed down from a challenge. She was always fearless when it came to caring for her family, and he realized now that it was time for him to be strong for her. "There's got to be something that was missed—some way we can find her."

Faith lifted her troubled gaze to her brother's. "I kept thinking the same thing, but we covered it all."

"We'll think of something. We can't give up. Abbie won't give up. Maybe she'll find a way to escape from them."

"If anyone can, it will be Abbie."

"How's Jake taking it?"

"Hard."

They shared a knowing look.

"I'd better go back and let them know how you are. They were waiting to hear. Everyone's worried about you."

"Tell them I'm fine," Mason answered.

"Are you?"

"I'm as fine as I can be."

Their gazes met in understanding as she got up to leave the room.

Coyote Canyon

Trent had been taking it easy. He'd been resting and trying to figure out where he was headed next. He made his way down to the Ace High Saloon to pass the evening. He saw Cal there and joined him at the bar.

"Trent, it's good to see you," Cal said. "You been enjoying your time here in town?"

"Yes, it's a nice, quiet little town you've got here."

"Sheriff Fike works hard to keep it that way."

Max, the barkeep, came up to take Trent's order. "What'll it be?"

"Whiskey. You need a refill?" Trent asked Cal.

"Sure. Thanks."

Max set about pouring their drinks and looked at Cal. "You two know each other?"

"This is Trent Marshall. We hired him to hunt down Matt Sykes, and he just completed the job a few days ago," Cal explained as he picked up his glass and took a deep drink of the potent liquor.

"You did?" The bartender looked at Trent with renewed respect. Sykes's reputation as a cold-blooded killer was well-known throughout the area.

"That's right," Trent replied, not offering any more. He rarely made small talk. He didn't see the need. In fact, he'd been in the saloon several times over the last few days and had managed to keep his conversation to a minimum by sitting alone at one of the tables in the back of the room. In his line of work, it was important that he be able to see and not necessarily be seen.

"How'd you manage that?"

"Trent's good—real good," Cal said, lifting his glass to Trent. "That's how he managed it."

"You must be," Max agreed. "Your drink's on me. The world's a safer place with Sykes not running loose anymore."

"I appreciate it."

"Max! We need some liquor down here—fast!"

Max heard the roar and looked over to see Sheriff Fike coming through the swinging doors, followed by the other men who'd ridden with him on the search for the missing girl out at the Lazy R. He heard the edge of anger in the lawman's voice and hurried to serve them.

"How did it go?" Max asked as he lined glasses up on the bar before the weary group.

"Don't ask," Sheriff Fike growled.

The lawman had planned to go straight back to his office and check in with the deputy he'd left in charge, but the lure of a drink had waylaid him. The men needed some liquor after their endless days of searching and turning up nothing.

Max poured them shots of whiskey and watched as they quickly drank them down.

"Did you find the girl?"

"No. We lost the trail after the first day out. We kept looking for two more days, but we were never able to pick it up again."

The barkeep understood their frustration. "What's the family going to do?"

"I don't know," Sheriff Fike answered sadly, thinking of Faith and how brave she'd been during the search, and what she had to face now that she was back home with her wounded brother. "Right now, I can't offer much hope that Abbie will ever be found."

"Who's missing?" Cal asked, having heard only a part of their conversation.

The lawman glanced over to where Cal was

standing with a stranger at the bar. "You didn't hear about the trouble out at the Ryan place?"

"No. What happened?"

He quickly told them about the raiding party's attack. "It's been four days now. We got on their trail as fast as we could, but they still got away."

"And you're sure it was Apache?" Trent asked.

"That's right," Sheriff Fike answered, looking him over questioningly. "Why do you ask?"

Trent reached into his pocket and took out one of his business cards to hand to the lawman.

Sheriff Fike took the card and read it—MARSHALL'S LAW—TRENT MARSHALL, GUN FOR HIRE.

He looked back up, sizing the stranger up. "Being fast with a gun is one thing, but how good are you at tracking?"

"He's the best," Cal claimed. "He's the one who just hunted down Matt Sykes in Silver Mesa."

"So, you're the one who found him. Good job." The lawman's expression showed respect. He'd heard from Cal that Sykes had been brought in the other day, and that was some of the best news he'd had in a long time. "That man was one mean bastard. That's for sure."

"And thanks to Trent, here, he won't be robbing or killing anybody ever again," Cal said.

"That's the kind of news I like to hear." Sheriff Fike was thoughtful. "But there's a lot of difference between tracking down an outlaw like Sykes and going after Apache."

"I know," Trent said.

"So you've done this kind of thing before? Tracked renegades?" There was an edge to his voice.

"Yes." Trent's answer was firm, but he didn't elaborate.

"Well, if you're as good as Cal says you are, you might be the Ryan girl's only hope. You interested in taking on another job? Do you want to ride out and talk to the family?"

The thought of an innocent girl in the hands of a savage raiding party deeply troubled Trent. "Where's the ranch?"

"Not too far out of town. I'll ride along with you," Sheriff Fike offered. Weary though he was, he didn't mind making the trip back to the Lazy R if it would help Abbie in some way.

Any thoughts Trent had had about relaxing were gone. He now had a feeling he knew what his next job was going to be. "How soon do you want to leave?"

"Let me check in with my deputy and then I'll be ready to go." Sheriff Fike drained his glass and threw some money on the bar to cover their drinks. "Meet me at the sheriff's office."

"I'll be there." Trent left the saloon and went straight to the hotel to get his things together. If he took on this search for the girl he would have to ride out right away. There would be no time to come back into town to get his few belongings.

* * *

Jake and Faith walked outside the ranch house.

"Thank you for staying," Faith told him.

Jake had known how hard it was going to be for her to tell Mason what had happened on their search, so he had remained behind after the sheriff and the other men had returned to town to offer her what moral support he could.

"I just wish there were something more I could do to help find Abbie." Jake was thoroughly disheartened by their failure.

"I keep thinking that we must have missed something on the trail, but we went over the area so many times and found nothing. It was almost like they vanished off the face of the earth. . . ." The torrent of her emotions threatened to overwhelm her again. With an effort she fought it down. She didn't want to appear weak or vulnerable in front of Jake.

"If you need me or if you hear anything new, just send word."

Faith nodded and stepped back as he took his reins and swung up into the saddle. "Thanks, Jake."

Jake nodded to her and started to turn his horse, about to leave when he saw two riders in the distance. "Faith, someone's coming."

"It looks like Sheriff Fike, but I don't recognize the other man." She tensed, surprised that the sheriff should be returning to the ranch so soon.

"I don't either." Fearing that the lawman might be bringing bad news, Jake dismounted to stay with her. If there was news about Abbie, he wanted to hear it.

CHAPTER EIGHT

Faith waited, anxiously watching the two men ride in. Her gaze was fixed on the man riding beside the sheriff. Even at this distance, something about him seemed vaguely familiar, but she wasn't sure why. As they drew ever closer, Faith suddenly came to realize who the man was—none other than the darkly handsome stranger named Trent who'd danced with her at the social.

"It's Trent," she said, surprised to see him, and her heartbeat actually quickened at the sight of him. For an instant she thought how dirty she was after all the days on the trail. When they'd met she'd been at her best, and now . . . As quickly as she had the thought, she put it from her. There was nothing she could do about the way she looked, and it didn't matter. What mattered was Abbie.

"Trent? You know him?"

"I met him at the social, but I don't even know his

last name. I wonder why the sheriff's bringing him out here?"

"I think we're about to find out."

"Afternoon, Faith, Jake," Sheriff Fike greeted them as he and Trent reined in before them.

"Sheriff, Trent." She was looking up at Trent in surprise.

"Faith." He nodded to her as he said her name. When Sheriff Fike had mentioned on the ride out that they'd be speaking to Abbie's sister, Faith, at the ranch, he'd realized she might be the same woman he'd danced with the other night. As they'd ridden in, the lawman had pointed her out, and he had recognized her at once. He gazed down at Faith now and could tell she was as startled as he was by the coincidence.

"You two know each other?" Sheriff Fike was caught off guard as they dismounted.

"We met at the dance," Trent offered.

Faith looked back at the sheriff. She pushed the memory of being in Trent's arms out of her mind. So much had gone on since that night, it seemed as if it had happened a thousand years ago.

"Why are you here, Sheriff Fike?" Faith asked nervously, concerned over his reason for returning to the ranch so soon and puzzled as to why Trent was with him. "Is something wrong?"

"Nothing's wrong, Faith. I thought it was important to bring Trent out here to meet you."

"Why? I don't understand."

"Trent's a hired gun. He just did some work for

Cal Harris and the stage line. He's one of the best trackers around. I thought he might be able to help you search for Abbie."

For the first time in days, Faith felt a glimmer of hope. She turned to Trent, a light shining in her eyes. "You're a good tracker?"

"Cal says he is," the lawman affirmed.

"Did Sheriff Fike tell you what happened to my sister?"

"Yes."

"And you think you can do this? You think you can find her?"

"I'll do my best."

"And his best is damned good," Sheriff Fike added.

Faith knew from what the sheriff had said that Trent wouldn't be doing this for free. She eyed him as she asked, "What do you charge?"

"Five hundred dollars."

It was a lot of money, but if hiring him meant they had a chance to save Abbie's life, then he was worth every cent and more.

"You're hired," she stated. "Let's go up to the house, so we can talk."

"All right."

They all started toward the house.

"Faith." Jake drew her aside for a moment.

"What is it?"

"If you need any help getting the money to pay him, I'll be glad to give it to you," Jake offered. He had been troubled by his own failure to find Abbie, and was more than willing to do everything possible to bring her safely home.

Faith was deeply touched by his offer. She looked up at him and gave him a reassuring smile as she touched his arm. "You are a good man, Jake. Thank you, but I should be all right."

"Just know that if you do need any help, all you have to do is ask."

"I'll remember."

They hurried to catch up with Sheriff Fike and Trent, who'd walked on ahead of them.

As Faith moved past them to lead the way, Trent's gaze was drawn to her slender, pants-clad figure. Even dressed as she was, there was no mistaking she was female, and though in her current state she bore little resemblance to the delicate-looking beauty she'd been the night of the dance, she was still a lovely woman.

Recognizing the direction of his thoughts, Trent pushed them aside. He had to focus on finding her sister. He had no time to think about anything else.

When they reached the house, Jake stayed with Sheriff Fike outside on the porch.

"We'll wait out here for you."

They watched as Faith and Trent went indoors.

"Are you heading back to your ranch now?" the lawman asked Jake, thinking they could ride out together.

"No," Jake answered. "When Trent rides out, I'm going, too. Send word to the ranch for me, will you?"

"I'll let them know as soon as I get back to town," the sheriff promised.

They settled in to wait and see how Faith and Trent planned to track down Abbie.

Jake just prayed that Trent was as good as they said he was and that he would have the ability to find her.

"How do you want me to pay you?" Faith asked Trent as they went inside.

"You can have the money wired to my account at the bank in San Antonio."

"You're from Texas?"

"Originally. I get back when I can, but that hasn't been too often lately."

"Well, I'm just thankful you were in town. We have to do everything possible to find my sister," she told him.

Rose was waiting anxiously to find out what was going on, and Faith quickly explained everything to her.

"Tell Mason we'll be back to see him in a few minutes."

Rose hurried off to do her bidding while Faith led Trent into the small room she used as an office.

"Have a seat," Faith directed as she sat down at the desk.

He took the chair in front of the desk and gave her the information she needed to have the money transferred.

"I can be ready to leave within the hour," Faith

began when the financial arrangements had been made. "I want Hank to go, and Jake will probably want to ride with us, too."

Trent was surprised by her announcement and quickly wanted to set things straight. "You don't understand. . . ."

"What don't I understand?" She looked up at him in irritation.

As he met Faith's challenging green-eyed glare, Trent realized again what a good-looking woman she was, and he grew even more annoyed. The last thing he needed was her kind of distraction while he was trying to work.

"I work alone," Trent stated firmly. It was his one hard-and-fast rule. When he was on his own, he could move quickly and quietly. He didn't need any help from anyone when he was working, and working by himself, he didn't have to worry about anyone else.

"What are you talking about?" Faith's regard turned into a cold-eyed glare across the desk. In the years since she'd taken over running the ranch, she'd dealt with all kinds of men. She hadn't backed down from any of them, no matter how arrogant or demanding they were, and she wasn't about to start now—not when her sister's life was hanging in the balance.

"You've hired me to do a job, and I'm going to do it—my way. I work alone. It's better like that."

"No, *you* don't understand," she countered in a

tone that brooked no argument. "Like you just said—I hired you to do a job, and that means I'm your boss." She paused for effect. "You work for me. When you head out, you won't be going alone. I'll be riding with you, and so will Jake and Hank."

Trent was not happy. He had to be free to do his job the way he liked to do it, but before he could argue any further, Faith went on.

"I don't doubt that you're good at what you do, but according to my brother, there were at least three, maybe four warriors in the raiding party. When you catch up with them, you just might need some help."

He was tempted to refuse the job right then and there. Only the thought of an innocent young woman in the hands of murderous renegades kept him from getting up and walking out the door. He didn't want Faith Ryan and the other men riding along. They would only slow him down and make things more awkward, but it looked like he had no choice.

"When I travel, I travel hard and fast," Trent said tersely, hoping that might discourage her.

It didn't.

"Good. That's what I expected from you. We've got a lot of ground to cover and a lot of lost time to make up for. They've got a four-day head start on us already. How soon do you want to ride out?"

"Whenever you're ready."

"I can get the supplies we need together and be set to leave in an hour."

Trent only nodded. He had nothing more to say,

though his gut instinct was telling him this woman would mean trouble for him.

"Come with me," Faith said, standing up. "I want you to meet my brother, Mason."

Trent got to his feet. "Sheriff Fike told me he was shot during the attack."

"He was, but he's doing all right now."

Trent followed her from the office to the back of the house. They went into a bedroom to find the young man braced up in his bed, his chest tightly wrapped with thick bandages.

"You're Trent Marshall?" Mason asked as they came in."

"That's right," Trent answered.

"I'm Mason Ryan." He extended his hand to the hired gun as he met his gaze straight-on. "Rose was just telling me about you."

They shook hands.

Then Mason added, "Find my sister."

"I intend to do just that," Trent said. "Tell me everything you remember about the attack."

Mason began to relate the events of that fateful day to Trent while Faith left them to get ready. She met with Rose to tell her what supplies they would need, then went out to speak with Jake and Sheriff Fike. As she'd expected, Jake was ready to ride with them, so she took him with her to find Hank. She told Hank to get her horse ready, and to be prepared to ride himself. They sought out the foreman, Tom, next. Faith knew he wanted to go with the search party, too, but she insisted he stay behind and run the ranch. She had no idea how long they'd be on the trail, and Mason was in no condition to take charge.

Faith returned to the house. The first thing she knew she had to do was get cleaned up. She bathed quickly and washed her hair. She left her hair unbound for the time being, wanting it to dry before she plaited it into a more practical braid. Faith donned clean clothes, wearing pants again. She packed a few extra things, and then returned to Mason's room, where Trent was still talking with him.

"I'm ready," Faith announced as she came to stand in the doorway.

Trent glanced over toward Faith and had to be careful not to do a double take at the sight of her standing there with her long blond hair loose and falling about her shoulders in a soft cascade of still-damp curls. Had she been wearing a gown, he would have thought her the image of feminine beauty, but she was dressed in pants again. Even so, he had to admit to himself that he admired the view.

"All right. Let's go," Trent said tersely. He glanced back at Mason. "Thanks for your help. We'll be back."

"With Abbie," Mason added.

When Trent had stepped from the room, Faith went to her brother to kiss his cheek.

"Do you want me to help you lie back down?"

"No, I'll be all right," he told her, meeting her gaze. He took her hand as he said, "Be careful."

"We will be, and you do everything you can to get better." She was still worried about him.

"Hurry back."

She gave him a tight smile and left. She paused only long enough to quickly plait her hair into a manageable braid, then strapped on her sidearm, got her rifle, and put on her hat.

It was time to go.

She was riding out with a hired gun in a last desperate attempt to find her sister.

Faith started outside where Trent, Jake, Hank, and the packhorse were ready and waiting.

"I'll tell you what I told your boss lady, here," Trent was saying to the other two men as she joined them. "I usually work alone. I ride hard and I ride fast. I don't wait for anyone. If you can't keep up, don't bother coming along."

"We'll keep up," Jake said firmly.

"You'd better. If you get lost or we're separated, you're on your own. I'm not going to waste time backtracking to find you. I'm after the raiding party."

Jake and Hank understood what he was saying, and they didn't doubt for a moment that he meant every word.

"All right. Let's head out to the scene of the attack." He looked impatiently back at Faith, who was finally getting ready to mount up. "Are you coming?"

"Try leaving without me," she replied, swinging up in the saddle. She didn't say another word as she led the way from the ranch house.

CHAPTER NINE

They made the ride to the scene of the attack without speaking. Faith reined in at the spot where they'd found Mason. She quickly explained to Trent what they'd done the first day out, then showed him the trail they'd followed.

Trent dismounted and studied the tracks, looking for anything unusual. He stood up and stared off in the direction the trail led.

"We still have a few hours of daylight left. Let's keep going," Trent directed.

They pushed on, traveling at a ground-eating pace. They followed their earlier tracks until darkness forced them to halt. They made camp and then settled in to eat. Little was said while they made short work of the food Rose had packed for them.

An almost tangible sense of tension prevailed, because it was obvious that Trent resented their presence, but Faith didn't care. There was no way she was going to change her mind and stay behind. She could keep up with him, and she could shoot as straight as any man. There was no way she could just sit back at the ranch and do nothing while she waited for word of her sister's fate—word that might take weeks or even months to reach her.

"What do you think the odds are that we'll find them?" Jake finally asked, breaking the silence.

"If I were a gambling man, I'd say the odds weren't good after so many days, but I'm not much of a gambling man," Trent answered. "I mean to find them, but it's not going to be quick or easy."

"I hope you have more luck picking up the trail than we did," Hank told him.

"How far out did you lose it?"

"About another half day's ride," Jake offered.

Trent nodded. It was good to know that they would have plenty of daylight left once they reached that location. "Be ready to ride at dawn. We've got a lot of ground to cover tomorrow."

Everyone bedded down for the night.

Trent lay in his bedroll, his thoughts on all that had happened during the day and what they faced over the days to come. Restless and on edge, he got up sometime later and walked away from the campsite. He stood there in the darkness, studying the lay of the land and trying to get a feel for where the raiding party might have been headed. When he heard someone coming, he tensed, ready to draw his gun.

"Trent," Faith quietly called to him when she saw him standing there, staring out across the land. Trent was an intimidating, solitary figure. Tall and broad-shouldered, he was a man to be reckoned with. She'd been hoping to have the opportunity to speak with him alone, and after seeing him get up and move away from the camp, she realized this was probably going to be the only chance she would have for a while.

Trent relaxed a little when he discovered it was Faith—not that he was glad to see her. He didn't want or need the distraction she presented while he was tracking the renegades. He let his hand fall away from his sidearm as he waited for her to come to him.

Faith made her way across the rocky ground toward Trent's imposing figure. What she had to say wasn't going to be easy for her, but she wanted no conflicts between them while they were on the trail.

"There's something I needed to say to you," she began.

"What?" He waited, unsure what she was leading up to.

"I wanted to thank you."

Trent was surprised. "For what?"

"For taking the job." She faced him squarely. "Back at the ranch, when I insisted we ride along with you, you could have refused. You could have walked away and never looked back, but you didn't, and I appreciate that."

He was impressed by her unexpected display of humbleness. "It really hurt you to say that, didn't it?"

"You have no idea," Faith said stiffly. It wasn't often she had to swallow her pride, but for Abbie's sake, she would do anything.

"We haven't found her yet."

"Not yet, but judging from what Sheriff Fike told me, if anyone can find her, it will be you."

They fell silent for a moment as they looked out over the night-shrouded landscape.

"She's out there somewhere," Faith said, emotion lowering her voice to a whisper. "I just hope she's still alive."

Trent recognized her pain, for an instant, was almost tempted to take her in his arms and comfort her. Angered by his own reaction to her momentary display of vulnerability, he stated, "So do I." Then he turned away from her. "We'd better get some rest. You coming?"

For some reason, Faith felt bereft for a moment; then she managed to get a grip on her emotions. She hardened her heart so she could deal with what the future might hold. "Yes."

Faith followed Trent back to the campsite to bed down for the night.

It would be dawn soon.

Abbie lay huddled beneath the blanket. She was pretending to sleep, but every fiber of her being was aware of her surroundings—of the flickering campfire and of the warriors drinking the whiskey they'd stolen from the two men they'd attacked and killed on the trail earlier that day. They had left her behind, bound and gagged, when they'd launched their assault, so she hadn't witnessed the actual murders, but she had seen the victims' bloodied bodies afterward.

Abbie had silently mourned their deaths. She hadn't realized her captors had the whiskey until they'd stopped for the night. Only then had she come to understand the possible horror that awaited her there in the darkness. So far during her captivity they had left her untouched, but she knew that if the warriors got drunk and went wild, anything could happen. She shuddered at the thought. The one hope she held on to was that they would drink so much they might pass out. If that happened, she would have the opportunity to escape. She had no doubt Faith was out there searching for her somewhere. Abbie would do everything she could to get away and try to find her way back home.

Home . . .

Memories of the Lazy R and her brother and sister were all that were keeping her sane. She hung onto them tightly as she waited to see what was going to happen next. If the renegades drank themselves insensible, she would be able to sneak off and have a good head start on them before they even realized she was gone.

Abbie could hear the sounds of drunkenness in the warriors' voices, and, not for the first time, she wished she understood their language. Being ignorant of their plans for her put her at a disadvantage, but in their drunken condition, she figured their only plan for the night was to stay put until morning.

Black Cloud took another deep drink of the firewater, then handed the bottle to Little Dog.

"It is good," Black Cloud declared in a slurred, drunken voice.

"Very good," Little Dog agreed, chugging even more of the potent whiskey.

"It is a shame Crooked Snake will not let us take the Golden One for our pleasure," Black Cloud said as he looked over to where their captive lay sleeping nearby.

"You are right. She would please me greatly," Little Dog agreed, handing back the bottle. "But the firewater pleases me, too."

"You are right. The firewater gives more pleasure than that one would," Black Cloud slurred, smiling as he took a drink.

Little Dog didn't know if he agreed with Black Cloud, but he didn't argue. He just let his gaze linger on the woman as he continued to enjoy the liquor.

The two warriors continued to drink heavily until they both fell back on their blankets, dead to the world around them.

Lone Eagle took a swig from the bottle he and Crooked Snake were sharing, and then offered the bottle back to him.

"This is a good night," Crooked Snake said, celebrating the success of their raids. They had the woman and now they had whiskey.

"Yes, it is," Lone Eagle agreed.

"We have done well, and there is yet another ranch ahead, just three days' ride from here," he told Lone Eagle, already anticipating their next raid. "Perhaps we will find more women there." He smiled at the thought and looked over to where the Golden One was sleeping. He drank eagerly from the bottle.

As Abbie lay there, biding her time, she began to believe that the moment would never come when it would be quiet at the campsite. Finally, though, long into the night, the last two warriors fell silent. Encouraged by the stillness, she carefully lifted the edge of her blanket and peeked out from underneath it to find that they were all sprawled around the campfire, passed out and oblivious to their surroundings. They may have been celebrating earlier, but now she was the one with something to celebrate.

This was her chance.

Now was the time.

She was going to make a run for it.

Abbie had been chewing at the rope that bound her wrists and had made some progress loosening it. Sitting up, she was finally able to free her wrists, and then quickly untied the binding at her ankles.

Abbie wished she had a gun. She looked around,

hoping to see one somewhere close by, but the warriors had kept their weapons beside them, and she didn't want to risk getting caught trying to take one.

Carefully brushing her blanket aside, she checked the campsite one last time to make sure she hadn't missed anything, then piled her blanket up in a mound to make it look as if she were still sleeping there. That done, she began to move slowly and silently. She couldn't afford to make any sudden, unexpected noise that might alert the drunken warriors to her escape attempt. Creeping ever farther from the campfire, she sought the dark, protective cover of the night.

The horses were tied a short distance away, and Abbie offered up a fervent prayer that they would not stir too much as she neared them. She held her breath as she made her way to the place where her own horse was hobbled. Stroking his neck, she freed him and took up his reins.

Abbie was thankful her prayer was answered. The other mounts did not cause any trouble as she led her horse away.

With infinite care, Abbie moved farther and farther away from the campsite. She didn't stop to mount up until she was certain it was safe. Only then did she swing onto her horse's back. She needed to get away fast. She needed to put as many miles between herself and her captors as she could. And she needed to do it as quickly as possible. She desperately wanted to put her heels to her horse's sides and gallop off at top speed into the night, but she didn't. She had made it this far by being cautious, and she wasn't going to do anything to ruin her escape. With a slight nudge, Abbie urged her mount on at a slow, quiet pace. Only when they were several miles away and out of earshot would she speed up. For now, silence was all that mattered.

Little Dog awoke suddenly in the middle of the night. Dreams of the white woman had left his body on fire with his need for her, and that need was throbbing within him. With liquor impairing his judgment, he gave no thought to anything but easing the demanding ache in his body.

The campfire had burned down low, and he was glad. The darker it was, the easier it would be for him to lead the Golden One away from the campsite without disturbing the others.

Getting to his feet, Little Dog drew his knife and staggered toward where she lay sleeping. He believed that when she saw the knife, she would be terrified and obey him without a fight. That was what he wanted—a submissive woman who would do exactly what he wanted her to do.

The thought heated his need even more.

He was ready.

Any concerns he had about Crooked Snake were forgotten in his drunkenness.

His animal desire driving him on, Little Dog knelt beside the sleeping woman and picked up the corner of her blanket. The warrior lifted the blanket a little so he could see the Golden One. In his drunken state, it took him a moment to realize she was missing.

"She is gone!" he raged.

At his shout, the other three warriors came awake. Crooked Snake got up and staggered to his side.

"Where did she go?" he demanded, looking around in confusion.

"I don't know," Little Dog told him. "I thought something looked strange, so I came to check on her."

Black Cloud and Lone Eagle joined them there.

Lone Eagle knelt to pick up the ropes that had bound her. "I'll check the horses."

He moved off to see if her horse was still there. It didn't take long for him to find out.

"She has taken her horse," Lone Eagle told them when he returned.

Crooked Snake was in a drunken fury. He looked at the eastern sky. "It is not long until dawn. I will track her down then—and when I find her, she will pay."

As the angry warrior waited for first light, he slowly sobered up, becoming more furious and determined with every passing minute.

CHAPTER TEN

Abbie had kept her pace slow as she continued on ever farther away from the campsite. The cover of the night had been both a blessing and a curse. She had escaped unseen, but finding her way in the darkness was not easy. She would have liked to have ridden faster, but she did not want to risk injuring her horse.

At sunup, Abbie quickened her pace. She had tried to pay attention on the previous days, wanting to keep a sense of which direction they were going, and she was glad now that she had. She kneed her horse to a gallop, heading back the way they'd come.

For the first time in days, her spirits were filled with hope.

She was going home.

She was going to be safe.

Crooked Snake was relentless in his pursuit. Anger and humiliation motivated him. He had known the

Golden One was a fighter from the first, when she had resisted him so violently. He had been careful in the succeeding days not to be harsh with her, but no more. When he found her—and he would find her—she would pay the price for her defiance.

Lone Eagle and the other warriors kept pace with Crooked Snake. As the miles passed and they still saw no sign of her, Lone Eagle found that he was growing impressed by the Golden One's daring and riding skill. He was confident that they would catch up with her eventually, but he admired her stamina and bravery.

Abbie had been making good time in her desperate race to freedom. She had no idea how much of a head start she had on the warriors, and she couldn't worry about it. All that mattered was to keep going. In her heart, she prayed she would come upon trackers from the ranch searching for her, but she knew not to count on anyone coming to her rescue.

She was on her own.

She had to save herself.

It was late in the afternoon when the raiding party finally caught sight of the woman. They had just topped a hill and could see her some distance ahead of them in the valley below.

Crooked Snake was determined to catch up with her before dark. He raced after her, intent on making her pay for daring to defy him.

At first Abbie was not aware that she had been

spotted and that the renegades were closing in on her. She kept her gaze fixed on the trail. Each mile she covered brought her that much closer to home. She remembered that there was a small stream not too far ahead of her, and she planned to stop there and let her horse rest and have a drink.

Abbie never got the chance.

The eerie, frightening shouts of the warriors as they closed in echoed around Abbie and sent a terrified chill down her spine. She put her heels to her horse's sides and leaned low over his neck, hanging on tightly as she raced on.

She refused to give up.

She refused to surrender.

But Crooked Snake was as determined as she was.

He rode up beside her and reached over to grab her. He dragged her off her horse and hauled her bodily over in front of him.

"*No!*" Abbie screamed in abject horror. She had been so close! And now . . .

Crooked Snake reined in as she fought violently against him. Her blouse ripped, and a piece of it was torn off in the struggle. He was so infuriated that he threw her to the ground. He dismounted, and, in a rage, he took her by the arm and pulled her up, hitting her. At her cry of pain, he hit her again.

The other members of the raiding party quickly reached the scene.

Lone Eagle had known Crooked Snake was angry, but he hadn't thought he would be so cruel. He could see that Golden One was suffering from

Crooked Snake's punishing blows. For just an instant the Golden One looked up at him, and across the distance their gazes met. He could see the hatred, desperation, and pain revealed there. Something stirred within him, and he felt driven to take action.

"Crooked Snake!" Lone Eagle dismounted and grabbed the other warrior's arm to stop him from beating his captive anymore.

Abbie was stunned to be released so suddenly, and she collapsed to the ground, battered and bleeding. She clutched at her torn blouse in an attempt to cover her breasts. She looked up to see that the other warrior had stopped the first from beating her.

Furious that Lone Eagle had interfered, Crooked Snake drew his knife on him. "You dare to stop me?"

The two warriors faced off.

"Look at her," Lone Eagle countered. "You were the one who said she would be worth more unharmed."

Crooked Snake glared down at the bloody captive. His rage was still powerful within him.

"Then you take her and make sure she does not escape again," he directed. He did not wait for Lone Eagle to respond. He walked away to get his horse.

Lone Eagle picked up the beaten girl, who resisted only slightly.

"No," Abbie cried out weakly.

"Be still," he said to her in English as he carried her to his horse and lifted her up onto its back. He mounted behind her and kept his arms around her for support and restraint, just in case she might try to escape again. He knew now just how smart and resourceful she was.

Once Black Cloud had claimed her horse, they started off again, riding back the way they'd come.

It was getting near sundown, but Trent didn't even consider stopping. They'd followed the trail as far as it had led, and then he'd circled out, looking for any clue that would give him a hint of his quarry's direction. He hadn't found anything new, but his instincts were telling him the raiding party had headed south, and he'd been at this long enough to know when to trust his instincts.

"They headed south—toward the border," Trent said, staring off in the distance.

"How do you know? How can you be sure?" Jake pressed him.

Trent was scowling darkly as he glanced back over his shoulder to where Jake stood with Faith and Hank. "It's what I get paid for," he said tensely. "Let's get a few more miles in before we stop for the night."

As they continued on, Jake rode beside Faith.

"I hope he knows what he's doing," Jake said to her.

"He does."

Faith trusted Trent's judgment.

She had to.

He was her only hope.

Faith's gaze lingered on Trent as he rode ahead of her. She could tell he was alert and completely focused on their surroundings. He was ready for trouble, should anything happen.

Faith found herself wondering about his past—whether he had any family, and how he'd come to be a hired gun. Silent type that he was, she didn't know if she'd ever find out. The one thing she did know about him was that he was a good dancer. The memory made her smile for just a moment; then she frowned, wondering where that thought had come from.

Darkness had enveloped the land when they finally set up camp for the night near a small watering hole. They took care of their horses, then settled in and ate. All were appreciative of the food Rose had packed for them.

Hank and Jake hadn't had much to say. Both men were still uneasy about Trent's decision to head south.

"Why do you think they're heading for the border?" Hank asked finally, breaking the silence around the campfire. He'd always considered himself a good tracker, and had seen no sign indicating the raiding party had come this way.

Trent looked over at Hank. "There are men there who would pay a lot of money for a girl like Abbie. Since we haven't found her dead on the trail, it's a good possibility that's where they're taking her."

Faith was sickened by the thought. "Do you think we can catch up with them in time?"

"We have to," Jake said quickly.

Unable to bear thinking about what might be in store for Abbie, Jake got up and stalked away from the campfire. It was difficult enough for him imagining what Abbie might be suffering at the hands of her captors, but the thought of her being sold into that kind of slavery tormented him to the depths of his soul.

Faith started to go after him, but Trent spoke up, stopping her.

"Don't."

She paused, giving him a questioning look.

"Trent's right. Sometimes a man needs to be alone," Hank finished.

"It's time to bed down if we're going to be ready to ride out at dawn," Trent said.

Faith looked off into the darkness in the direction Jake had gone, then moved to spread out her bedroll. After the long day they'd had in the saddle, there was no denying she was exhausted. She slipped beneath the blanket and sought what comfort she could find there on the unforgiving hardness of the ground.

Lone Eagle brought his blanket and a length of rope with him as he walked over to where the Golden One was sitting. Lone Eagle looked her over for a moment, studying her bruised face in the light of the campfire. He hoped she was as smart as she was spirited. He hoped she had learned her lesson. She could not escape. She belonged to them now. He spread out his blanket and then knelt beside her. She started to scoot away from him, but he stopped her. He tied one end of the rope to her right ankle and then tied the other end to his own left leg. He would make sure she did not get away again.

Abbie was in pain. She ached all over from the brutal beating she'd received earlier. When she'd seen the warrior coming toward her with a blanket and a rope, she hadn't been sure what to expect. When he'd knelt beside her, she'd feared the worst, and now that he'd bound her to him, she was even more uncertain of what was to come. She believed he wasn't as savage as the other warrior who'd beaten her earlier, but he was still one of her captors.

"What are you going to do with me?" she asked, terrified of what was to come.

Lone Eagle ignored her question. He could sense the near panic in her, so he simply stretched out on his blanket beside her.

"Sleep," he directed tersely, and then he closed his eyes.

Relief flooded through Abbie that he hadn't tried to touch her. She shifted as far away from him as she could and then lay down herself. The rope that bound them together was pulled taut, and she knew he would be aware of every move she made all night long. She closed her eyes and prayed for sleep to come. It would be the only peace and solace she would find.

Across the campfire, Little Dog's gaze was hot upon their captive. He had been glad that no one had suspected his true motive when he'd discovered she had escaped the previous night. He just regretted that he hadn't been able to take her for himself. Now that she was bound to Lone Eagle, he realized he would never get the chance. The knowledge left him frustrated and angry, but there was little he could do about it. He bedded down, wondering what females they would find on the ranch they were going to raid in a few days.

Mason lay in bed in darkened bedroom, staring out the window at the night sky. He longed to be riding with the search party, not lying there so helplessly. Though he did thank God he was alive, he cursed his weakened condition. He wanted to save Abbie.

It seemed to Mason that he had been lying there for an eternity. He was a man of action, and being bedridden this way was pure torture for him.

A soft knock at the door drew his attention.

"Yeah?"

Rose opened the door to check on him, and light spilled into the room from the lamp she was carrying with her. "I just wanted to see if you needed anything before I call it a night."

"The only thing I need is to be able to get up out of this bed and go help look for Abbie."

She heard the frustration and anger in his voice.

She understood it, but Mason was going to have to learn to accept the fact that he would not regain his full strength for some time.

"Don't even think about trying to get out of that bed without help," Rose ordered. "The doctor will be out again tomorrow or the next day to see how you're doing. Until then, you're to stay right where you are."

Mason knew she was right, but it didn't make his helplessness any easier for him to accept.

"Yes, ma'am," he replied, using the tone he'd used as a boy whenever she'd corrected him.

"I'll see you in the morning, then," she said. "Good night."

As she closed the door and left him, Rose was glad for his show of spirit. She hoped it meant he was getting some of his strength back.

Long hours passed before Mason fell asleep. And though he badly needed the rest, his sleep, when it finally came, was fitful. It was filled with images of the day of the raid and his last vision of Abbie, being thrown from her horse and lying motionless on the ground.

CHAPTER ELEVEN

Determination and hatred filled Ward Sykes as he rode out of Tucson. Word had reached him the day before that his son Matt had been killed by a hired gun named Trent Marshall up in Silver Mesa.

It didn't matter to Ward that Matt had been a killer—a wanted man with a price on his head.

Vengeance was all he cared about.

He set out for Coyote Canyon. He'd heard that was where the hired gun had gone to turn his son's body over to the stage line authorities, so he was going to start looking for him there. Ward didn't know how long it would take, and it didn't matter to him. He was going to kill Trent Marshall—he was going to get his revenge.

Little Dog was up before the sun. He made no sound as he walked closer to the Golden One to watch her as she slept. Her blanket had fallen away, exposing the curve of her breast where her blouse

109

had been torn the previous day. Again, fiery need grew within him. He wanted her, and it infuriated him that Lone Eagle and Crooked Snake were both watching over her.

Lone Eagle had been lying quietly with his eyes closed, waiting for the dawn, when he heard someone moving about. He glanced up to see Little Dog standing close by, staring down at their captive. Lone Eagle looked over at the Golden One and realized why the other warrior was there.

"What do you want, Little Dog?" he demanded, knowing full well what was on the other warrior's mind.

Little Dog was startled to find Lone Eagle was awake. "It is almost dawn. It is time to ride out." He let his gaze rake over the woman one last time, then turned and stalked off.

Abbie had come awake at the sound of their voices so close by. When she'd opened her eyes to find the warrior staring at her, she'd instinctively covered herself with the blanket.

Lone Eagle knew what Little Dog was like, and he knew what he had to do. Untying the rope that bound Abbie to him, he got up and went to pull the blanket away from the captive. He wasn't surprised that she resisted, clutching at the blanket and struggling to hold on to it, but he managed to get it away from her.

Abbie was frightened by the warrior's move. She held the fabric of her blouse up as she watched him warily. When he took out his knife, her heartbeat quickened, and she knew a moment of true terror. She thought he might be planning to punish her for not letting go of the blanket. She began to tremble.

Lone Eagle ignored her as he cut off a section of the blanket, made a slit in it, and then walked over to her. Abbie stared up at him in abject horror, not knowing what to expect. He could see fear in her expression as he approached, but didn't care. He simply slipped the makeshift garment over her head to cover her.

Abbie's relief was profound as she looked up at her captor. She was completely surprised by his act of kindness.

"Thank you," she said.

Lone Eagle saw the change in her expression and nodded to her. He turned away to get the horses ready.

Crooked Snake and Black Cloud had awakened when they'd heard the others talking. They'd watched what had happened and understood why Lone Eagle had taken such action. They both knew that Little Dog was not to be trusted around female captives.

They ate what little food they had and then got ready to mount up.

Abbie had been hoping to ride her own horse this day, but the warrior led her to his. It had been awkward for her riding in front of him the day before. She'd struggled not to lean back against him, but pain from the beating and weariness had made her give up the fight. She expected him to ride the same way today, but instead he untied the rope at her wrists, then mounted and reached down to bring her up behind him. Abbie instinctively put her arms around his waist, clinging to the hard, lean strength of him as they rode off.

Larissa Murray was up early and waiting for her father when he came downstairs to have breakfast.

"Papa, are you going to go out to the Lazy R today to see Mason?"

"You heard me talking to your mother last night, didn't you?" he asked with a smile.

"Yes, and I was wondering . . . Could I come along, and maybe Katie and Zach, too?"

Richard Murray was thoughtful for a moment, thinking back to the last time he'd seen Mason. "I think we can arrange it. Mason should be strong enough to have visitors by now. What do you think, dear?" he asked his wife, who was busy cooking his breakfast.

"That's fine. I know they've all been worrying about him."

"All right, I plan to leave around ten o'clock. Can you get Katie and Zach here by then?"

"We'll be ready!" Larissa pressed a quick kiss to his cheek as she started to hurry from the room. She had to go tell Katie and Zach the news. Pausing at the door, she looked back at her father. "Thank you."

"Go on—get your friends," he encouraged.

Larissa was thrilled and relieved. It was going to be a wonderful day! She was going to see Mason.

She had been in love with Mason for what seemed like forever, and when she'd first learned that he'd been shot and Abbie had been kidnapped, she'd been heartsick. Then, when she'd heard that Faith had ridden out with the searchers, leaving Mason in the care of their housekeeper, she'd longed to go out to the Lazy R and nurse him herself. She'd known she couldn't, though, since she was no relation to him, but now that he was improving there was no reason he couldn't have a visit from friends. Larissa rushed off to get Katie and Zach, and by ten o'clock they were ready to go.

Dr. Murray decided to take the carriage on this trip, so the girls could ride with him while Zach rode along on horseback.

"I want you to remember Mason has been through a lot. The wound was serious, and it's going to take a while for him to make a full recovery. Keep your visit short. We don't want to wear him out," her father advised.

"Do you think he'll be glad to see us?" Katie asked.

"I'm sure he will," Dr. Murray reassured her. "This is a very troubling time for him—for his whole family. We need to do whatever we can to try to lift his spirits. It won't be easy, though—not with what he's facing—but just knowing he has friends like you will help."

* * *

Mason heard the sound of a carriage coming in. Rose had told him Dr. Murray would probably be out that day, so he wasn't surprised when he heard a knock at his bedroom door a short time later. He was feeling a little stronger, and hoped the doctor would give him permission to get up out of bed for a while.

"Come in," Mason called out.

The door opened and, as he'd expected, Dr. Murray came in with Rose.

"Good morning," Dr. Murray greeted him. He had wanted to make sure Mason was properly situated in the bed before he admitted the girls to the bedroom. "I have a surprise for you this morning."

"A surprise?" Mason frowned.

"It's all right to come in now," he called to Larissa and the others.

"Who's here?" Mason asked.

When Larissa appeared in the doorway, Mason smiled for the first time since the attack.

"Larissa."

"Mason." She breathed his name as she got her first glimpse of him. She was used to him being strong and vibrant. Her father had warned her of his condition, but still, the sight of him looking so pale, with his chest swathed in bandages, startled her. Her heart ached for him.

"Larissa's not the only one who showed up," Zach said, coming to stand with her. "I'm here, and so is Katie."

"Come on in," Mason invited.

Dr. Murray was pleased to see that Mason seemed a bit stronger. "I'll wait until after your visit to change your bandages."

He left them alone to talk for a while.

Larissa wasted no time pulling a chair up to sit beside the bed. "We've been so worried about you. How are you? How are you feeling?"

He looked over at her, his dark-eyed gaze meeting hers.

"I've been better," he answered, not wanting to admit just how bad he really was feeling.

"Will you be up and around soon?" Zach asked.

"Doc hasn't said yet. I'm hoping I won't be stuck here in bed too much longer."

Katie asked the question that was on everyone's mind: "Have you had any word back from your sister yet?"

"No. Nothing. I tell you, this waiting and not being able to do anything is hard—real hard," he admitted in frustration.

Impulsively, Larissa reached out and took his hand in hers. "We're here for you if you need anything."

"I know—and I appreciate it. Just seeing you today helps; believe me. I'm not used to sitting around waiting for things to happen."

"I heard Cal Harris talking about the man you hired to do the tracking, and Cal seems to think that Trent Marshall is the best," Zach offered.

"I hope Cal's right," Mason said.

They changed the topic to try to lighten the mood of their visit. They spoke of events in town for a few more minutes until Dr. Murray returned.

"I think that's enough excitement for Mason on this trip," he told them.

"We'll be back to see you again," Larissa promised, getting up to leave.

"I'm glad you came. It was really good to see you."

Dr. Murray closed the door once they were gone from the room.

"So, how have you been feeling?" he asked as he unwrapped the wound.

"I'm a little stronger, I think. How soon can I start getting up and moving around?"

"I know you're in a hurry, but don't push yourself too hard. You're better off in the long run to take it slow."

His advice wasn't what Mason wanted to hear, even though he knew the doctor was probably right. He'd never been shot before, and it was troubling to him to discover he was, after all, human. He'd always believed he was strong enough to do whatever he wanted to do when he wanted to do it, and up until now he had been. It wasn't easy for him to accept his limitations.

Dr. Murray checked his wound. He cleansed it and rebandaged it.

"If you want to try to get up and sit in a chair for an hour or two each day, start with that. I'll come back again toward the end of the week and we'll see how you're holding up."

"Thanks, Doc."

"You take care."

Dr. Murray stopped to talk with Rose for a minute while Larissa and the others went back in to say good-bye. When they came out again, it was time for them to go.

It had been hard for Larissa to leave Mason. She could see the pain and sadness in his eyes, and she wanted to stay there with him, to try to cheer him, but she knew she couldn't. She was only a friend to him—nothing more.

As they were riding home in the carriage, Larissa asked, "Is Mason really going to be all right?"

"As long as no infection sets in, he should be," her father reassured her.

"You can tell this has been really hard on him," Katie said. "Do you think they'll ever find Abbie?"

"I hope so," he answered. "Faith is a strong woman to be out riding with the tracker herself. She won't give up as long as there's any hope of finding her sister."

At that moment, Faith wasn't feeling very strong, not that she would admit it to anyone. Trent had been serious when he'd told them at the onset that he rode hard and fast. He was proving to them just how tough he was, and she had to admit to herself that she was impressed. Faith had always considered herself just about any man's equal, and she was determined not to show any weakness around Trent. She knew he hadn't wanted her along, and she wasn't about to give him any reason to ride off and leave her behind. The endless hours in the saddle were taking their toll on her, but she would make it. What she was going through was nothing compared to what Abbie had to be suffering.

"How did you come to be a hired gun?" Faith asked as she rode beside Trent.

Trent glanced over at her as he answered, "Some years back, I caught a killer and got the reward for bringing him in. I was glad to see justice done, and getting paid just made it that much better. It seemed a good way to make a living, so I've been at it ever since."

"Where did you learn how to track?"

"A friend—Old Jim. He was part Comanche. He taught me everything. He rode with me for quite a few years early on."

Faith understood where his confidence came from now. "Do you know this territory? Have you ridden this way before?"

"Once, a few years ago. There's a ranch not too far ahead. We can stop there and see if they've had any run-ins with the raiding party."

"What if they haven't?"

"Then we'll keep riding."

CHAPTER TWELVE

Trent had to admit to himself that he was impressed by Faith's stamina. She was keeping up with him without complaining. He could tell just by looking at her that she was tired, but she never suggested that they rest.

Trent saw them first. He didn't want to believe it, but there they were—buzzards circling in the distance over some unseen carcass. A sense of dread filled him as he imagined what their party was about to come upon. He reined in, drawing puzzled looks from the others.

"What's wrong?" Jake asked quickly.

"Stay here with Faith while Hank and I ride ahead," he ordered.

"Why?" Faith demanded. She could tell by his tone that something was wrong.

Trent looked over at her. He knew there was no way to break it to her gently. There never was with this kind of news. "There are some buzzards up there—"

"No!" It was torn from her.

"They're circling just over that rise. Wait here." He said no more, but urged his horse on.

Hank looked over at Faith. "Trent's right. You stay here."

Trent and Hank disappeared from sight, leaving Faith and Jake tense and uneasy.

"It can't be Abbie," she said, trying to convince herself. "It can't be."

"I'm praying you're right," Jake said solemnly.

Trent led the way, keeping an eye on the buzzards overhead. He wasn't sure what he was going to find, but whatever it was, it wasn't going to be pretty. As they drew nearer, Trent realized there had been horses through the area not too long before, and he was torn between excitement that he might have picked up the trail again and fear of what he was about to discover.

"Do you think it's Abbie?" Hank asked grimly. Tracker that he was, he'd seen the trail, too.

"With the trail here—" He broke off uneasily.

Both men fell silent as they continued on.

And then Trent spotted them—the naked bodies of two men.

"It's not Abbie."

They dismounted and went to examine the bodies.

The scene was horrible. They could tell the battle had been fierce and bloody, and then the buzzards had set upon the dead men. Their flesh was torn, and their eyeballs were missing.

Trent was glad he'd ordered Faith to stay behind with Jake.

"It was the raiding party, all right," Trent said with certainty as he looked over the area, studying which direction they'd ridden out.

"What should we do with these two?"

"We'll bury them."

Hank had thought Trent would want to ride on immediately, and he was surprised that the other man was willing to take the time to do the right thing. "Any idea who they were?"

"No. There's nothing left to identify them. Ride on up and tell Faith and Jake what we've found, while I start digging the graves. You might want to keep Faith away as long as you can."

"I'll try, but you know how she is."

"I'm finding out," Trent said grimly, then set to work.

Faith and Jake had been waiting tensely to hear what the others had discovered. They saw Hank on his way back, looking grim, and shared a troubled look. They weren't sure what he was going to tell them.

Hank knew what they were thinking and wanted to ease their worry. As soon as he was within earshot, he called out, "It's not Abbie."

"Thank God." Faith was so relieved she almost burst into tears. Somehow she controlled herself.

"Who was it?" Jake asked.

"Two men. The raiding party killed them."

"So we've found their trail again?" Faith asked quickly, torn by terribly conflicting emotions. A part of her mourned the murdered men, but a part of her rejoiced that they might have found the trail again.

"It looks that way. Trent wants to bury them before we head out."

"We'd better help him," Jake said, then looked at Faith. "Do you want to wait here?"

"No. I'll come with you."

It was a gruesome task, but they managed to bury the dead. They stood quietly over the unmarked graves as they each offered up a silent prayer for the brutally murdered men.

"Let's ride," Trent said.

They were soon heading out.

"Looks like you were right to trust your instincts," Hank told him.

Trent ignored his praise. They hadn't found Abbie yet.

Faith had been deeply shaken by the events of the day, and she could tell that Jake had been, too. When they made camp for the night, Jake wandered off to be alone for a while, but this time Faith went after him. She understood far too well what was troubling him.

"Jake." She said softly as she found him sitting on a rock, staring off into the darkness.

"What is it, Faith?" His shoulders were slumped as if they carried the weight of the world upon them.

"Do you want to talk?"

Jake drew a ragged breath as he glanced over at her. "I thought Abbie was dead today. I thought we were going to find her there."

"But we didn't," she reassured him. "There's still hope."

He looked away again. "I should have told her. . . ."

"Told her what?"

"The night of the social . . . I should have told her that I loved her," he said, agony plain in his voice. "I wanted to propose to her, but I was afraid she wasn't ready to hear it yet, so I waited."

"Oh, Jake—I'm so sorry." She understood his pain. "But we're going to find her. I know we are, and when we do, you can tell her then."

"I want to believe what you're saying, but with every day that passes, the chances of finding her get worse. Who knows how far ahead of us they are?"

"It doesn't matter. We're going to catch up with them. Trent's going to lead us to her, and she's going to be fine. You'll see," she said, voicing the hopes she held in her heart.

Jake only nodded and got up to return to the camp. "You coming?"

"In a while," she answered.

Faith watched him walk away, her heart filled with great sadness. The events of the day suddenly and completely overwhelmed her. A pain deep in her heart wrenched at her, and she knew she needed to be alone for a while. She told herself she had to be strong—that there was no alternative. But in spite of all her determination to stay in control of her fragile emotions, the memory of the fear that had jolted through her when Trent had pointed out the circling buzzards left her devastated.

Unable to stop herself, Faith started to cry. She tried to muffle the sound, not wanting anyone to know of her torment. Alone in the night, she wept, giving vent to all the sorrow she had tried so hard to deny.

When Trent saw Jake returning, he asked, "Where's Faith?"

"She said she was going to sit out there by herself awhile."

Trent understood the torment she was going through. He got up and went to find her. As he walked in the direction from which Jake had just come, he heard her crying in the darkness. She hadn't heard his approach, and he stood there silently behind her for a moment, giving her the time she needed.

"Faith," he finally said softly.

"Oh . . . I didn't hear you coming," she said, nervously turning to face him.

"I didn't mean to sneak up on you. I was just worried about you. I know it's been a rough day."

"I'm all right," Faith said, trying to deny the pain she was feeling.

"Are you sure?"

"No . . . no, I'm not sure. I don't think I'll ever be

sure of anything again. I was so scared this afternoon when you saw those buzzards." A shudder racked her at the torturous memory. "I was so afraid it was Abbie."

She felt totally vulnerable as she relived that horrible moment in her mind.

"But it wasn't," he reassured her.

"I know, but those poor men . . ."

"There's nothing more we can do for them. We have to concentrate on finding your sister."

"If we can ever find her." The despair within her could not be denied.

"We will."

She looked up at him. He sounded so confident, so sure. She wanted to believe him. She had to believe him. "Oh, Trent . . ."

Trent saw her need and closed the distance between them. Without saying another word, he took her in his arms and held her close.

Faith had never known such a safe haven. Trent was strong and powerful. He was a shelter against the harshness of the savage world that surrounded them. Weary of her own struggle to be strong, she clung to him, needing the strength and reassurance she felt in his embrace. Her troubled spirits eased as she gave herself into his keeping.

Trent sensed her surrender, and he gathered her even closer, holding her to his heart. A shuddering breath racked her as she surrendered to the peace that came with being in his arms. He sensed the change in her as he held her close, and lifted one hand to her cheek to tilt her face to him.

"Are you all right?" he asked, his voice husky with emotion.

"I am now," she whispered, looking up at him.

In that moment, as their gazes met there in the quiet peace of the night, she felt drawn to him. Trent felt it, too, and without speaking, he bent to her and claimed her lips in a soft, tender kiss.

It was heaven—a pure sanctuary being close to him, and she lifted her arms to encircle his neck.

At first Trent had been hesitant to deepen the kiss, but at her move he gave in to his need for her. He kissed her hungrily, his lips moving over hers in a possessive exchange.

Excitement coursed through Faith. She'd been kissed by other men before, but no kiss had ever affected her like this. Trent's kiss was pure ecstasy. Lost in the pleasure of his embrace, she responded eagerly.

Trent had known from the first moment he'd seen her at the social that he was attracted to Faith, but he'd never known how much until now. His body ached with his desire for her. He could feel the enticing crush of her breasts against his chest, and her hips nestled against his.

His need for Faith was powerful, but Trent was a man who prided himself on being in control. He knew he had to end the kiss and put her from him. He didn't want to. He wanted to hold her and kiss her and make love to her, but this was not the time.

They were on a hunt to find her sister. He

couldn't take advantage of Faith's emotional vulnerability by making love to her now. She might hate him afterward if he did.

Reluctantly, Trent ended the kiss and set her away from him.

Faith had been caught up in the passion of his embrace, and she was confused when he ended it. She looked up at him—at his ruggedly handsome features and firm, sensuous lips—and wanted to go back into his arms and kiss him again.

And then reality returned.

She was glad it was dark, so he couldn't see that she was blushing. She was embarrassed to have lost control the way she had.

"We'd better get back," he told her.

"You're right . . . we'd better."

She started back toward the campsite, leaving Trent to follow.

CHAPTER THIRTEEN

Mason knew something was wrong when he awoke just before dawn the following morning. He felt disoriented and confused, and weaker than he'd ever felt before. He realized he needed help.

Struggling to maneuver himself out of the bed, he managed to get to his feet and stagger through the open bedroom doorway. Waves of dizziness swept over him. He braced himself against the wall and shook his head, trying to clear it, but it did little good. Keeping one hand on the wall to steady himself, he moved on down the hall toward the front of the house. He made it to the front door and had just managed to open it when his strength completely gave out and he collapsed.

Tom and some of the ranch hands were already up and working. They noticed that the front door was open, and, realizing that they hadn't seen Rose up at the house yet, Tom went to see if there was anything wrong.

"It's Mason! Somebody go get Rose!" he shouted the minute he caught sight of Mason lying on the floor. "I'm going to need some help here!"

Two of the men ran to help him while another went to get Rose.

"Take it easy with him," Tom directed as they carefully lifted Mason to carry him back to his bed. Tom feared Mason's gunshot wound might reopen if they tried to move him too quickly.

"What happened to him?"

"I don't know, but he seems awful warm."

Mason let out a low groan as they laid him back on the bed.

When Rose came rushing in, she took one look at his flushed features and knew what was wrong.

"He's got a fever." She had feared this would happen. "One of you ride to town and get Dr. Murray out here."

She took charge, trying to cool Mason down as best she could while she awaited the doctor's arrival.

Larissa was home alone when she heard someone pounding on the front door and calling out for her father. This wasn't an unusual occurrence. There were a lot of times when emergencies brought people to the house at all hours of the day and night. In fact, a ranch hand from the Nolan spread had come to the house just past midnight the night before. He had told them that Mrs. Nolan had been in labor for a long time and was having a difficult time delivering her baby. Both her father and her mother had ridden in the carriage together out to the Nolan ranch. Her mother's talent as a midwife was well known.

Now Larissa wondered who else was in need of her father. When she opened the door to find Burt, one of the men from the Lazy R, standing there, she was struck by the fear that something might have happened to Mason.

"Is the doc home?" Burt asked, looking past her in hopes of catching a glimpse of her father. "We need him out at the ranch."

"What's happened?" she asked. "What's wrong?"

"It's Mason," he began. "He's taken a fever, and it's bad."

"My father's not here." Her mind was racing as she tried to decide what to do. She knew she could send word to the Nolan place about what had happened, but there was no guarantee that her father could get out to help Mason anytime soon.

"Where is he? I'll go get him."

"He's out at the Nolan ranch. Mrs. Nolan's delivering her baby. Ride out and tell him what happened, and tell him I've gone to the Lazy R to help with Mason."

"You're going?" he asked, surprised.

"I know some of what my father does to treat fevers. I'll do what I can until he can get there."

Larissa had always been fascinated by her father's healing ability. He had taught her a lot about caring for the sick and infirm, and she knew that knowledge was going to come to good use right now.

"Don't you need somebody to ride out to the ranch with you?"

"I'll be all right. You just hurry and get word to my father."

Burt hastened to leave. It was a long ride out to the Nolan ranch.

Larissa went into the room where her father kept some of his medicine and supplies. She gathered the few things he'd told her were used to treat fevers and got ready to go. Since her parents had taken the carriage, she knew she was going to have to ride out on horseback. She quickly changed into her riding clothes and went to saddle up her horse. There was no time to waste. Mason needed her.

Dottie lived next door to Dr. Murray and his family. She was never intentionally nosy, but she'd been awakened by all the noise of the emergency in the middle of the night and had been unable to fall back asleep. She'd been up ever since, wondering what had happened. When she'd seen Burt pounding on the door at the doctor's house just now, she'd feared something was terribly wrong out at the Lazy R, and hurried over to find out. Just as she reached the front of the house, where Larissa's horse was saddled and waiting, Larissa came outside dressed for riding and carrying one of her father's small black tote bags.

"Larissa, what's happened?" Dottie asked.

Larissa quickly explained about her father's absence and Mason's suddenly worsening condition and high fever. "I'm going to see if there's anything I can do to help Mason until my father gets there. I don't know if I can do much, but I'm going to try."

"You say he's running a really high fever?"

"That's what Burt told me."

"Then let me get you the ammonia compound I've got. It helps with dangerous fevers."

"Thank you, Dottie." She knew of her elderly neighbor's past history, that she'd worked as a nurse during the war.

Dottie rushed into her house to get the compound, then hurried back out to give it to Larissa. "Wipe him down with this. It will help cool him off, and some say it even eases the pain."

"I will."

"Hurry on, now. He needs you."

Dottie stood back and watched as Larissa mounted up and rode out of town. She'd known for a long time how Larissa felt about Mason, and she could well imagine the anxiety the young woman was feeling. She started back inside, offering up a silent prayer for Mason and Mrs. Nolan.

Rose heard a rider coming and hoped it was Dr. Murray. She rushed to the front of the house to let him in, only to discover it was his daughter, Larissa, and she was riding in all alone.

"Where's your pa?" Rose demanded as she went outside to meet her.

"He's out at the Nolan place. I'm sure he'll be here as soon as he's finished. I brought some of his medicines with me. I thought I could help until my father arrives."

"Well, come on in," Rose said, quickly ushering her inside. "Mason is not doing well."

Rose went on to tell Larissa what had happened that morning as she led her back to Mason's bedroom. "It was lucky his wound didn't reopen when he fell, but his fever is high."

Larissa followed the housekeeper into Mason's room and stood for a moment, just staring at him as he lay in bed. He was flushed, and she could tell his breathing was fast and labored.

"I've been keeping a wet towel on his forehead, and wiping him down to try to cool him off."

"That's good. I brought quinine. I know the dosage my father always gives, so we can start with that, and Dottie gave me an ammonia compound that she says will help cool him down, too."

Larissa went to Mason's bedside and quickly set about preparing the medicine the way she'd watched her father do. A pitcher of water, a basin, and a glass were on the nightstand, so she mixed up the solution there. It wasn't easy, but with Rose's help she lifted his shoulders up enough so she could get him to swallow the medication. She was relieved that he managed to get most of it down.

"What more do you think we should do?" Rose asked.

"I think you've been doing the right thing, trying

to keep him as cool as possible. I can take over for a while, if you want to rest."

"Thanks. If you need anything, I'll be in the parlor."

When Rose had gone, Larissa emptied the water from the basin and got out Dottie's compound. She poured it in the basin, then soaked the small towel Rose had been using to cool Mason off and began to wipe it across his forehead and down the side of his neck. With stroke after gentle stroke, she wiped his shoulders and arms. She could feel the heat emanating from him and hoped her efforts would work quickly to break the debilitating fever.

"Mason Ryan, you have got to get well," Larissa ordered in a low voice as she continued to lovingly stroke his neck and shoulders with the wet towel. The horror of his being shot was terrible enough to deal with, but to think that now she might lose him from a fever was too much for her to bear.

She stared down at the broad, tan width of his chest. Though it was heavily bandaged, there was still no doubt he was a strong man. He'd been through a lot, but she believed he could make it. She offered up a prayer that the fever would break soon. She didn't want him to suffer any more than he already had.

It was about an hour later when she heard someone come into the house, and then the sound of a man speaking with Rose in the parlor. She thought she recognized the voice as belonging to Rose's husband, Tom, who was the foreman on the Lazy R.

She found out a few minutes later that she'd been right, when Rose came down the hall with him to check on Mason.

"How's he doing?" Tom asked quietly.

"I got a dose of quinine in him, and I've been trying to cool him down," Larissa explained.

"He's burning up; that's for sure." Tom could tell just by looking at Mason. "Do you have any idea when your father might get here?"

"I wish I did," she answered. "I sent Burt out to the Nolan place to let him know he was needed here."

Mason emitted a low groan just then, and she quickly turned back to sponging him down with the cloth.

"What are you using?" Tom asked.

"It's a special ammonia compound. Sometimes it helps reduce a bad fever like this. Dottie gave it to me when I told her about Mason."

"I hope it works," Tom said gravely.

"I do, too."

"Is there anything else we can do to help until your father shows up?"

"I don't think so. I'll stay with him and keep sponging him down," she answered.

"All right. If you need anything, just let me know. I'll be out in the kitchen," Rose said.

As they started from the room, Tom paused to look back at Mason one last time. He gave a slow nod toward Larissa, his expression grave, then walked out.

Larissa pulled the chair up next to the bed and sat

GET UP TO
4 FREE BOOKS!

You can have the best romance delivered to your door for less than what you'd pay in a bookstore or online. Sign up for one of our book clubs today, and we'll send you **FREE* BOOKS** just for trying it out...**with no obligation to buy, ever!**

HISTORICAL ROMANCE BOOK CLUB

Travel from the Scottish Highlands to the American West, the decadent ballrooms of Regency England to Viking ships. Your shipments will include authors such as CONNIE MASON, SANDRA HILL, CASSIE EDWARDS, JENNIFER ASHLEY, LEIGH GREENWOOD, and many, many more.

LOVE SPELL BOOK CLUB

Bring a little magic into your life with the romances of Love Spell—fun contemporaries, paranormals, time-travels, futuristics, and more. Your shipments will include authors such as LYNSAY SANDS, CJ BARRY, COLLEEN THOMPSON, NINA BANGS, MARJORIE LIU and more.

As a book club member you also receive the following special benefits:

- **30% OFF** all orders through our website & telecenter!
- **Exclusive access to** special discounts!
- **Convenient** home delivery **and 10 day examination period to return any books you don't want to keep.**

There is no minimum number of books to buy, and you may cancel membership at any time. See back to sign up!

*Please include $2.00 for shipping and handling.

YES! ☐

Sign me up for the **Historical Romance Book Club** and send my TWO FREE BOOKS! If I choose to stay in the club, I will pay only $8.50* each month, a savings of $5.48!

YES! ☐

Sign me up for the **Love Spell Book Club** and send my TWO FREE BOOKS! If I choose to stay in the club, I will pay only $8.50* each month, a savings of $5.48!

NAME: _____

ADDRESS: _____

_____

TELEPHONE: _____

E-MAIL: _____

☐ **I WANT TO PAY BY CREDIT CARD.**

☐ VISA   ☐ MasterCard.   ☐ DISCOVER

ACCOUNT #: _____

EXPIRATION DATE: _____

SIGNATURE: _____

Send this card along with $2.00 shipping & handling for each club you wish to join, to:

**Romance Book Clubs
20 Academy Street
Norwalk, CT 06850-4032**

Or fax (must include credit card information!) to: 610.995.9274. You can also sign up online at www.dorchesterpub.com.

*Plus $2.00 for shipping. Offer open to residents of the U.S. and Canada only. Canadian residents please call 1.800.481.9191 for pricing information.

If under 18, a parent or guardian must sign. Terms, prices and conditions subject to change. Subscription subject to acceptance. Dorchester Publishing reserves the right to reject any order or cancel any subscription.

JOIN NOW!

down beside Mason. Her gaze went over him, tracing a loving visual caress over his ruggedly handsome features and the broad width of his shoulders. There was no doubt in her mind how she felt about him. She loved him. She always had and she always would. She didn't know if he felt the same way about her, but right then it didn't matter. All that mattered was getting the fever to break and making sure he recovered. Reaching out, she took his hand in hers and then stayed quiet, waiting and hoping that he had enough strength left in him to battle back.

Another hour passed, and Larissa noticed that Mason seemed to grow tenser as he lay there. It happened suddenly. Caught up in the grip of the fever, he began to toss restlessly about on the bed, fighting some unseen enemy and shouting out as visions of the hell he'd lived through began to torment him.

The memory of the bullet slamming into him tore at him. . . .

The agonizing knowledge that he hadn't been able to help Abbie when she'd need him the most . . .

Devastating images of his sister helpless at the hands of the murderous renegades . . .

"Abbie—no!" he groaned, thrashing and twisting about. Then, suddenly, he tried to sit up.

Fearful that he would injure himself even more, Larissa put her hands on his shoulders and tried to press him back down on the bed. "Mason, Mason—it's all right!"

But Mason was beyond reason. He knew only

that someone was trying to restrain him—to stop him from reaching Abbie. He reached up and grabbed her wrists and shoved her away from him.

"I have to get to Abbie."

Larissa staggered backward from the bed. She couldn't believe the strength Mason had mustered to push her away. Again he tried to get up, and she went back to his side.

She spoke to him soothingly, not wanting him to hurt himself even more. "Mason, it's all right—you're home."

His eyes were open, but even though he was looking straight at her, she could tell he didn't see her. He was delirious in the grip of the fever. Then, as quickly as his violent moves had come on, they stopped, and he collapsed back on his pillow and went still, closing his eyes again.

Rose had heard Mason's shout and rushed back to the bedroom to see what was wrong and whether she could help. She came in just as Larissa was trying to get him to lie still.

"What happened?"

"He's delirious," she explained, close to tears as she realized there had been no improvement in his condition.

"You go rest for a while. I'll stay with him," Rose said.

Larissa wanted to stay with Mason, but seeing him this way was breaking her heart. She went to stand in the parlor and, unable to help herself, gave vent to her tears. She tried not to make any sound. She didn't want Rose to know how distraught she was.

And then she felt a gentle, comforting hand on her shoulder.

"Larissa." Rose spoke softly to her. She understood what the young woman was going through.

Larissa drew a ragged breath and turned to give Rose a teary half smile.

"He's quiet now, and hopefully that won't happen again."

"It's just so hard to see him this way and not be able to do anything to help." She looked past the housekeeper toward his bedroom doorway.

"Oh, but you are helping. You came here all on your own, when there was no one else available." Rose could see the pain in Larissa's eyes. "Go on back in there and stay with him. That's where you want to be. That's where you need to be."

Larissa knew Rose was right. She wiped away her tears and returned to keep her vigil at Mason's side.

Burt came back from his long trek to the Nolan ranch with word from her father that the baby had been born but that both the mother and child were sickly, and that he would get there as soon as he could make it.

The rest of the day passed slowly. Several times, different ranch hands came up to the house to check on Mason and see how he was doing. They kept hoping for some good news, but there was none. His condition had not changed.

As evening drew near, Rose got the meal ready to serve, and Larissa came out of the bedroom long enough to eat with her at the kitchen table.

"Will you be staying the night?" Rose asked, hoping Larissa wasn't planning to leave.

"I'll stay at least until my father arrives," she promised.

"Thank you. I know Faith will be forever indebted to you when she learns what you've done, and I am, too." Rose looked back down the hall toward Mason's room. "I just hope to God he doesn't get any worse overnight."

She had voiced the fear that gripped them both.

"So do I."

They shared a worried look across the table and said no more. Larissa found she couldn't eat much, even though the food was delicious. She left most of her dinner on the plate and went back to keep watch over Mason.

CHAPTER FOURTEEN

Mason's thoughts were jumbled, and nothing seemed real as he slowly came awake. His head hurt and he ached all over. He tried to remember what had happened during the day, but his mind was blank. He opened his eyes to look around, wondering what time it was, and it was then that he saw her.

Larissa—asleep in a chair beside his bed in the dimly lit bedroom.

For a moment Mason thought he'd died and gone to heaven and that she was an angel, but then he realized he wasn't dead. He felt too bad.

And with the recognition of the pain came memories.

Mason frowned, confused, wondering why she was there . . . with him.

"Larissa." He managed to say her name, though his voice was hoarse.

Larissa awoke instantly at the sound of his voice and quickly went to him. "Mason, you're awake."

"What time is it?" he asked, trying to get oriented.

"It's late—after midnight, I'm sure," she told him.

"Why are you here?"

"You had a bad fever. Rose sent for my father, but he wasn't home, so I came out to help her."

"How long ago was that?"

"Early yesterday morning." She gazed down at him, all the joy she was feeling over his obvious improvement shining in her eyes. "Thank God you're better."

"It was that bad? I don't remember much."

"Be glad that you don't—it was terrible."

"And you stayed?"

"My father still wasn't back from the Nolan ranch, and I didn't want to leave Rose here by herself. I was too afraid for you."

Mason looked up at Larissa, seeing her beauty, and her kindness, and her generosity. Until this moment he hadn't realized just how much he cared for her, but her devotion touched him, and he knew then the truth and depth of his feelings for her. He lifted his hand toward her, and he was glad when she didn't hesitate to take it, holding it tight. Ever so gently, Mason drew her to him.

"Thank you," he whispered.

"Oh, Mason."

He slowly pulled her down close and kissed her.

Rose had chosen to sleep at the main house in the extra bedroom that night, just in case something happened. The sound of voices awakened her, and she feared Mason was delirious again. She got up, threw on her robe, and hurried toward the bedroom.

"Larissa? Is something wrong?" she asked as she rushed into the room, only to find Mason alive and well, giving Larissa a kiss. She stopped and stood still near the doorway.

"Oh, Rose." Larissa shifted nervously away from Mason, embarrassed that Rose had caught them kissing. "I . . ."

Rose's shock gave way to pure happiness, and she broke into a bright smile as she looked at the two of them. "Well, of all the things I expected to see when I came rushing in here, that wasn't one of them." She looked at Mason. "I think it's safe to say you're back among the living now . . . ?"

"Thanks to you and Larissa," he told her.

"I'm just glad your fever's finally broken," Rose said. She came in and stood at the opposite side of the bed from Larissa. "How do you feel? Do you think you could eat something?"

"Food sounds good—real good," he answered.

"Now, that sounds like the Mason I know." Rose laughed. "I'll be right back with some broth for you."

"I was thinking of something more like a steak," he called after her as she turned to go.

"You *are* feeling better."

"Rose."

Rose looked back at Mason.

"Has there been any word from Faith?"

Her gaze met his across the room. "No. Nothing."

She left them alone while she went to prepare his broth.

Mason gave a slow shake of his head. "I wonder where they are. I wonder if they're even getting close."

"I heard my father and mother talking, and they were saying they'd heard Trent Marshall was every bit as good as his reputation claims."

"I hope what they heard is true. I was impressed with him when I talked to him that day, but with the big head start the raiding party had, it's going to take the best to track Abbie down. If they've had any luck at all, they should be closing in on the renegades by now."

Abbie had lost all track of time, and she was beginning to lose any hope that she would ever be rescued. With every mile they covered, she grew ever more mentally and physically drained. She merely existed, trying not to think beyond the moment. She'd been relieved when she was finally allowed to ride her own horse again. When she'd been forced to ride double, the unavoidable close contact with the warrior had been unsettling for her.

They had been riding since dawn, and she knew something strange was going on when they stopped late in the morning.

"Black Cloud and Lone Eagle, ride with me," Crooked Snake ordered. "We will check on the ranch. It is only a short distance ahead. Little Dog, tie up the captive and be ready. If all is as it should be, we will come back for you and then we will attack."

"Where do you want me to leave the Golden One when we go on the raid?" Little Dog asked.

Lone Eagle had been looking around and saw a place among some rocks that would shield her from view and from the sun. He wanted to make sure she would still be there when they got back.

"Tie her up and leave her there, where she will be hidden," Lone Eagle told him, pointing out the place.

Little Dog dismounted and went to pull her down off her horse.

"What are you doing?" Abbie demanded, resisting his efforts. Something about this warrior troubled her, and she didn't want his hands upon her. She had noticed how they had all been looking around the area, and couldn't imagine what they were planning.

Little Dog ignored her protest and forced her to dismount.

"Stay with him," Lone Eagle ordered, knowing Little Dog spoke no English.

Abbie did as she was told and watched helplessly as her captor rode off with the other two warriors, leaving her alone with the one who frightened her.

Little Dog got a rope to restrain her, then grabbed her by the wrist and hauled her after him. He led her to the spot they had chosen and pushed her down to sit on the ground. He knelt down before her and quickly bound her legs, then untied her wrists and twisted her arms behind her to tie them there.

"Why are you doing this? Stop!" Abbie tried to break away from him, but his hold on her was unyielding. She knew that if he was restraining her this way, they planned to leave her behind for some reason.

Little Dog finished tying her, then gagged her. He was smiling as he watched her struggling against her bonds.

He liked that she was helpless before him.

He liked that she could not fight him or scream now.

His smile broadened even more at the thought. The others were gone, and they would never know. . . .

Abbie realized from the tightness of her bonds that she would not escape them. She looked up at the warrior, and, in that moment, she saw the evil lust in his expression. Her breath caught in her throat, and she went completely still.

Little Dog reached out and brushed aside the makeshift top Lone Eagle had made for her. With the blanket out of the way, he pushed her ripped blouse down off her shoulders as far as it would go, pawing at her as he did so. He could see the swell of her breasts above her undergarment, and he slipped his hand beneath the chemise to grope her intimately.

Abbie let out a squeal of disgust and tried to twist away from him, but there was no escape. She shuddered as he ran his hands over her, down her hips and thighs, touching her in intimate ways she'd never been touched before. She felt violated and sick. She wanted to fight back, to force him to leave her alone, but it was useless. There was no way she could defend herself, no way she could escape his abuse. She began to cry soundlessly as she prayed for deliverance. She did not know what he might do to her next, and she was terrified.

Little Dog was truly enjoying himself as he tormented the captive. He hated whites with a passion and wanted to do all he could to destroy them. Heat was rising up within him as he continued to fondle the Golden One. The need within him grew ever stronger, so he leaned closer and rubbed himself against her.

A part of him wanted to take the Golden One right then and there.

He wanted to bury himself inside her.

Animal passion was driving him; only the thought of what Crooked Snake would do to him if he did rape her stopped him, turning his passion to fury. With near violent intensity, he thrust himself away from her and got up. In disgust, he stalked away and didn't look back.

Abbie's revulsion was so fierce, she couldn't stop shaking as she watched him go. She could only wait there in misery to see what was going to happen to her next.

Little Dog returned to where he'd left their horses to wait for the others to come back. He was surprised when they showed up rather quickly, and he realized then what trouble he would have been in if he'd given in to his need for the Golden One.

"You have bound her well? You are certain she will not get away?" Crooked Snake asked.

"She will be here when we return," Little Dog said with confidence.

"Good. Then it is time," Crooked Snake said.

Little Dog quickly mounted up to ride with them.

Lone Eagle wanted to check on the Golden One, but knew there was no time.

With their weapons ready, the raiding party rode for the ranch house.

Having scouted the area before, they knew how many men were working there, and they also knew two women lived on the ranch as well. They moved in close, taking care not to be seen. They needed the element of surprise on their side, and they had it. They launched their attack suddenly, catching the workers completely off guard. They brutally slaughtered most of the ranch hands as they tried to run for cover.

At the first sound of gunfire, Ellie Gray and her sixteen-year-old daughter, Caroline, were shocked to see a raiding party attacking. They ran for the house, hoping to get their guns and fight off the attackers.

"Hurry!" Ellie screamed to Caroline.

They raced inside, shutting and barring the door behind them. Neither spoke. They had always feared something like this might happen—and now it had.

Ellie prayed for help to come, but knew it was unlikely. Her husband, John, and most of their men were on a trail drive and not due back for several more days. They had only themselves to rely on, and, after they'd witnessed the cold-blooded slaughter of the few hands who'd been there, that prospect was frightening.

Black Cloud and Little Dog saw the women flee into the house, and they went after them.

Ellie and Caroline heard gunfire still erupting outside, and they were relieved to know that at least a few of the men had survived the initial attack.

"Get the windows!" Ellie ordered, wanting to make sure none of the raiding party could get into the house. She didn't know how long they could hold the attackers off, but they had to try.

Caroline ran to shutter the windows while her mother got rifles down from the gun rack, took their handguns from the locked desk drawer, and gathered up whatever ammunition she could find. They were going to need it—all of it.

Ellie gave Caroline a rifle and a handgun when she returned to join her. She took one of each for herself. They carried all the ammunition with them and took up positions at the two windows at the front of the house.

"How many Apache were there?" Ellie asked.

"I only saw three," Caroline answered, "but from

the sound of all the gunfire there could have been more—a lot more."

"What about the men? Do you know how many of them made it to the stable or out to the bunkhouse?"

"No."

Mother and daughter shared a look of pain at the knowledge that many of the men who worked for them were dead.

They turned back to face the reality of what was happening outside. Gunfire was still going on down by the stable. Ellie and Caroline couldn't see any of the fighting now, but they could see the bodies of at least two of their men, lying unmoving in the dirt.

Then suddenly it went eerily quiet outside.

A chill of terror went through the two women.

"Be ready," Ellie warned, instinctively tightening her grip on the rifle she was holding.

They were as ready as they could be to fight off the Apache, but when they smelled smoke, their terror grew still greater.

"What's burning?"

"I don't know." Caroline ran to check the back of the house. "It's not the house."

"Yet."

Their gazes met, and they knew that even though they were safe for the moment, the house would be next. Unless help came, their fate was sealed.

Crooked Snake watched in satisfaction as the stable went up in flames. They'd already run off the stock and were now ready to go after the women.

"Black Cloud, it is time. Set fire to the back of the house."

Black Cloud understood Crooked Snake's plan. They would force the women to flee the burning house and take them captive as they ran outside. He hurried off to start the fire.

Inside, Ellie and Caroline waited tensely to see what would happen next, but they didn't have to wait long. They heard noises at the back of the house, and then their worst fear came into being. Smoke began to billow into the house as the fire grew.

"What are we going to do?" Caroline was hysterical.

"There's only one thing we can do—we've got to try to make a run for it."

"Where are we going to run to? What if they've set everything else on fire, too?"

"We don't have any choice. We have to get out of the house while we still can. Are you ready?"

"Yes."

They had heard the stories of what happened to women who were taken by the Apache, and they knew it would be terrible, but they had no choice. To stay in the house meant certain death. Smoke and heat were already filling the room.

"I love you, Caroline," Ellie told her daughter, taking her in her arms for one last, deeply emotional embrace.

"I love you, too, Mama," Caroline said, crying.

"Take your handgun. At least we can get off some shots while we're running. And Caroline . . ."

Her daughter looked over at her, hearing the grave tone of her voice.

"No matter what happens, you keep running. Don't worry about me. Don't worry about anything but saving yourself. Do you understand me?" She pierced her daughter with a serious look.

"Yes, Mama." The words were choked from her.

"All right. Let's go—and remember, don't look back!"

They could wait no longer. The smoke and heat were overpowering.

Ellie threw open the door and ran out of the house, gun in hand, firing as she went.

"Run, Caroline! Run!" she shouted, leading the way from their burning home.

CHAPTER FIFTEEN

The warriors were waiting as the two women escaped the burning house. Black Cloud and Little Dog had hidden alongside the building, and they ran after the fleeing women.

Caroline caught sight of the warriors first and screamed. She turned and tried to fire her gun at them, but Black Cloud was too quick. He threw himself at her, knocking her to the ground. The gun flew from her grip.

"Caroline!"

Ellie had told her daughter not to stop running no matter what happened, but that didn't apply to her. There was no way she could abandon Caroline to the savages. Desperate to try to rescue her, Ellie turned and began shooting. She heard one of the Apache yell out in pain and hoped it was because her bullet had found its mark. She was so intent on trying to save Caroline that she didn't see Lone Eagle.

Lone Eagle had circled around behind the woman

and went after her quickly. She screamed when he grabbed her and tore the gun from her hand.

Both of the females fought to get away, but they were no match for the power of the warriors.

When Abbie had heard the gunfire so close by, she'd been shocked. She'd fought violently against the ropes that bound her, but knew it was useless. There was no way she would ever break free. All she could do was lie there and imagine what horrors were being played out somewhere nearby.

Abbie despised her captors. The memory of what had just transpired a short while before left her feeling filthy and degraded. As much as she hated the renegades, though, she realized that if they were killed in this raid, she would never be found. She would be left there alone, bound and gagged, to die. She was torn by conflicting feelings. She didn't want to hope for the warriors' return, and yet, the thought of dying there all alone was horrifying.

Abbie stared at the rocks that surrounded her. She was hot, miserable, despairing.

She had thought her existence couldn't get any worse.

And then she saw the rattlesnake slowly winding its way in her direction.

Abbie went completely still. She was helpless to do anything except pray that the snake didn't strike.

Lone Eagle and Little Dog rounded up the additional horses they needed to transport the women, while Crooked Snake and Black Cloud bound the captives and got them ready to ride. They forced the struggling females onto the horses and then rode away from the still-smoldering ruins of the ranch house and outbuildings, back to where they'd left the Golden One.

Ellie and Caroline were crying as they got what they feared might be their last look at what had been their home. They could see the bodies of the murdered cowhands and were filled with rage and sorrow. Ellie looked at her daughter and gave thanks that she hadn't been killed. As long as they were alive, there was hope.

"It was good that we raided the ranch," Crooked Snake said to the others, looking over the women they had just taken. He was certain they would bring a high price.

"Let us get the Golden One and cover many miles today," Black Cloud said. He suspected there were more men who worked for the ranch and feared they might try to come after the women once they discovered the ranch had been raided.

"You are right," Little Dog agreed.

They picked up their pace on their way to claim their other captive.

Lone Eagle was anxious to get back to the Golden One. Although Little Dog had said that he'd made sure she was tightly bound and wouldn't be able to get away, Lone Eagle wanted to make sure nothing had happened to her while they'd been gone.

At the sound of horses coming, Abbie was shocked to find she was almost relieved that the raiding party was back. But she had little time to think about her confusing emotions. Just then the rattlesnake that had curled up under a rock nearby emerged from its hiding place and began to move.

The warriors reined in close to the place where the Golden One had been left. Lone Eagle dismounted and went to get her as Black Cloud prepared her horse. There was no time to waste. They had to put as many miles as they could between themselves and the ranch before sundown.

Abbie was nervous. She wasn't sure which one of the warriors would be coming for her. If the one who'd abused her earlier showed up, she wasn't going to reveal anything about the snake. If the rattler struck him, she would be glad. He deserved that—and more.

Only when Abbie saw it was the other warrior coming to get her did she worry about how she could warn him. Fearful of being bitten herself, she didn't dare make any sudden moves. Instead she called out to him in grunting sounds to alert him as she nodded in the direction of the rattler.

Lone Eagle had been concentrating only on getting the Golden One back on her horse as quickly as possible, but he realized something was wrong by the way she was acting as he came upon her. He spotted the snake just as it was about to strike, and in one quick, smooth, accurate move, he drew his knife and threw it, killing the rattler instantly.

Abbie's eyes were wide with amazement as she looked up at the warrior. When the rattlesnake had prepared to strike, she'd feared that one or both of them would be bitten, but he'd killed it with one unerring strike.

"You did it," she gasped, once he'd knelt down beside her and removed her gag.

As she was speaking, Little Dog came running over. He had seen the way Lone Eagle had reacted, throwing his knife so quickly, and thought he had thrown it at the captive. When he got close enough, he could see that the Golden One was unharmed and talking, and he was puzzled by Lone Eagle's actions.

"What happened?" he asked.

"Rattlesnake," Lone Eagle told him, pointing it out.

Little Dog bent down to pick it up. He was smiling as he tossed the knife back to Lone Eagle and then stood up, holding the nearly severed snake by its tail. He took a step closer to the Golden One and enjoyed the look of fear that showed in her eyes as he waved the rattlesnake close to her. Little Dog's smile broadened. He walked away, carrying the dead rattler.

Lone Eagle untied the Golden One's ankles and helped her get to her feet. He unfastened her wrists and retied them in front of her so she would be able to ride.

"Come. We must go."

"What was all the gunfire about? What did you do?" she asked.

He ignored her questions as he led her down to where the others were waiting. Abbie had not known what to expect after hearing all the shooting, and she was startled to see that there were two other female captives sitting on horseback with their wrists tied before them, just as hers were. Their clothing was torn as hers had been, and they had been beaten, but they did not look too seriously injured. She noticed that they seemed just as surprised to see her, but none of them spoke. Abbie looked at the older of the two women and saw pain and devastation in her eyes. Abbie acknowledged her with only a slight nod before mounting her own horse. She hoped that later, when the warriors stopped for the night, they would have the chance to talk.

"Over there!" Faith shouted. "I think I see something!"

She wasn't sure what it had been—just a quick glimpse of color—but it had stood out on the rocky landscape. She rode away to check on it, leaving the men to follow.

The piece of cloth was caught in a low-growing shrub, but Faith recognized it as she got closer, and distress filled her. She jumped down from her horse and ran to tear the material out of the bush. She began to tremble as she stared down at the piece of cloth. There was no doubt it was from the blouse Abbie had been wearing the day she'd disappeared.

Trent, Jake, and Hank were there beside her in what seemed like an instant.

"Is it Abbie's?" Hank asked.

"Yes," was all she could manage in a choked voice as she lifted her gaze to stare off in the direction they were heading.

Abbie was out there somewhere close.

Now there was no doubt.

After a moment, Faith looked over at Trent. "You are as good as everyone said you were. Let's ride."

She tucked the cloth into her pocket and went to mount her horse.

Trent looked around the area, studying the ground before mounting up again, too. "Let's spread out, and keep a close lookout for a trail. Abbie was around here not too long ago."

They circled out, searching for the tracks from the raiding party, and Jake shouted excitedly when he came upon them leading off to the southwest.

Trent studied the trail, and he had a feeling he knew where the renegades were headed. A part of him hoped for the sake of the folks on the ranch up ahead that he was wrong, but he didn't think so.

Faith's heart had been racing ever since she'd found the cloth. She told herself to stay calm. She told herself not to get too excited, but this was the first real proof that they were closing in on Abbie and the raiding party. Faith couldn't deny that she was worried about Abbie's blouse being torn, but there was no blood on it, and she hung onto that consolation.

Jake had been furious when he'd first seen that Abbie's blouse had been torn. Had someone's hands been upon her, abusing her? He was filled with the driving need to protect and guard her. After his initial anger over the discovery passed, he was able to calm himself down. He reassured himself with the realization that it was a relief to know they were heading in the right direction, and that Abbie was still out there somewhere—alive.

"What's ahead?" Jake asked Trent as they rode on.

"There's a ranch. We'll reach it in the next day or two."

"Do you think they attacked them, too?"

"I guess we'll find out." He was grim.

Jake understood his mood and fell silent.

They rode until dark, making camp near a watering hole.

"This is the first time since we've been on the trail that I've really believed we'll be able to find her safe and sound," Faith offered, holding the scrap of material in her hands. "I've always held on to the hope that Abbie was still alive, but now, after finding this piece of her blouse, we have evidence that she came this way."

"How close do you think we are, Trent?" Jake asked.

"They've still got at least a day and a half on us."

"But we're closing on them," Hank added.

"Yes. We are," Trent said, believing it.

* * *

Abbie and the two new captives were forced to sit close together, bound hand and foot before the campfire. She hadn't had the chance to say much to the other women yet, but she could tell they understood just how dangerous their situation was. Only when the warriors moved off to tend to the horses did they finally have the opportunity to talk.

"I'm Abbie Ryan," Abbie told them softly.

"I'm Ellie Gray, and this is my daughter, Caroline. They raided our ranch today and killed our ranch hands," she said in a strained, emotional voice.

"What are we going to do?" Caroline whispered. She had been crying almost nonstop since she'd been taken.

"There's not much we can do right now," Ellie whispered back. "Just pray that your father gets home quick and comes after us." She looked at Abbie. "Where did they capture you?"

"On my family's ranch up near Coyote Canyon. They shot my brother and took me. We've been riding south ever since."

"Was your brother killed?"

Abbie paused as the pain of the memory assailed her. "I don't know."

"I'm sorry," Ellie told her. "What do you think they're going to do with us?"

"I wish I knew."

"They've beaten you." Ellie could see the bruises on her face.

"I tried to escape."

"You were brave to try that all by yourself."

"I had no choice, but it didn't matter. They caught up with me."

Ellie looked down at Caroline and then over at Abbie. Fearing for her daughter's innocence, she asked, "Did they . . . ?"

"No," Abbie answered quickly before Ellie could say more.

They fell silent as one of their captors returned.

Little Dog had heard the women talking and wanted to frighten them. He took out the dead snake from where he'd stowed it and, keeping it hidden from view, he walked toward them. He could see the fear in their eyes as they watched his approach, and he enjoyed the feeling of power their terror gave him. He particularly liked taunting the Golden One. She was watching him warily, her hatred for him open in her gaze, so without warning, he threw the rattlesnake directly at her. He laughed aloud when she cried out in shock.

Lone Eagle heard the Golden One's cry and rushed back to find out what had happened.

"What have you done, Little Dog?" he demanded. The longer they rode together, the less he trusted the other warrior.

Little Dog was still laughing as he pointed to the dead snake. "I gave her a present."

Lone Eagle didn't respond. He just walked over and picked up the snake. He carried it away from the campsite and threw it into the brush.

The three women stared up at Little Dog, unsure what he might try next. Their relief was great when he walked away.

"What are we going to do? How are we going to get away from them?" Caroline asked her mother.

"Your father will save us. He'll come after us," Ellie said reassuringly, hoping all the while that what she was saying was the truth.

Chapter Sixteen

It was the middle of the night when Faith awoke. She lay there on her bedroll, staring up at the clear, moonlit night sky. It was a heavenly sight. The stars twinkled brightly and the half-moon gave off a soft glow.

Faith had always considered herself a fit woman. She knew she could ride with the best of her men and keep up, but after all these days on the trail, traveling so hard and fast, she was coming to recognize her limitations—not that she'd ever let Trent know. She'd told him she could keep up with him, and she was going to—no matter what.

She admitted to herself that she was sore all over. Every inch of her body ached, but what bothered her more was that she hadn't had the chance to wash up properly since they'd left the ranch, and she knew she was filthy.

An inspiration came to Faith as she lay there, thinking about the long, hot, dusty days to come on the trail, and she knew what she wanted to do. Quietly sitting up, she looked around and was glad to find that Trent, Jake, and Hank were all sound asleep. She knew then that her timing was perfect. Since they'd camped near a small watering hole and the men were all sleeping, she would have the privacy she needed to sneak off and wash up without their ever finding out.

The watering hole wasn't big enough or deep enough for a real bath, but Faith didn't care. She would be satisfied with just washing off what trail dust she could for now.

Ever so carefully, she took what she needed out of her saddlebags. She got her handgun, too, just in case she ran into trouble, and then stood up and moved silently from the camp to the watering hole which was only a short distance away. When she got to the water's edge, she took one more quick look around to make sure she truly was alone, and then stripped off her blouse and knelt down to start scrubbing herself clean as best she could.

The cool water felt glorious, so she took her time. Bathing this way was a far cry from her usual warm soak in the bathtub at home, but she was still enjoying every minute of it. Just having some time by herself away from the men helped to make the moment special. Faith sighed in contentment and continued to work at washing away the many days' worth of dirt and grime.

* * *

Trent wasn't sure what woke him, but he suddenly found himself wide-awake in the middle of the night. He lay still, listening and waiting, trying to figure out what had roused him from his sleep. All seemed quiet. He heard nothing unusual, yet his instincts were telling him something was wrong.

Troubled, Trent sat up and looked around the campsite. Though the campfire had burned down low, it still gave off enough light for him to be able to see, and he noticed right away that Faith was missing from her bedroll. He realized it was probably her moving about that had awakened him, so he stretched out again to await her return.

When Faith hadn't come back after a few minutes, Trent grew concerned. He got up and decided to take a look around to make sure nothing had happened to her. He grabbed his sidearm and moved carefully off into the darkness.

Trent hadn't gone far when he heard a faint splashing down by the water. He moved cautiously toward the watering hole. He was hoping that it was Faith, but he didn't let his guard down, keeping his gun in hand—just in case. He had learned that a smart man was always careful.

The sight that greeted Trent when he reached a vantage point over the water stopped him in his tracks. There before him, bathed in the soft glow of the moonlight, was Faith, and she was partially undressed.

Trent didn't move. He remained where he was,

gazing down at Faith, visually caressing her. He'd known from the first moment he'd seen her at the dance that she was a tempting beauty, and as he watched her now, he felt the heat of his need for her rise up within him.

Trent knew he should turn away and give her the privacy she needed. He knew he should return to camp and wait for her there, but he couldn't. He moved forward.

"Faith." He said her name quietly, so as not to awaken the others.

"Trent." Her heart jolted at the sound of his voice so near, and she turned quickly to find him there. Trent's tall, broad-shouldered presence sent a shiver of sensual awareness through her. He was a strong man, a powerful man, and she was drawn to him as to no other. Memories of the kiss they'd shared the last time they'd been alone played in her thoughts.

"When I woke up and found you were gone, I got worried about you," he explained, coming to stand before her. His gaze went over her, over the slender slope of her bared shoulders and down across the tempting swells of her breasts revealed above the simple yet enticing undergarment she wore.

Logic told Trent to walk away from her, to go back to camp and bed down again, now that he knew she was safe. He was a man on a mission. He had no time for any distractions while he was on the trail of the raiding party. Yet a more powerful force than logic had him in its grip.

"I couldn't sleep, so I thought I'd clean up a bit," she explained, feeling breathless at being partially unclothed before him. The heat of his gaze upon her excited Faith. "I guess I'd better . . ."

She started to reach for her blouse to cover herself, but Trent stopped her. He set his gun aside and took her by the arm, drawing her very gently, very slowly to him.

The touch of his hand on her arm sent a shiver of excitement through Faith, and she didn't resist. She went into his embrace willingly. She wanted to be near Trent. She wanted to be in his arms again.

His mouth covered hers in a demanding, hungry kiss, and she responded fully and without reserve. Wrapped in each other's arms, they shared kiss after passionate kiss. They clung together, caught up in their need for each other.

When his lips left hers to press heated kisses to her throat, the fire of desire began to grow deep within her, and when his caress swept over her, she thrilled to his touch. Faith had never experienced such passion or delight. She felt alive in ways she'd never known before. She eagerly clung to him, loving the feel of his lean, hard body against her.

Trent rose up and claimed her lips again as he caressed the soft curve of her breast. Faith gasped at the sensations his intimate touch aroused within her, and an ache grew within her. She arched to him, instinctively offering herself to him.

The heat in his body driving him, Trent crushed her closer and kissed her passionately. There was no denying he wanted her. He did, badly, but one last fragile thread of sanity kept him from giving in to his burning desire for her.

This was not the time. . . .

It took all his willpower to break off the kiss. He didn't put her from him right away. He just stood there, holding her in his arms as he fought with himself to bring his raging passion under control.

For a moment Faith wondered why Trent had broken off the kiss, and then she realized just how caught up she had been in the moment. His touch and his kiss had left her mindless in her need to get ever closer to him. The knowledge that he could affect her this way unnerved her. She had never responded to any man the way she did to Trent. He challenged her and he aroused her. She wasn't quite sure what to think as she drew back away from him, and she was almost disappointed when he let her go.

Neither of them spoke as she quickly donned her blouse.

"Are you ready to go back?" Trent asked, gazing down at her and fighting the desire to take her back into his arms. She was the most spirited woman he'd ever known, and the most beautiful. It came as a revelation to him that he was falling in love with her, and the revelation startled and troubled him. He put the thought from him. This was not the time, he reminded himself again.

Faith wanted to tell him that she wasn't ready to go back, that she wanted to stay right there with him. While she was in his arms, she could forget about all her troubles and the ugliness of life.

"Thank you for coming to check on me," she said softly as she moved past him.

"I'm glad I did."

Faith stopped and looked up at him. She smiled at him. "I am, too."

She walked ahead of him to the campsite and settled back into her bedroll, making sure not to disturb Jake and Hank. She turned on her side so she could watch Trent as he bedded down across the fire from her.

Faith had never known a man like Trent before. From the first moment they'd met at the dance, she'd known he was special. She'd never dreamed they would meet again after that night, but then he'd ridden back into her life on that terrible day when she'd lost all hope of ever finding Abbie. Because of Trent, hope had been reborn within her, and now she realized there was more to what she felt for him than she'd ever suspected. His kiss and his touch were ecstasy for her. His very nearness filled her with excitement. He had brought hope back into her life—and he had brought love.

She loved him.

She smiled in the darkness as she accepted the truth of her feelings. She knew she couldn't say anything yet. She would have to keep the knowledge of her love for him to herself for now. For the moment, all that mattered was rescuing Abbie.

Trent stretched out and got as comfortable as he could in his bedroll. He was tired, but after those few intimate moments with Faith, he knew sleep was going to be hard to come by tonight. The memory of her kiss and embrace were going to keep him awake for quite a while.

The recognition of the truth of his feelings for Faith ate at him. The dangerous life he had chosen for himself didn't allow for settling down. He stayed on the move, tracking down bad men and bringing them in. He worked hard at his job, and he enjoyed seeing justice done.

Trent closed his eyes as the memory of her kiss returned, and he stifled a groan of annoyance at the wayward direction of his thoughts. He needed to concentrate on tracking the raiding party. He told himself that was all that mattered—and he tried to make himself believe it.

It was late in the afternoon when Ward Sykes rode slowly down the main street of Coyote Canyon, looking the town over. He'd been there some years before, and it seemed like not much had changed while he'd been away. He was hot, tired, and hungry as he reined in before the town's only hotel and went in to take a room for the night.

"Afternoon. Need a room?" the clerk asked.

"Yes."

"How long will you be staying?"

"I'm not sure yet. I'm just passing through," he answered as he signed the register.

"Well, welcome, Mr. . . ." The clerk turned the register so he could read his signature. "Tucker." He got a key and handed it to him. "Upstairs, third door on the right."

"Thanks."

Sykes went to the room to get washed up, and then he left the hotel and headed to the local saloon. He wasn't going to ask any questions today. He was just going to have a few drinks and listen to the talk. He deliberately took the long way to the saloon, passing by the stage office to get a look at the man who'd paid Marshall to bring in his son. The office was still open, and he could see a man sitting at the desk inside. Sykes knew that when the time came, he'd be paying that fellow a visit, too.

The Ace High Saloon wasn't crowded, so he got a drink and settled in at a table to pass the time. One of the saloon girls approached him, but he was in no mood for female companionship, and he let her know it right away. He was glad when she left him alone. He had some serious listening to do at the bar, and he didn't want anyone interfering.

Sykes was glad to find out that the saloon served food, so he sat there for a while just eating and drinking, but heard nothing that would help him. Not that he'd expected to hear something about the hired gun right away, but he'd been hoping for a fast break once he got to Coyote Canyon. Sykes didn't want to risk bringing up Trent Marshall's name himself, so he continued to bide his time, joining in a poker game to make a few friends and try to win a pot or two. That didn't help either, because he didn't win any money and didn't learn any news about Marshall. Frustrated and tired, he finally called it a night.

The easy part of getting his revenge was over—he'd reached Coyote Canyon. Now came the hard part—tracking down Trent Marshall. Sykes never even considered that he might be forced to give up. One way or another, he would find the hired gun and make him pay.

CHAPTER SEVENTEEN

"You're up and moving," Rose said in surprise as Mason appeared in the kitchen doorway, dressed and looking almost like himself. She was there cooking his breakfast and had fully expected to be taking it to him in his room.

"I've had enough of staying in bed," Mason told her.

"Are you sure you're strong enough to be moving around?" she asked, still worried about him.

"Yeah, it feels good to be up. I figured if I got outside in the sunshine for a while today that might help, too."

"It sure can't hurt. Sit down here at the table, and I'll get you your breakfast."

"That's what I like—fast service."

They were both smiling, enjoying the normalcy of the moment. Rose watched with satisfaction as Mason ate his usual fare. His appetite was back, she noted, and he truly was getting stronger.

Larissa and Dottie entered the general store together.

"How's Mason doing? Has your father been out to see him again?"

"Not since the other day. He told Rose to let him know if there were any problems, so not hearing anything is good."

"What about Abbie? Has there been any news about her at all?"

"Nothing that I know of."

"Hello, Dottie, Larissa," called out Alnette Scribner, the town's biggest gossip, when she saw them come inside. She hurried up the aisle from the back of the store to talk with them.

Dottie and Larissa knew there was no escaping her, so they girded themselves for the conversation to come as Alnette headed their way.

"How are you, Alnette?" Dottie asked politely, knowing full well that she was going to find out— and probably in detail.

"I'm doing just fine," she answered, and then looked at Larissa. "I was just wondering if your father learned anything new about Abbie Ryan when he was out at the Lazy R?"

"The last any of us heard was that there had been no word."

Alnette shuddered visibly for dramatic effect. "This is all so horrible. Can you imagine what poor Abbie is going through?"

"I try not to think about it," Larissa answered.

"I do too," Dottie added for emphasis, not wanting the conversation to deteriorate into lurid speculation.

"Why, being taken hostage by those horrible savages . . ." Alnette went on emotionally. "I've heard talk that that tracker the Ryans hired is real good. He just brought in that outlaw named Sykes the stage line was after, and if he can track down someone as elusive and dangerous as Sykes, he should be able to find Abbie."

"I hope you're right," Dottie said.

"It's hard on Mason, though," Larissa added. "I feel so sorry for him. He wants to be out on the trail helping to search for her."

"How is he?"

"He's getting better, but he won't be able to do any regular work for another few weeks, and with Abbie gone, and Hank, too, they're shorthanded out at the Lazy R."

"It's a difficult time for the family; that's for sure," Dottie said sympathetically. "We'll have to keep them in our prayers."

"I'll do that," Alnette said, moving on up to the front of the store to pay for her purchases. "You let me know if you hear anything new."

Larissa and Dottie just smiled and nodded as they started off to do their shopping.

None of them noticed the man in the back of the store who'd been listening intently to their every word.

Sykes couldn't believe his luck. After his failure

to learn anything about Trent Marshall the night before at the saloon, he'd been biding his time. It had been pure luck that he'd decided to come over to the store to get the supplies he'd need when he rode out again. And now he knew where Trent Marshall had gone. He had a hard time keeping from smiling as he finished gathering up what he needed and went up to the counter to pay for it.

Sykes headed back to the hotel to drop off the supplies. Once he was in his room, he tried to decide what action to take. He knew now where Trent Marshall had gone. He was off tracking down a renegade raiding party that had taken a local girl hostage. Sykes knew he could try to go after Marshall, but decided right away against that. It would be far easier to sit tight in Coyote Canyon and wait for Marshall's return. Then he had an even better idea. The woman had said the rancher who'd hired Marshall was shorthanded. He decided to go down to the saloon again and check in with the bartender to find out exactly where the Lazy R was and to see what his odds of getting hired on there would be.

It was certainly worth a try. If it all worked out the way he hoped, he'd be right there at the Lazy R, ready and waiting, when Trent Marshall rode back in.

Sykes was smiling as he entered the saloon. Some days were better than others.

"You're looking mighty happy today," the barkeep told him.

"Gimme a whiskey," Sykes ordered.

"You got it." The barkeep quickly poured him a shot and pushed it across the bar. "So you're enjoying your stay in our fine little town?"

"The longer I'm here, the better I like it. Trouble is, I need to find some work. I was just over at the general store and heard some ladies talking. They said a ranch called the Lazy R was shorthanded right now. Do you think I could get hired on out there?"

The barkeep frowned slightly, thinking of all the trouble the Ryans had had lately. "The way things have been going for them, they probably could use another able-bodied man or two out there for a while."

"The women said something about a raiding party kidnapping someone?"

The barkeep told him the story of what had happened, including how the Ryans had hired a tracker to go after the renegades.

"They are having some rough times. Do you think it's worth my while to ride out and talk to them?"

"Couldn't hurt. Mason Ryan's the man you need to talk to—if he's able. I heard he was doing better, but I don't think he's back to work yet. Tom Jackson's the foreman. He's a good man."

"Where is the place?"

The barkeep gave him directions. "Just tell them you talked to me. My name's Max. Tell them I told you to ride out."

"Thanks. I appreciate it."

"Let's just hope they find the girl soon."

"Real soon," Sykes said, nodding in agreement. The sooner, the better.

Mason went out and sat on the small bench on the front porch in the sunshine. He'd pushed himself a little too hard that day, and he needed to take it easy for a while. He hadn't been there long when he noticed a rider coming in. He didn't recognize the man and wondered who he was and what he wanted.

Out by the stable, Tom saw the stranger, too. He left what he was doing and walked up to the house so he could be with Mason when the man arrived.

"What do you think?" Tom asked as he joined Mason on the porch.

"I don't know, but I think we're going to find out real soon," Mason responded.

The stranger reined in before them.

"Afternoon," Sykes said, tipping his hat to them.

"What can we do for you?" Mason asked.

"Is this the Lazy R?"

"It is," Mason answered, not offering any more. Something about the man troubled him, but he had no idea why.

"You must be Mason Ryan, then. My name's Tucker, Charley Tucker."

"I am Ryan, and this is my foreman Tom Johnson. What brings you to the Lazy R?"

"I was in town, and I heard some talk at the saloon that you might be running a little shorthanded right now. Max, the bartender, told me to tell you he sent me out to see if you wanted to hire on an extra hand."

"Where are you from?" Mason asked.

"No place in particular. I like to keep moving."

"If you like to keep moving, what makes you think you'd want to work here?"

"I've been down on my luck for a while and could sure use a few paydays right now."

Tom had a feeling Mason didn't like the man, but they were shorthanded and could definitely use the help. He spoke up. "We could use an extra man until Hank gets back."

"The barkeep told me about your trouble with the raiding party. I'll work hard for you."

Mason had his doubts, but realized Tom did need help. "All right. We'll give you a try, but I'm hoping it'll only be for a short time."

"For your sake, I hope so, too. I'll take whatever work you can give me," Sykes told him, playing humble.

"Come on out to the bunkhouse," Tom said, taking charge. "I'll show you around."

"Thanks."

Mason remained where he was, watching the two men walk away. He didn't know why Tucker put him on edge, but he did. For now, he'd trust Tom's judgment, but if he noticed anything strange— anything at all—he would call Tucker on it.

* * *

Trent had been keeping an eye on the clouds gathering in the distance, and knew harsh weather was headed their way.

"We need to ride for higher ground," he told them. "There's a bad storm coming in, and it's coming fast."

Faith had seen the threatening clouds, too, and feared the tracks they were following might be washed out.

"But we need to keep on the trail for as long as we can," she argued. "It might get washed out."

"Staying on the trail won't do us any good if we end up dead," Trent countered.

"Trent's right, Faith," Hank concurred, studying the sky. "The storm's moving quick."

"But if we lose the trail . . ." She stared off in the direction they'd been traveling, knowing Abbie was out there somewhere.

"If it gets washed out, we'll just have to find it again," Trent told her, meeting her gaze.

Faith saw the calm determination in his eyes. She had learned to trust him during their time together, and she put her trust in him now. "All right. Let's ride."

They started off toward higher ground, looking for a place to seek shelter from the coming storm.

Trent had been right. It wasn't long before the wind picked up and the rain began. It had been storming for some time in the mountains, and the water was already washing down and surging through the arroyos. Fierce lightning split the sky as the deluge gained strength.

Trent saw there was another arroyo ahead that they had to cross to reach safety. The water was rising, but he thought they could make it in time. He led the way, urging his reluctant horse on.

"We have to hurry before the current gets any stronger!" he shouted as he forded the rushing waters.

His horse balked and came close to losing its footing, but finally made it up the other side.

Faith followed next. True fear gripped her as lightning struck nearby and the deafening crack of thunder exploded around them. Her horse shied and stumbled as it struggled against the power of the onrushing water.

"Come on, Faith! You can make it!" Trent shouted to her over the roar that surrounded around them.

Faith held on tight as her horse braved the fast-moving water and finally managed to pull itself up to safety.

Hank and Jake were ready to follow behind her. Just as Hank reached the water's edge, though, lightning erupted again and his horse reared wildly, backing away in complete and total terror, refusing to cross the flooding arroyo. Hank tried to regain control, to force his horse across the raging waters, but it was no use. The lightning and the deadly current made it impossible.

"We're not going to make it!" Jake shouted to

Trent and Faith over the roar of the storm. "The water's too deep and it's moving too fast!"

Trent knew they were right.

"Find shelter!" he called back. "We'll meet up when it's over!"

Hank and Jake didn't need to be told twice. They quickly rode away, looking for a safe place to wait out the storm.

"Come on!" Trent called to Faith.

She followed him as he rode up the rocky hillside, searching for a haven from the rain.

Trent couldn't be certain, but he thought he saw what looked like a small cave about half a mile ahead of them.

"Up there, Faith!" He pointed it out to her and then led the way toward the place he hoped would offer them shelter from the fierce weather.

It was hard riding, but they finally managed to reach the spot. They wasted no time dismounting and, after tethering the horses and grabbing their bedrolls, they sought what safety they could find inside the shallow cave.

CHAPTER EIGHTEEN

Faith and Trent were drenched as they took shelter in the small cave. Tossing their gear aside, they turned back to stare out at the torrential downpour scouring the land.

"I wonder if Jake and Hank are all right?" Faith worried.

"They're smart men. They'll find someplace to wait it out, just like we did."

"I hope so."

"It looks like we're going to be here for a while," Trent said, taking a look at the sky.

"I know," she said in disgust as she turned away from watching the storm to try to figure out how to find any comfort in their cramped surroundings. At least the cave was deep enough to protect them from the bad weather. She was even more glad to discover that there were no snakes curled up anywhere. "I guess we might as well try to get comfortable."

Trent joined her and unrolled his bedroll so

they'd have something to sit on while they bided their time. Lightning continued to split the sky with ferocious intensity, and the deafening roar of the thunder that followed echoed around them as they sat down on the bedroll. It was damp, but it was still better than sitting on the rocky ground.

"Do you think we'll be stuck here all night?" she asked. It was late in the afternoon already.

"It looks like it," he answered.

"We were closing in on them," she said sadly.

"We were. The only good thing about this is that it's a big storm."

"And you think that's good?" Faith asked in disbelief.

"Yes, it means the raiding party will have to hole up somewhere, too. We'll find them."

She heard the confidence in his tone and looked over at Trent, studying his lean, darkly handsome profile as he sat beside her. His very nearness sent a shiver of sensual awareness through her. She was attracted to him as she'd never been to any other man. There was a quiet inner strength about him that drew her to him. From the first moment they'd met, she'd known he was special, and she found herself wondering how he'd come to be a hired gun—a man who worked alone to bring in wanted killers.

"Trent?"

He glanced her way.

"How did you get started doing this? Tracking people down?"

"About ten years ago down in Dry Gulch, two outlaws—Charlie Hunt and Will Anderson—killed my brother, Brett. Brett was the sheriff there in town, and they set him up and shot him in the back. The people from town were so afraid of them, they wouldn't even form a posse to go after them, so I did it myself."

"Did you have any other family to help you?"

"No. Our folks had died some years before."

"But you did it. You found them." Her respect for him grew even greater as she realized all he'd been through, and at such a young age.

"Yes. Old Jim, one of our ranch hands, was a real good tracker. He rode with me. It took us a while, but we caught up with them. Their days of killing are over."

She didn't ask for details. His emotionless tone told her all she needed to know. Gently, she reached out and touched his arm. "Good."

"It didn't bring Brett back, but it did feel good turning them in."

Faith could see the steely look in his eyes as he remembered that time in his life, and she understood, now, how he'd come to be the man he was.

"That's why I stayed at it," Trent went on. "Old Jim worked with me. He taught me everything he knew about tracking."

"What happened to him?"

"He died a few years back."

"So you've been working by yourself ever since?"

"I've come to like working alone."

Faith couldn't resist teasing him. Trying hard not to crack a smile, she said, "I've heard that about you."

"You have, have you?" Trent countered, his mood lightening. He gave her a devilish grin.

Faith realized it was one of the few times she'd ever seen him smile. Trent looked so handsome, her heartbeat quickened in response. She returned his smile as their gazes met.

From the beginning, Faith had been a distraction for Trent, and right now she was proving to be one again. This time, though, holed up as they were because of the storm, he found he actually appreciated the distraction. His gaze went over her in a visual caress, lingering on her lips as he remembered the sweetness of her kiss, and then dipping lower to take in her wet blouse clinging revealingly to the full curve of her breasts. Trent lifted his gaze to her lips again, and, unable to resist, he leaned toward her and kissed her.

Faith had been a bit chilled by her wet clothes, but the moment his lips touched hers, a fire of longing was ignited within her. When he took her in his arms, she went willingly into his embrace. Trent guided her back down onto the bedroll, covering her slender body with his. That intimate contact was thrilling. Faith gave a low moan as she felt the heat of him upon her like a searing brand. His lips left hers to trail heated kisses down her throat, and she clutched at his shoulders and held him tightly to her. When he rose up over her again, she drew him down to her and kissed him hungrily.

Her fiery response urged him on. Excitement trembled through Faith as Trent began to unbutton her blouse. He brushed the garment aside and then slipped the straps of her undergarment down her shoulders, baring her breasts to his caress. She gasped at the intimacy of his touch and arched instinctively against him.

Faith began to caress him, sculpting the hard-muscled width of his shoulders and chest, working at the buttons on his shirt. He was strong and lean and all man, and she wanted to be closer to him. Trent drew back to finish shedding his shirt and then helped her strip off her blouse and undergarment before taking her back in his arms again.

She gasped at the thrilling sensations that vibrated through her at that intimate contact. The hard crush of his bare chest against her left her restless and aching for something more. She shifted her hips against his, seeking some unknown fulfillment that, instinctively, she knew only he could give.

Trent wanted her. There was no doubt about that. His body was aching with the need to make her his own, but one last thread of sanity remained. He told himself he should stop. It took an effort, but he did it. He broke off the kiss and shifted slightly away from her.

"Faith." He said her name in a husky whisper.

She looked up at him, wondering why he'd stopped kissing her. "Trent? What's wrong?"

"Nothing's wrong." He drew a ragged breath as he gazed down at her. Faith was everything he'd ever wanted in a woman. She was beautiful and spirited and smart, and he wanted nothing more than to make her his own in all ways, but . . . "And that's the problem."

She frowned in confusion. All she wanted was to kiss him again. "I don't understand."

Trent moved even farther away, needing to distance himself from the temptation she represented. "We have to stop—now."

Faith realized he was trying to protect her, and her love for him grew even more. "Trent . . . kiss me."

He hesitated, knowing full well that one more kiss might shatter the tenuous control he had over himself. He looked down at her, and their gazes met and locked.

"I love you," she whispered, reaching out to draw him back down to her for a passionate kiss.

Her words touched Trent, but, though he wanted nothing more than to make love to her, he couldn't allow himself to give in to his desire for her—not here, not now.

Trent reluctantly ended the embrace and sat up to stare off into the night. He didn't trust himself to look at Faith again. He had to get hold of his emotions. He had always prided himself on being a man in control. He hadn't survived in dangerous situations all these years by being weak, and this night could be no exception.

The struggle deep within the heart of him was fierce. His desire for Faith was almost overpowering, but it was the fact that he cared for her that gave him the strength he needed to stop. Tracking this raiding party was one of the most dangerous situations he'd ever been in. Her sister's life was threatened, and Faith's very safety depended on his being at his best. As painful as it was for him to deny himself, Trent knew that if he gave in to his passion, it would cloud his judgment and affect his ability to remain focused on the very job she'd hired him to do.

He couldn't do anything that would put them at risk.

He had to be strong.

Faith had never known such intimacy with a man before, or such excitement. She had been caught up in the rapture of Trent's embrace and had wanted to stay in his arms forever. Now, as her sanity slowly returned, she understood why Trent had drawn away from her. A part of her still longed to go back into his arms, but she knew she would be forever grateful that he'd been strong enough to stop when he had. The knowledge deepened her love for him even more, and she quickly moved to cover herself.

As Trent sat there staring out at the storm-swept land, he finally admitted to himself that he loved Faith, but acknowledging it left him even more frustrated. From the beginning, he had never wanted her to come along. He'd wanted her to stay behind, to be safe and out of harm's way. He considered sending her back home, but even as he thought it, he knew it was too late. They were too far out. It would be too dangerous for her to try to return to the ranch now. He was going to have to keep her with him so he could make sure she was protected.

Trent found himself half smiling as he thought of how she would react if he told her he was going to send her back home.

"What are you smiling about?" Faith asked, seeing the slight curve of his lips. She was unsure of what he was feeling, and a little nervous because she'd been so brazen with him.

He turned to her, feeling slightly more in control now. "I was thinking about how you would react if I told you . . ."

Faith was waiting breathlessly for his next words. She was hoping he would declare his feelings for her—hoping he would tell her he loved her, too.

"That I wanted you to go back to the ranch," he finished.

"Go back to the ranch?!" She was shocked.

"I knew you would react that way, and that's exactly why I was smiling." He chuckled. "Don't worry. I'm not going to send you away. I'm going to keep you right here with me."

"But why would you even have thought of it?"

Trent's gaze met hers and his expression turned

serious as he answered her. "Because I want to make sure you're safe."

At his words, all the tension she'd been feeling melted away. "I am safe—as long as I'm with you." And she knew that was even truer now that he'd proven what a strong man he really was.

"We'd better try to get some rest."

"I know."

They sought what comfort they could find on their bedrolls, lying close together without touching.

Outside, the storm continued unabated.

Hank and Jake had taken refuge beneath a rocky outcropping on higher ground some distance away from the arroyo. They were drenched and miserable, but at least they were out of the worst of the weather.

"I hope Faith and Trent are all right," Jake worried as darkness laid claim to the storm-ravaged land.

"I'm sure Trent found a place to wait it out."

"You trust him, don't you?" Jake looked at the older ranch hand, respecting his judgment.

"I do. He hasn't led us wrong yet."

"You think it'll be hard picking up their trail again?" His thoughts were on Abbie. He wondered if the raiding party had been stopped by the torrential rains, too, or if they'd gotten even farther ahead of them. He didn't want Abbie in any greater danger than she already was.

"It ain't going to be easy, but if anyone can do it, it'll be Trent. They don't say he's the best for nothing."

Jake let the conversation lapse.

It was going to be a long, miserable night.

Miles away, Trent lay beside Faith, watching her sleep and wondering what their future could be together.

Marriage . . .

The thought came to him, but he put it from him—for now.

Faith stirred and awoke in the darkness to find Trent asleep beside her. In sleep, he looked relaxed and at ease and even more handsome—if that were possible. A shiver of excitement coursed through her at the memory of his kiss and touch, and as she remembered the respect he'd shown her, heartfelt emotion filled her, deepening her love for him even more.

With the coming dawn, they would be reunited with Jake and Hank, and Faith knew the intimacy they'd shared this night would be lost. She was going to have to act as if nothing had happened between them, and she hoped she could do it.

CHAPTER NINETEEN

It was late as Abbie huddled with Ellie and Caroline in the back of the cave. Earlier that afternoon the warriors had seen the storm coming and had recognized its power. They had tried to outrun it, but when it had overtaken them, they'd taken shelter in this cave to wait for it to pass. The warriors had bound the captives' wrists behind them and had forced them farther into the back, while they'd remained near the entrance to keep watch and stand guard. As night had fallen and the storm had shown no signs of letting up, they'd bedded down.

When Abbie realized that the warriors were going to stay closer to the front, she'd been glad. She'd been hoping for a chance to speak with the other women, but she didn't want to risk being overheard by the warrior who understood English. She'd managed to fall asleep for a short time, and then awoke to find that Ellie and Caroline were awake, too.

An occasional flash of lightning gave Abbie enough light to see that the warriors appeared to be sleeping, so she knew this was the time she'd been waiting for.

"I have an idea," Abbie whispered to the other captives.

"What?" Ellie asked nervously. She was nearly hysterical in her terror, and barely staying in control of her emotions.

"We need to try to escape."

"You're crazy!" Ellie's voice was hushed yet terrified.

"No, I'm not," Abbie argued. "I'm crazy if I just sit here and do nothing. I want to go home, and the only way that's going to happen is if I find a way to outsmart these Apache."

"You think we can?" Caroline asked eagerly. It was the first ray of hope she'd had since they'd been taken.

"There are four of them and three of us. We can figure out a way to do it. The hardest part is getting free. After that, it's just a matter of trying to grab their guns so we can defend ourselves and fight back if we have to. You know how to use a gun, don't you?"

"Yes." Ellie was still hesitant.

"How are we going to do it?" Caroline was ready to try anything.

"If one of us can get free, then it will just be a matter of untying the other two and making our move without waking them up. When the time comes, we're going to have to move fast."

"But you already tried escaping once, and they caught you. Why do you think it will work this time?" Ellie worried.

Abbie looked over at her, her expression grave and serious. "Because this time we're not running away. This time we're after their guns."

Ellie was scared, but she knew Abbie was right. It was up to them to save themselves. They couldn't wait for a rescue that might never come. She looked over at her daughter. She loved Caroline with all her heart and soul, and would do whatever was necessary to keep her from harm. "All right. When?"

"Now. Back up to me. Let's start working on these ropes."

Ellie shifted her position so they could try to untie each other's hands.

And it was then that it happened.

In one quick, savage move, Little Dog rolled to his feet, drew his knife, and threw it at them with unerring accuracy.

Abbie cried out in terror as his knife just barely missed her and hit the cave wall beside her.

The other warriors were roused by the disturbance and quickly got up.

"What is it, Little Dog?" Crooked Snake demanded as he saw him going to the women.

"They were trying to escape," he answered, coming to tower over the Golden One. As lightning flashed again outside, he could see her expression clearly and knew she was truly frightened. Her terror gave him a feeling of even greater power, and he was smiling ferally as he hunkered down next to her to get his knife.

Abbie held her breath as the warrior she despised reached across her to get his weapon. The fact that he was watching her so closely unnerved her, and though she fought for control, fear shone in her eyes.

Little Dog took his time retrieving his knife. He enjoyed being so close to her and feeling her tremble. He had her just the way he wanted her—helpless. Ever so slowly, he used the knife to push aside the makeshift garment Lone Eagle had made her, then ran the cold edge of the blade across her throat in an unspoken threat and then down lower to the tops of her breasts. He heard her gasp at the contact and savored the feeling of power that surged through him. She thought she was smart. She thought she could get away from them, but she would never escape him—never.

Caroline was watching the horrible torment the warrior was inflicting on Abbie, and she grew mindless in her fury.

"No!" she screamed. In a rage, she kicked out at him to try to knock him away from Abbie. She made contact, but paid the price.

Little Dog reacted instantly. He turned on her and pinned her to the ground, his knife at her throat. He was snarling with anger at her defiance. He wanted to make her pay.

Abbie and Ellie tried to go to Caroline's aid, but Lone Eagle was there, pushing them both back down to the ground. Crooked Snake went after Little Dog.

"Do not harm her!" Crooked Snake ordered.

Had he not spoken, Little Dog, in his rage, might well have cut her throat right then. Instead, he pulled away in disgust and stood up.

"I woke up and heard them whispering," he told Crooked Snake. "Then I saw the Golden One trying to get free."

"It is good that you stopped them." Crooked Snake checked the bonds on all three captives to make sure they were still tied tightly.

Lone Eagle left the women for a moment, then returned with a length of rope and his own blanket. As he had done before, he tied one end to the Golden One's ankle and the other to his own before stretching out on his blanket close beside her.

"You will not try to escape again," he told her.

The other warriors moved away.

Little Dog took one last look down at the Golden One's partially bared breasts. There were times like this when he would have enjoyed torturing and raping the captives much more than taking money for them. Trying to control his anger, he returned to bed down on his blanket. The night was going to be a long one.

Abbie lay unmoving in the darkness, all too aware of the warrior beside her. Her heart was broken, for she knew he would never leave her alone again, and that meant there was no hope for escape. Tears of misery traced silent paths down her cheeks as she gave in to her emotions. Unless a miracle happened, she would never be free again—she would never find out what had happened to Mason or see Faith or be with Jake.

Abbie closed her eyes against the darkness and the pain and listened to the rain falling. Her despair deepened even more, for the downpour sounded less harsh now, and that meant the storm was passing and they would soon be riding on again.

It was just starting to get light outside when Faith awoke. She rolled over, expecting to find Trent there beside her. She was startled to discover he'd left their shelter without her knowing it. Getting up, she went looking for him. She wanted to have a moment alone with him before they had to ride out.

Faith went outside and saw him standing a short distance away. He was looking off in the direction they'd come from the day before, no doubt watching for some sign of Hank and Jake. Her gaze went over him, taking in his broad shoulders and lean, powerful build, his dark, rugged good looks and the commanding way he carried himself. Her heartbeat quickened at the memory of his kiss and touch, and she made her way to join him.

"Good morning."

Trent turned to her. She had been in his thoughts ever since he'd awakened. He hoped things would be all right between them this morning. "Yes, it is. The storm is over."

"Thank heaven." Faith gazed up at him. "You know, this isn't going to be easy."

"Picking up a trail again after a rain like that never is." He looked back out over the landscape, deliberately trying not to dwell on the long, dark hours of the night just past.

"That, and trying to act like nothing happened between us."

He looked over at her, his expression serious. "I don't know which one will be harder, but right now we have to find your sister." Ever so gently, he bent to Faith and kissed her. "We'd better get ready to ride."

They moved apart reluctantly, trying to concentrate solely on what lay ahead for them that day.

"There's still no sign of Jake and Hank, so we're riding on without them," he told her after they'd eaten.

Faith understood. Trent had warned them back at the ranch that if they got separated, he wasn't going to waste any time looking for the other members of the search party.

"All right."

He was glad she didn't argue with him. "I've already got the horses saddled up."

They packed up the few things they had with them and rode out.

"How much farther is it to that ranch?" Faith

asked as they continued on in the direction they'd been heading before the storm had broken.

"We'll make it today."

"Good. I just hope we can pick up the trail again."

"I'll find it." He was confident.

And Faith believed in him.

Jake and Hank were up before dawn, and both men were thankful for the clear skies.

"Trent's not going to come looking for us, so we're going to have to catch up with them," Jake said.

"What are we waiting for? Let's go."

The two men saddled up and rode hard and fast after Trent and Faith. They knew Trent would not slow down in his quest to find Abbie. They found the arroyo where they'd been separated from the others by the fast-moving water the day before and crossed it with ease now. It took Jake and Hank a while to locate Trent and Faith's trail, but once they did, they rode at top speed, trying to catch up. It was late morning when they finally caught sight of them in the distance.

Trent had been keeping watch, too, and he spotted the two men at about the same time.

"Jake and Hank are coming," he told Faith, pointing them out.

"Should we wait for them?' "

"No. We'll keep riding for the ranch. I want to talk to the rancher to see if he's seen or heard anything of the raiding party. They can catch up with us there."

Faith said no more. She was as anxious as he was to reach the ranch.

"Pa! Get your gun!" twenty-year-old Pete Gray shouted to his father when he saw the riders appear at the top of the rise.

John Gray reacted immediately, dropping the shovel he'd been using to bury the dead and grabbing his rifle. Pete ran to his side, his own gun in hand. Both men were tense, their moods dangerous and deadly as they waited to see who was riding in.

They had returned a few days early from the cattle drive to find their ranch in ruins. The buildings had been burned to the ground, and all the ranch hands had been slaughtered. By the look of things, they had no doubt the attack had been carried out by an Apache raiding party.

John and Pete had searched among the burned-out ruins for any sign of Ellie and Caroline, but had found no trace of them. Afraid to think what might have happened to their womenfolk, they were intent on mounting a search, but decided to take the time to bury the dead before leaving. After such a severe storm, they knew finding Ellie and Caroline wasn't going to be easy.

Father and son were both ready for trouble as they watched the riders approach.

"Do you recognize them?" Pete asked.

"No." John didn't take his eyes off the incoming riders. "But it looks like one of them's a woman."

They lowered their guns a little, but didn't relax as the man and woman reined in before them.

"What do you want? What are you doing here?" John demanded aggressively.

"We're after an Apache raiding party," Trent began, looking around at the burned-out ruins of what had once been a prosperous ranch. He saw, too, the fresh graves the two men had been working on.

"They were here," John answered him in an emotionless tone.

"How long ago?"

"Must have been yesterday or the day before." He turned and looked at the devastation. "We were on a trail drive and weren't due back for several more days. We got done early, so we left the rest of our hands in town, and my son and I came on home. We just got here a few hours ago, and this is what we found." He paused again, trying to control his emotions and deal with his pain. "There's no sign of my wife or my daughter."

"We're so sorry," Faith said gently, understanding what the two men were going through.

John looked up at them again. "My name's John Gray and this is my son, Pete."

"I'm Trent Marshall, and this is Faith Ryan. This same Apache raiding party was up near Coyote Canyon and took Faith's sister captive. We've been tracking them ever since."

John and Pete exchanged a haunted look.

"That's what we were afraid of," John began in a tortured voice. "I was almost hoping to find them dead in the ruins of the house, but they're not here."

"You think they took Ma and Caroline, too?" Pete was horrified.

John looked at his son. His expression was grave as he answered, "It looks that way, son." John turned back to Trent. "We'll be going after them, too. We can ride with you or we can track them on our own. It doesn't matter to me as long as I find them."

"Ride with us," Trent told him. He didn't really want them along, but he didn't want them getting in his way, either.

"Trent, Jake and Hank are here," Faith announced as she saw the two men crest the rise.

"They're with you?" John asked.

Trent quickly put his concern to rest, explaining how the searchers had gotten separated in the storm.

"How soon can you be ready to ride?" Trent asked them.

"We'll be ready as soon as we finish burying our dead."

"Do you need any help?" Trent offered.

"No. We'll handle it." John and Pete continued their gruesome task.

Trent and Faith turned their horses away and rode off to meet up with Hank and Jake.

"I see you two made it through the storm all right," Faith said to Jake and Hank as they reined in before them. "We were worried about you."

"It was a bad one," Hank said.

Jake was looking past them to the ruins of the ranch and watching the two men at their grim task. "We may have lost the raiding party's trail, but we know now that they were here not too long ago."

Trent explained what John Gray had told them. "John and his son, Pete, will be riding with us once they're done."

The other two men understood.

"Let's take a look around while they finish up," Trent said.

They rode around the area, looking for anything that might give them an idea of where the raiding party was headed. The heavy rains had erased almost all traces of the trail, but Trent did manage to find some small rocks that had been dislodged—he believed by horses passing through.

When they saw that John and Pete had finished burying the dead, they rejoined them.

"Are you ready?" Trent asked.

"It's time," John said in a voice completely devoid of emotion as he took one last look at the graves of the men they'd just buried and his burned-out home.

"We're going to find 'em, Pa. I know we are."

"I hope you're right, son," he answered. He looked up at Trent. "There was some talk going around a month or so ago that renegades were selling women captives for a good price just across the border."

The thought sickened Faith, and Jake's expression grew even grimmer.

"Let's ride," Trent responded, leading off. "They headed out this way."

Faith was relieved to be back on the trail again. She didn't want the renegades to get any greater lead on them than they already had.

As they rode away, Faith was touched by Pete's fierce determination to find his mother and his sister. She thought of her own brother and wondered how his recovery was going. She hoped no fever had set in and that Mason was getting his strength back. He had always been a man of action, and she was certain being left behind at the ranch this way wasn't sitting well with him. She could imagine how frustrated and miserable he was. No doubt he blamed himself for not preventing Abbie's abduction, and so Faith offered up a silent prayer that they would be able to find the raiding party soon and bring Abbie and the other women home.

CHAPTER TWENTY

Mason was ready. His expression was serious, his concentration fierce. He squared off, ignoring the pain that ate at him. Then he drew and fired his gun.

The shot went wide.

Mason swore under his breath in disgust as he shoved his gun back in his holster.

He'd gotten up that morning determined to get back to his normal activities again. He'd had enough of taking it easy, waiting for his wound to heal. He was used to keeping busy and getting things done. Since he was feeling stronger, he'd decided it was time to test himself and see if he could still use his gun. He had his answer now, and it wasn't the one he wanted. He'd been practicing for close to half an hour and had yet to hit the target.

Angry and as determined as ever, he got ready to try again.

He was a Ryan.

He didn't quit.

* * *

Larissa and Dottie made the carriage ride out to the Ryan ranch together, enjoying each other's company and looking forward to having a visit with Mason. They wanted to make sure he was feeling all right and to find out if there had been any news concerning Abbie.

"What's that?" Dottie asked worriedly when she heard what sounded like gunfire in the distance.

"Here, take the reins."

Larissa handed them over and pulled out the rifle her father always insisted she carry with her for protection. As the shooting continued erratically, she appreciated his sage advice.

Dottie was uneasy as they continued on. When the ranch house finally came into sight and it looked like nothing was out of the ordinary, both women were able to relax a bit. They could still hear shots being fired, but realized it was not a gun battle of any kind. Larissa stowed the rifle back under the seat again.

Rose saw the carriage coming in and went out to greet them. "It's good to see you."

"You, too," Dottie returned. She knew that if Rose was calm, there was nothing wrong.

"What's all the shooting about?" Larissa asked.

"It's Mason." She quickly explained to them what he was doing. "I'll go let him know you're here. You can go on inside."

"That's all right, Rose. I'll get him," Larissa offered. "You and Dottie visit for a while."

The two older women went in the house while Larissa went to find Mason.

It didn't take her long. Mason had his back to her, so he didn't see her coming, and that was fine with Larissa. It gave her the opportunity to watch him, and watch him she did. He looked wonderful to her—so tall and broad-shouldered and powerfully built. Her gaze never left him as he squared off as if in a gunfight. He drew his gun and fired, his motion smooth and confident. He came close to the target he'd set up for himself, but he didn't hit it.

Mason's frustration was growing as he holstered his sidearm again. He was getting tired, and the pain was getting to him.

"You were close," Larissa said, coming up behind him.

Mason turned quickly to face her. His concentration had been so fierce, he hadn't heard her approach.

"Close doesn't count," he told her.

Larissa sensed his frustration and gave him an inviting smile as she stopped before him. She'd noticed there wasn't anyone else around, and she wanted to take full advantage of having a moment or two alone with him.

"Oh, I don't know," she purred. "I think being close counts a lot."

As Mason gazed down at her, he momentarily forgot all about his impaired shooting ability. He hadn't realized just how much he'd missed her until now. "You know, I think you may be right. . . ."

He didn't hesitate, but took her in his arms and kissed her. It was a deep, hungry exchange that left them both wanting more. He was reluctant, but managed to put her from him.

"I've been worrying about you," Larissa said as they finally moved apart.

"I'm better."

"I can tell," she said.

"There is something that might help me recover even faster, though."

"What's that?"

"Another kiss," he answered.

She obliged, and her heartbeat quickened at the intensity of the embrace. She clung to him in delight, thrilled and relieved that he was obviously well on his way to recovery.

Larissa would have stayed in his arms forever if they hadn't heard someone calling Mason. They broke off the kiss. Both were a bit embarrassed by the power of their need for each other, and they both regretted that the moment had to come to an end.

Mason looked over to see Tom and the new man, Charley Tucker, coming to speak with him.

"How's it going?" Mason asked.

"We're doing fine," Tom answered. "I was just talking with the boys, and they were wondering if it would be all right if they went into town tomorrow night. It's payday weekend, and they wanted to have some time off."

"I don't see why not," Mason agreed. "It's been a while since they've had the chance to unwind."

Tom turned to Tucker. "Why don't you go tell the rest of the boys the good news?"

"I'll do that." Sykes couldn't believe his luck. He couldn't have planned it better. He'd been afraid he was going to be forced to bide his time at the ranch, trying to find a way back into town to take care of the man at the stage office, but now everything was working out perfectly. In just a matter of days, he would start claiming his revenge.

Sykes was smiling as he and Tom walked away.

Mason turned back to Larissa. "Let's go back up to the house."

She smiled at him as she answered, "I like being out here alone with you better."

"So do I," he agreed.

They returned to the house to find Rose and Dottie sitting in the kitchen talking. They joined them there.

"So you haven't heard anything new from Faith?"

"There hasn't been a word," Mason answered.

Larissa looked across the table at him. "Then we have to hold on to the hope that no news is good news."

"That's what I keep telling myself," he said, meeting her gaze.

In his eyes she saw a flash of the emotional pain he tried to keep hidden from everyone, and she understood even more clearly just how hard it was for him to be forced to wait at the ranch while Abbie was facing possible death at the hands of the renegades. Her love for him grew even greater.

Dottie spoke up, hoping to cheer him. "We just need to keep praying for her safe return, and we need to start thinking about the celebration we're going to have when they do come home."

"That is going to be one big party," Rose agreed, wanting to be positive.

"I know," Larissa said. "And I can't wait."

They stayed on to visit for several hours before heading back to town. Larissa and Dottie were both relieved that Mason seemed to be doing so well physically.

As he worked stock the following day, Sykes was all but counting the hours until it was time to ride for town that afternoon. Since it was a payday weekend, he knew there would be a lot of free-spending cowboys in Coyote Canyon that night from the Lazy R and the other neighboring ranches, and he was going to take full advantage of the chaos to kill Cal Harris.

Sykes knew he had to plan things carefully, though. Getting even with Harris was important, but he couldn't take any chances. He couldn't risk getting caught. He had to be ready and waiting at the ranch on the day Trent Marshall rode back in. That was the most important thing.

"Tucker!" Tom shouted, motioning for him to ride over.

The fact that the foreman wanted to talk to him left Sykes edgy. He rode toward Tom, wondering what he had to say. Although Mason had given his permission for the men to go into town, as the newest ranch hand, Sykes was worried they were planning on making him stay behind and work.

"What do you need?" Sykes asked, reining in next to the foreman.

"Were you planning on going to town with the other boys tonight?"

"Yes."

"Then, here." Tom reached into his shirt pocket and took out a roll of money. He peeled off several bills and held them out.

"What's this for?" Sykes was surprised.

"Consider it an advance against your paycheck. I heard you telling Mason when you hired on how you were running short of cash, so this way you'll be able to have yourself a little fun tonight."

"This is mighty generous of you," Sykes said.

"It's not a gift. I expect you to pay me back."

"I'll do just that," Sykes said, smiling at him. But even while he was smiling, he was thinking that the way he was planning to pay Tom back was a far cry from what the foreman would be expecting. He believed the man was a fool to trust someone this way, and he'd show him why real soon.

"Be ready to ride for town in about two more hours. We're meeting at the bunkhouse."

"I'll be there. You don't have to worry about that."

Tom wheeled his horse around and rode off.

Tucker seemed to be working out all right. He hadn't had any complaints from the other hands, so he assumed the man was carrying his weight. He'd recognized Mason's hesitation in hiring him, but so far had seen no reason to doubt Tucker could give an honest day's work for his pay.

Sykes let out a sigh of relief as Tom left him. He wasn't quite sure what he would have done if the foreman had insisted he stay behind, but he didn't have to worry about that now.

Things were looking good.

Sykes and the other men reached Coyote Canyon and took rooms at the hotel before making their way straight to the Ace High Saloon, ready to have a good time. They'd been there ever since, drinking and gambling and being entertained by the saloon girls.

Sykes was sitting at the poker table now, smiling down at the three of a kind he held in his hand. He was certain he was going to win big this time and just wished he had even more money to bet so he could run the pot up still higher.

"I'll raise you twenty dollars," he told the other players as he pushed the money out into the center of the table.

"I'm done," Tom said in disgust, throwing in his hand.

"Your luck's running out?" Sykes asked him.

"No. My luck's the same as it's been all night— bad," he complained, sitting back. He looked over at Tucker and knew his hand had to be darn good for him to run the stakes up so high.

Sykes turned his full attention back to the game as it played out. Just as he'd hoped, his three of a kind won it all. His smile was even bigger as he raked in the pot. He did like having money.

The saloon girls were very aware that he was the big winner tonight, and they were eager to get his attention.

"You in the mood for something a little more exciting than card playing?"Ruby asked, leaning close to give him a view of her ample bosom, which was enticingly revealed by her low-cut bodice.

Sykes looked her over in appreciation, but answered, "There ain't nothing more exciting than winning a big hand at poker, darling."

"You want to bet?" she purred. She wanted to lure him upstairs and get her hands on some of his money.

"Yes, that's why I'm not leaving this table right now, but if you want to stay here with me and bring me even more luck, we'll see what we can do later on."

"I can do that," she said, leaning down to give him a hot, wet kiss right there in front of everybody.

The other men hooted loudly at her passionate display.

Ruby just smiled and sat as close to him as she could. He was not as young as the other cowboys, but that was all right with her. Because he was older, she believed he wouldn't be as mean or rough as the young ones were when they went upstairs with her.

Encouraged by her attention, Sykes took some of the money he'd just won and shoved it in her bodice right between her breasts.

"Keep that safe for me, darling."

"I will," she promised in delight.

He gave her a lewd smile before turning back to the poker game. While he was gambling, he kept an eye out for Cal Harris from the stage line. He hoped the man would show up at the saloon. He wanted to follow him home and find out where he lived, but as the night progressed Harris never appeared.

Several hours passed before Sykes finally quit gambling and took Ruby up on her offer of a good time upstairs. They went to her room, and once they were inside she locked the door behind them.

"Did I ever tell you I just love winners?" she purred, eyeing him up and down as she stood with her back to the door.

Sykes turned away from looking at the bed to look at her. "Well, you got yourself one tonight, darlin'."

Ruby gave him a decidedly wicked smile. "Want to come and get the money I've been keeping for you?"

"Oh, yeah."

Enticingly, Ruby reached up and pushed the straps of her gown down off her shoulders, giving him an even better view of her breasts.

He smiled and went to her, not needing any more of an invitation. It had been a while since he'd enjoyed himself with a woman, and he decided to take full advantage of what she was offering. His need was hot within him, so he didn't waste any time stripping off her clothing. He retrieved the money from her bodice, then picked her up, and threw her on the bed. He took off his gun belt and put it aside before lifting her skirts.

"You in a hurry?"

"When I see something I want, I take it."

And it didn't take him long to get what he wanted right then. Unconcerned about her pleasure, he collapsed back on the bed, satisfied.

"You were mighty fast on the draw, big guy," she told him in a sensuous tone, wanting to arouse him again.

"I don't believe in wasting time," Sykes replied, reaching over to paw at her breasts.

"Neither do I."

And they didn't. They quickly stripped off their clothes and enjoyed themselves again.

It was after midnight when he finally left her. They were both smiling. Ruby had her money, and Sykes was ready to go after Cal Harris.

CHAPTER TWENTY-ONE

As Sykes left Ruby's room he could hear the noise of the rowdy drunks below. He figured it was safe for him to just disappear, so he left by the back way, completely avoiding the crowded saloon area. No one from the ranch saw him, and he was glad. Where he was headed was nobody's business but his own.

Slipping off down the dark alley, he stayed in the shadows as he made his way toward the stage office. He wasn't sure what he was going to find there, but it was the best place to start looking for Cal Harris.

Cal didn't like working late, especially on a Friday night, but tonight he had no choice. The work had to get done, and he was the only one who could do it. He was concentrating intensely as he pored over the stage line's books. He'd pulled down the shades on the office windows, but hadn't bothered to lock the door. He figured there would be no one around this time of night, since no stages were scheduled to arrive in town until the following afternoon.

Cal was surprised when the office door opened. He looked up quickly, startled by the interruption, and he watched as a stranger came in and closed the door behind him.

"Good evening," Cal said, wondering what the man was after.

"Evening," Sykes responded as he looked around. He wanted to make sure they were all alone.

"We are closed right now," Cal began.

"Oh, sorry—I know the shades were drawn, but I saw the light and thought you might be in here. I wanted to speak with you." He walked over toward where Harris was sitting at the desk.

"Well, it's late now, and there are no stagecoaches due until tomorrow." He got up to face the stranger.

"So things are quiet for you tonight, are they?"

"Right now, yes, but it'll be real busy tomorrow. What can I help you with?" Cal was in no mood to make conversation with a man who had obviously been drinking. He just wanted to get his work done and call it a night. He came around the desk, intending to usher the other man out of the office.

"You're Cal Harris, aren't you?"

"Yes, I'm Cal Harris."

Sykes's manner was deceptively genial as he reached out to shake hands with him. "It's good to finally get to meet you face-to-face."

"It is?" Cal was growing even more puzzled by the stranger's behavior as they shook hands.

"That's right." Sykes smiled.

When Cal tried to pull his hand away and the stranger wouldn't release his grip, he realized the man was more than just an ordinary drunk wandering the streets of town. This man meant trouble.

"What's this all about?" Cal demanded. "If you're thinking of robbing the place, there's no money kept here."

"I'm not here to rob you. Let me introduce myself. My name is Sykes—Ward Sykes."

Cal went completely still when he heard the stranger's last name.

Sykes saw the change in his expression and knew he had the stagecoach man right where he wanted him. "And you're the one who had my boy killed."

Before Cal could react to that statement, Sykes drew his knife from where he wore it in his belt and stabbed him violently. He stepped back and watched the man collapse and lie unmoving on the floor. After a moment, he checked to make certain the man was dead, then wiped the blood off the knife and stood back up to look around the office. The lamp burning on the desk was just what he needed to conclude this transaction.

Sykes locked the front door and then used the lamp to set the office on fire. He wanted to make Harris's death look like an accident. Once he was certain the blaze was not going to go out, Sykes made his escape out the back. He ran silently down the alleyway, wanting to distance himself from the fire as quickly as he could.

Cal Harris was dead.

He felt some satisfaction in claiming this part of his revenge, but Trent Marshall was still out there alive somewhere. Sykes wasn't going to rest until the hired gun was dead, too.

Sykes emerged from the alley some distance away from the stage office. He kept his head down and staggered a little, acting like a drunken cowboy as a carriage passed by. He made his way to the hotel. It was so late, there was no one at the desk when he went in. He hurried on up to his room, glad that he'd been able to move about the town undetected.

Sykes had just locked himself in his room when he heard the first shouts in the streets about the fire. Looking out the window, he could see the eerie glow of the blaze in the distance. He made no effort to go help fight the fire. The longer it burned, the better. He didn't want anyone to discover that Harris had already been dead when it had started.

Larissa and her father had just reached their stable when they heard someone yelling, "Fire!"

"Where is it?" Dr. Murray asked the man who was running by, spreading the word.

"The stage office!" he shouted back as he continued on, wanting to rouse the townfolk and make them aware of the danger.

"Let's go see if we can help," her father said.

He led the way from their stable to join the people running toward the fire. They began to line up so they could pass buckets of water from the watering troughs to fight the blaze.

The sheriff and his deputies joined in.

"Where's Cal Harris?" Sheriff Fike was asking.

"Nobody's seen him around anywhere," someone called back.

"Then send somebody over to his house to get him. He needs to know about the fire!" the lawman ordered.

One man ran off to do as the sheriff had ordered, while the rest stayed there and continued to battle the fire. Their efforts proved herculean as they struggled to prevent the flames from spreading through the town.

The man who'd gone to get Cal returned quickly with Cal's wife, Sarah.

"Sheriff Fike! Cal was working late tonight at the office—he hadn't come home yet." Sarah Harris was frantic as she stared at the burning building. "He wasn't trapped inside, was he?"

The lawman stopped for a moment to speak with her. "I don't know. We've been looking for him, but no one's seen him."

Sarah Harris was numb with fear for her husband's safety as she joined in to help.

It wasn't easy, but they finally put the fire out. Sheriff Fike and his deputies went to take a look through the ruins to see if they could find any clues to the cause of the blaze.

"Did anyone ever find my husband?" Sarah was asking as she wandered around in a tortured daze. "Has anyone seen Cal?"

"Oh, God . . ." One of the deputies had been sifting through what was left of the building and found what appeared to be the remains of a body buried under the rubble.

"What is it?" Sarah demanded, starting to rush to the place where he was standing.

The deputy reacted quickly, though, and blocked her view.

She went still as horror filled her. When her gaze met his, she knew what he'd found, and she began to sob.

One of the ladies from town hurried to her side and put an arm around Sarah's shoulders to guide her away from the scene.

Sheriff Fike came over to join his deputy, and together they began to examine the remains. It wasn't pretty. Finally the sheriff stood up and looked around at those who'd helped to extinguish the fire.

"It's Cal," the lawman told them sadly. "Somebody go get the undertaker."

"How did this happen?" one of the men asked. He was puzzled by how Cal could have been trapped in his own office this way.

"I don't know," Sheriff Fike answered. Then he ordered his deputies, "Start talking to everybody who was here helping tonight. Find out if anyone saw or heard anything unusual right before the fire was discovered."

"You think the fire was set intentionally?" one deputy asked, shocked at the notion.

"Cal was too smart a man to get caught in his own office like this."

His men moved off to start asking questions.

When Dr. Murray heard that a body had been found, he went to speak with the sheriff. "Is there anything I can do to help?"

"No. I've sent for the undertaker."

Their mood was grim.

"Were you out at all tonight?" Sheriff Fike asked him.

"As a matter of fact, Larissa and I had just gotten back from making a call when we heard the shouting about the fire."

"Did you notice anything unusual on your drive back in?"

He thought back over their return trip to the house. "You know, the only thing we saw was a drunken cowboy staggering down the street, and there's nothing unusual about that on a payday weekend."

"Was the man anywhere close to the stage office?"

"He was a block or so away, I think." The physician frowned, trying to remember more.

"Do you know who it was? Would you recognize him again if you saw him?"

"Honestly, I'm not sure, but Larissa might. I'll ask her if she remembers who it was."

"I'd appreciate any help you could give me. I'm going to find out how this happened if it's the last thing I do."

Dr. Murray moved away. There was nothing more he could do to help. Larissa had already gone home and was probably in bed. First thing in the morning, he was going to check with her to see if she remembered anything about the man they'd seen on the streets. Perhaps she would recall something that might help the sheriff identify him.

Sykes had been enjoying himself in his hotel room. From the window he had been able to see the glow of the fire in the distance and had known his plan had succeeded. If anyone bothered to question him, his alibi for the night was good. He hadn't been seen near the area except by the two people who'd driven by in the carriage, and it had been so dark, he seriously doubted they would be able to identify him even if they did remember seeing someone on the streets.

Turning away from the now-dark view of the town, Sykes stretched out on the bed. His thoughts turned to Trent Marshall, and he began to plan how he was going to get his revenge on the hired gun, now that he'd taken care of Harris. Eventually Marshall would return to the Lazy R. When he did, Sykes knew it was going to be hard for him not to just pull his gun and shoot the man down the first time he set eyes on him. He hoped to come up with a better plan than that before the day came, but for right now, he was satisfied to know he would be ready whenever Marshall showed up.

Vengeance was going to be his.

As Sykes closed his eyes and tried to get some sleep, he wondered just where Trent Marshall was and how soon he'd be back.

CHAPTER TWENTY-TWO

The following days on the trail were torturous. The heat grew ever more intense and the terrain more desolate. With Trent leading the way, they covered seemingly endless miles until darkness claimed the land each night and they were forced to stop. At the first light of dawn they were mounted up again and riding out.

It was on the third day that Trent's mood grew tense.

"Don't build a fire tonight," he ordered when they started to make camp.

"So we're that close?" Jake asked. He had noticed how serious Trent had become with each passing mile that day and had suspected that they were closing in.

"Yes. With any luck at all, we'll be able to spot their campfire tonight," Trent told them.

"And if we do?" John asked.

"If they're within range, we'll go after them."

"Tonight?" Faith asked excitedly.

"Tonight," he confirmed.

Any exhaustion she'd been feeling vanished at his answer. She was ready.

Trent was glad to have good news for the group, but he had mixed emotions about what was to come. He'd been in dangerous situations like this before and knew things didn't always turn out the way he hoped. No matter how they approached the raiding party's campsite, there was going to be a shoot-out, and the captives were going to be caught right in the middle of it.

"What do we need to do to get ready?" Hank asked, on edge.

"For right now, let's just get some rest and stay quiet. Sound travels out here, and we don't want them to know anyone is after them. If and when I spot the campfire, I'll figure out what we're going to do next."

They tried to stay calm as they settled in, but they all were anxious. The moment they'd been waiting for was almost upon them. They were going to do whatever was necessary to rescue the women.

They would get no second chance.

Trent moved off into the night to keep watch.

Jake sat down by Faith to share some of their meager fare.

"We could have Abbie back with us by morning," Jake told her. The long days of imagining what Abbie might be suffering at the hands of her captors had left him angry and eager to take action.

"I know." She looked over at him, the hope she

was feeling shining in her eyes. "I can't wait to see her again."

"It won't be long now. We were really lucky Trent was in town when she was abducted. He knows what he's doing."

"Yes, he does."

They fell silent, intent on controlling their excitement. The enemy they were up against was fierce and deadly. It wasn't going to be easy freeing the women, but they would find a way.

After a time, Faith got up and went to seek out Trent. She found him a short distance off, staring out across the land.

"Did you see anything yet?" she asked quietly as she joined him.

"Nothing yet." Trent cast a quick glance her way. He knew he couldn't relax his vigil, but he was glad to have a moment alone with her. They hadn't had any private time together since the night of the storm.

"Thank you," she told him sincerely.

"For what?" He frowned, puzzled.

"For never giving up on finding Abbie. You could have turned back any number of times when we ran into dead ends, but you didn't, and now we've almost freed her."

"We haven't rescued her yet."

"Not yet, but we will. I know it." Faith put her hand on his arm and looked up at him. When Trent turned to her, she moved closer and kissed him. It was a soft, cherishing exchange.

Trent would have liked nothing more than to lose himself in her embrace, but he couldn't. Faith was a temptation he could ill afford right then. He had no time to think of anything but saving the captives. He reluctantly put her from him. "When the time comes and we do go after them, I want you to stay with Hank. I don't want to be worrying about your safety while I'm trying to free Abbie and the other women."

"All right," she answered, ready to do whatever was necessary to help out.

She agreed to his order so quickly, he had to grin. "That's a first."

"What is?"

"Your being willing to do what I tell you without an argument."

She was about to say more when she noticed Trent suddenly go still as he looked off in the distance.

"There." Trent pointed out a faint glow several miles out.

Faith saw it, too, and her breath caught in her throat. "It's them."

"Let's go tell the others. We've got to move fast."

They hurried back to their campsite.

The men saw them coming and hoped Trent had good news.

"We've spotted the campfire!" Faith told them anxiously.

"Let's get ready to ride!" John insisted.

"Wait." Trent's order was stern.

"What for?" John demanded.

"We're not riding in on them without a plan. If they hear us coming, they'll kill the women. We have to be very careful."

Everyone was sickened by what they realized was a very real possibility, and caution replaced eagerness. They listened intently to Trent's directions.

"We'll leave the horses a distance away from their campsite and approach on foot. We know that there are at least three female captives, and from what I could tell by their trail, there are four warriors."

"How can we be sure this is their campsite?" Jake asked.

"We're going to find that out real soon," Trent answered. "Once we're certain it's them, we'll split up. Jake, you come with me. John, you keep Pete with you, and Faith will stay with Hank. We want to surround them so they can't slip away. Make every shot count, and watch out for the women. Take all the ammunition you have with you, because once the shooting starts, there will be no turning back."

The mood was solemn as they shared a look of understanding. They knew the danger they faced.

"Let's ride—and be careful."

They mounted up and moved out.

After the failed escape attempt, the pain of accepting that she would never go home again was more than Abbie could bear. She lost all hope and fell into a silent existence, as did Ellie and Caroline. They were helpless to save themselves. The future stretched bleak and horrifying before them. Their lives as they'd known them were over.

Huddled beneath her blanket, her ankle bound to the warrior's, Abbie closed her eyes and tried to sleep. Sleep was the only haven she had in her life. Only in her dreams could she escape the torment her life had become. Only in her dreams was she back in the loving safety of Jake's arms at the dance.

Though she tried to hide from the truth of what was coming, Abbie knew things were only going to get worse. She didn't even try to imagine what the renegades were going to do to her. It was too horrible to think about.

Trent kept their pace slow as they rode in. No one said a word. They didn't want to risk being heard. About a mile out, he signaled the others to stop. They reined in and left their horses tied up where they were. Silently, they covered the final distance through the rocky terrain on foot. As they drew near the clearing, Trent directed the others to stay where they were while he moved in to check things out.

Drawing upon all the lessons Old Jim had taught him, Trent made his way in close enough to observe the scene below. He had been almost certain the campsite belonged to the raiding party, and he was relieved to find he was right.

Trent could make out the four warriors he'd expected to find there, along with the three female captives. Trent recognized Abbie and frowned when he saw how her leg was bound to the warrior bedded down beside her. He knew that meant she must have tried to escape before, and the thought that she was so spirited made him smile slightly. Abbie was a lot like her sister. He also saw the women he assumed were Ellie and Caroline Gray. They were huddled together on the far side of the fire, their wrists bound. The women were being kept right beside the warriors, and Trent realized there was no way he could sneak in and free them without a fight. They were going to have to attack.

Trent went back to tell the others what he'd learned. As he described the situation they would be facing, tension filled the group. What happened in the next few minutes would mean the difference between life and death for Abbie, Ellie, and Caroline. The rescuers got their rifles and quietly moved off to take up the best positions they could find around the camp.

A terrible sense of fear and unease ate at Faith as she followed Hank toward the camp. She refused to give in to it, though. If ever there had been a time in her life when she needed to be strong, this was it. The shooting lessons her father had given her all those years ago had never been as important as they were now. Her sister's life depended on it.

John and Pete made their way toward the far end of the campsite. As they sought the best cover, they spotted Ellie and Caroline bedded down near the fire. Seeing that they were alive elated them, and they were ready to do whatever was necessary to bring their women safely home.

Trent looked over at Jake.

"This isn't going to be easy," he said quietly.

"Nothing worth doing ever is," Jake countered. "Let's go."

Trent nodded and led the way up into the rocks that overlooked the campsite. Their weapons ready, they settled in there and waited, to give the others time to get in position.

Little Dog had been sleeping soundly, but he suddenly found himself awake. The fire had burned down to a low flame, and all seemed quiet, but his instincts were telling him something was wrong. He got up cautiously and, taking his rifle with him, walked over to where the two women were bound together. They seemed to be asleep on the ground.

Little Dog had just come to stand over the captives when the first shots rang out. He heard Black Cloud and Crooked Snake scream in pain, and he ran for cover, forcing the two terrified women along with him.

At the sound of the gunfire, Lone Eagle reacted instinctively. He grabbed his knife and severed the rope that bound him to the Golden One. She began to scream and tried to fight him as he dragged her along to the place where Little Dog and the other captives were crouched, hiding out behind some rocks.

"Did you see who it is?" Lone Eagle asked him.

"No," Little Dog answered as he began returning fire.

Both warriors realized they were surrounded and outnumbered. They knew their only hope was to try to get away.

"We have to get to the horses!" Little Dog said. He grabbed the youngest girl, believing she would be the easiest to control. "She is going with me!"

"Leave her!" Lone Eagle told him.

"No! She will give me cover! They will not shoot at me if I have her with me!"

Both warriors started to run toward their horses. Lone Eagle went first, and Little Dog followed, taking Caroline with him.

Jake had seen one of the warriors forcing Abbie to go along with him into the rocks. He had come a long way to rescue the woman he loved, and he wasn't about to stand by and let something happen to her now.

"I'm going down there!" Jake told Trent.

Trent joined him, and, together they cautiously worked their way down toward the place where the renegades were holed up. They were just closing in on them when Jake caught sight of one warrior running for the horses and the other following behind him, dragging along the girl he thought was John's daughter. Just then, more shots rang out from John and Pete's direction, and the warrior who'd reached the horses first was wounded.

* * *

At the sound of the gunfire, Abbie looked up to see that the warrior had been shot. A torrent of conflicting emotions tore through her. A part of her was concerned about him, worried that he might have been killed, yet even as she found herself worrying about his safety, she kept praying that she would be rescued. Abbie was relieved when she saw the warrior slowly get to his feet and, with great effort, mount a horse.

Caroline's frantic cries for help forced Abbie's attention away from the wounded warrior. She knew that, no matter what else happened that night, she couldn't let the cruel one escape and take Caroline with him. Abbie looked over at Ellie. If they were going to save Caroline, they would have to work together.

"We have to stop him!" Abbie told Ellie.

"He can't take my daughter!"

Even though their hands were bound and gunfire was still raging around them, the two women were determined to take action.

Little Dog had seen that Lone Eagle had been wounded, and he knew he needed the girl with him now more than ever. He brutally forced her along.

Abbie and Ellie were as ready as they would ever be when he passed by them. They knew they couldn't stop him completely, tied up as they were, but they hoped they could slow him down long enough to give their would-be rescuers a chance to get to him and save Caroline. When he walked in front of them the women made their move. They threw themselves at him with as much force as they could muster, hoping to jar him and possibly knock him to the ground. They knew he was armed and they might suffer for their actions, but Caroline's life was more important than anything else.

Their ploy worked.

Little Dog was caught off guard by their unexpected assault. He stumbled and almost fell.

Caroline took advantage of their help. With all her might, she shoved him and broke free of his painful hold. She scrambled to escape, wanting to get as far away from him as she could.

Little Dog was furious. He swung around, bringing his gun to bear on the women who'd dared attack him. He smiled coldly as he stared down at the Golden One. He had never had the satisfaction of taking her the way he'd wanted to, but now he would have the satisfaction of knowing she would never escape from him.

He would kill her.

He would make her pay.

Abbie watched in pure horror as the evil warrior took aim at her. She could see the hatred in his eyes, and she held her breath.

She was expecting pain and death.

She was expecting her life to end.

And then a shot rang out.

Abbie could only stare in disbelief as Little Dog collapsed to the ground and lay unmoving before her.

"Abbie!"

The completely unexpected sound of Jake's call sent a thrill of pure ecstasy through her.

"Jake?" she cried aloud in disbelief. Hearing her beloved's voice, she felt her heart swell with emotion.

Jake was there!

Jake had come to save her.

Abbie suddenly realized that it had grown quiet. The gunfire had stopped. Looking out toward the place where the Indians had left their horses tied up, she could see that the other warrior was still there and that he was looking her way. She saw, too, that he was bleeding severely from a gunshot wound to his shoulder.

In that instant, across the distance, their gazes met and held.

"Abbie! Get down! There's another warrior!" Jake shouted as he ran up to her, his rifle in hand. He lifted his weapon, ready to take aim at the last surviving member of the raiding party, who was about to escape.

But Abbie reached out and stopped Jake, putting her bound hands on his arm to keep him from getting off a shot.

"No—don't, Jake. Let him go," she told him.

"But . . ." After all the murdering the raiding party had done, Jake wanted to make sure this last renegade never hurt anyone again.

"He didn't hurt me." She looked up at Jake, loving him. "And you're here now."

Jake looked down at the woman he loved and saw the intensity of her emotion. He lifted his gaze to look in the wounded warrior's direction again, only to discover that he was gone.

CHAPTER TWENTY-THREE

While Jake took care of the captives, Trent went to check on the warriors. He wanted to make sure the gun battle was really over.

"She's alive!" Faith cried out excitedly to Hank when she saw Abbie with Jake. Tears of joy filled her eyes, and she rushed down from their vantage point to be reunited with her sister.

John and Pete realized the shooting was over and started down, too.

Jake helped the other two women to their feet and then quickly freed all three of them from their bonds. Caroline was the first one he cut loose, and she looked up right then to see her father and brother running toward them.

"Ma, look!" Caroline called joyfully.

Ellie turned, and her heart ached at the sight of her husband and son. She had feared she would never see them again. Together Ellie and Caroline rushed to meet them.

Abbie was standing quietly beside Jake, watching their excitement when she saw her sister. "Faith?"

"Oh, Abbie!" Faith ran as fast as she could to throw her arms around her little sister. "We found you! Thank God, we found you!"

Jake looked on as they embraced and began to cry, holding each other close. He stepped away to give them time together.

"Faith, how's Mason?" Abbie asked, drawing away from her sister and searching her expression for some clue to their brother's well-being.

"He's alive and recovering," Faith told her.

Abbie began to cry even harder at the news. "I was so worried about him—I thought he might be dead."

"He'll be waiting for you when we get home," her sister promised, and they hugged each other again.

When Trent had finished his gruesome task, he made his way over to stand with Jake.

"You're as good as they said you were," Jake told him, extending his hand with respect and admiration.

Trent shook his hand, and replied, "Thank you, but some days a man just gets lucky." Watching the families being reunited touched him in ways he didn't want to admit.

"It takes more than luck to do what you do." Jake turned to him. "Thanks."

Trent only nodded.

Faith finished hugging her sister. "Come here. There's someone you have to meet."

She led her sister over to Jake and Trent.

"Abbie, this is Trent Marshall. He's the one who helped us track you down. We couldn't have done it without him," Faith said.

At first Abbie didn't say a word. She went to stand before Trent and looked up at him, all the admiration and thanksgiving she was feeling evident in her expression. "You saved our lives. Thank you."

"You're the one who tracked us down?" Caroline asked excitedly after overhearing their conversation.

"He's the one," Faith answered.

Caroline didn't care what anyone else thought. She was just so excited to be free that she went straight to Trent and impulsively hugged him. "Thank you for helping my pa and my brother find us. Thank you for saving us!"

Trent was touched by the young girl's display of emotion, and he returned her hug. "You're welcome."

John came over to thank him, too, then returned to his own family.

Trent stood back then, watching Abbie with her sister. He saw the deep love between them, and remembered a time long ago when he'd had a family. He knew Faith and Abbie were blessed to have each other, and their brother, Mason, too. He needed some time alone with Faith, but that would have to be later, once things had calmed down. He noticed Jake wasn't saying much and looked a bit troubled, so he went to speak with him.

"Something bothering you?" Trent asked.

"The other warrior—the one who got away. I know he was wounded, but do you think he'll try to come after us?" Jake didn't want to risk letting his guard down just yet.

"No. He knows what he would be up against. He won't be back," Trent assured him.

Relief flooded through Jake at his words. "You about ready to ride?"

"Yes."

Trent and Jake went to where Faith and Abbie were standing together.

Jake looked down at Abbie and smiled tenderly at her. "Let's go home."

Abbie had never known such happiness as she was feeling right then. Looking up at him, she said right there in front of everybody, "I love you, Jake."

Jake didn't hesitate. He'd been waiting for this moment. He swept her up into his arms and held her to his heart. "Thank God we found you." He drew back to gaze down at her and then told her, "I love you, too, Abbie."

Everyone was touched by the emotional moment.

"Jake's right. It's time for us to head home," John spoke up. "Pete, come with me. We'll get the horses."

While they went after their horses, Hank got the women's mounts from where they were tethered near the camp. John and Pete weren't gone long. By the time they returned, everyone was more than ready to ride out. They turned the renegades' horses loose to fend for themselves and then rode for their original campsite, where they would spend the night.

Faith and Abbie traveled side by side, following Trent and Jake, who were leading the way. The others brought up the rear.

Not much was said on the trek back. They were all beyond exhaustion, but they were happy. The torturous miles of tracking had paid off. They had rescued the women, and the raiding party had been stopped. The murderous savages wouldn't be terrorizing the area anymore.

When they reached the site, they quickly spread out their bedrolls and got ready to sleep. The worst was over, but they still had a long way to go before they reached home.

The others seemed to fall asleep quickly, but Trent lay awake, staring up at the moonless night sky. He knew it had to be at least two in the morning, or maybe three, but sleep was proving elusive for him. He found himself mentally reliving the treacherous events of the hours just past, and, though everything had turned out the way they'd hoped, the memories left him tense and on edge. Unable to fall asleep, Trent finally got up and moved silently away from the camp. He was dead tired, but needed to unwind before he could rest.

Faith had almost been asleep when she'd heard what sounded like someone moving about. She looked up to see Trent walking off alone into the night. She'd been desperately wanting some time alone with him, so she took advantage of the moment. She slipped out of her bedroll and went after him. She found him sitting in the same place he'd been earlier that evening, when he'd been watching for a sign of the raiding party.

Trent sensed he wasn't alone and turned to see Faith coming toward him.

"You should be resting," he told her.

"I know, but I needed to talk to you first. We didn't get much of a chance earlier, and I wanted to thank you for saving Abbie." Her voice was full with emotion.

He smiled up at her, and her heartbeat quickened in response.

"You're welcome," Trent said softly. "You know, you're a very lucky woman to have such a wonderful family."

"Yes, I am lucky—but I'm also lucky because I have you." Her gaze met his.

Trent stood up to face her. He knew the time had come to tell her the truth of his feelings for her. "I'm lucky to have you, too," he said with quiet intensity. "I love you, Faith."

Faith's heart was racing, and tears filled her eyes at his words of love. She lifted one hand to caress his cheek, and he pressed a warm kiss to her palm.

"I didn't think this night could get any more wonderful," she said breathlessly, "but it just did."

Trent drew her to him and kissed her. It was a hungry, passionate kiss that told her without words how much she meant to him. They clung together, treasuring the beauty of the moment and the knowledge of their feelings for each other.

There in Faith's arms, Trent found the peace his soul had been seeking. Faith was innocence and beauty. She was everything he'd ever wanted in a woman. He did love her.

When at last they ended the kiss and moved apart, Faith felt almost lost. She longed to stay close to him, but knew this was not the time. Not with her sister and the men so nearby.

"We'd better try to get some rest. It's going to be light in a few hours," Trent said regretfully, feeling the same way Faith did.

"I know you're right, but if I had my way, this night would last a lot longer," she whispered.

Trent gave her one last, gentle kiss; then, together, they made their way back to the camp. He watched until Faith was safely bedded down before seeking out his own solitary bedroll. The sweet memory of Faith's kiss stayed with him, and the knowledge that they loved each other stirred thoughts within him of what the future might hold for them.

Trent frowned in the darkness, wondering what he should do. He'd made his living as a hired gun for so long now, he wasn't sure he knew how to do anything else. He never stayed in one place for any length of time. He went where he was needed, and then he moved on. Since his brother's death, he'd had no family, no home.

But now, because of Faith, all that had changed. He found himself wondering if maybe the time had come for him to give up his wandering lifestyle, to get married and settle down.

The thought of spending the rest of his life with Faith left him smiling. He'd never met another woman like her. She was beautiful and smart. He'd learned firsthand that once she set her mind on achieving something, she did it. She let nothing get in her way. Faith was one special woman.

Across the campsite, Faith lay quietly, offering up a silent prayer of thanks. When they'd started out on the trek to find Abbie, she'd hoped she would be able to rescue her sister, but she'd also known how dangerous the situation really was. Their search had been successful because of Trent. It was his expert tracking ability and his unfailing determination that had led to her sister being found alive and well, along with Ellie and Caroline, too.

Faith's heart swelled with emotion at the memory of Trent telling her he loved her. He was the man she'd always dreamed of. The recollection of dancing with him in town that first night sent a shiver of awareness through her. They hadn't even known each other's names when they'd parted. She'd thought she was never going to see him again, and now she knew she loved him—and he loved her.

Faith wondered what the future held for them. He had made no mention of marriage, but she hoped he would—and soon. There was nothing she wanted more than to spend the rest of her life with him, loving him. With that last happy thought, she drifted off to sleep. It was to be her first good night's sleep in weeks.

In the bunkhouse at the Lazy R Ranch, Sykes woke up. It was the middle of the night, and he lay in his bunk trying to figure out what had awakened him. No one else was stirring in the bunkhouse, and he was glad.

He didn't want any conversation.

He didn't want any companionship.

He just wanted his quest for revenge to be over.

He wanted Trent Marshall dead.

The satisfaction he'd gotten from taking care of Cal Harris had appeased his need for revenge for a time, but Trent Marshall was the man he really wanted to face down. Sykes hoped nothing had gone wrong on the search for the raiding party and the missing woman. He hated to think some renegade Apache might have gotten to Marshall before he did.

Roused now by the direction of his thoughts, Sykes got up and pulled on his pants. He left the bunkhouse and went outside, walking a short distance away from the building. Sykes stopped there and looked up at the star-studded sky. The night was clear and moonless. He would have thought it was a pretty sight, if he hadn't believed that somewhere out there, the hired gun was probably staring up at the same view.

The rage that he barely managed to keep under

control flared back to life within Sykes, and he swore violently and impatiently under his breath.

He wanted this to be over.

He wanted Trent Marshall to pay for what he'd done.

CHAPTER TWENTY-FOUR

Everyone's mood had been good on the ride back, but as they neared the Grays' ranch on their third day of travel, the group grew somber. When the ruins came into view, they all fell silent. Memories of the horror that had happened there haunted them. They slowed their pace as they rode in and finally reined in near the burned-out remains of the main house.

John, Ellie, Pete, and Caroline all dismounted and just stood there, staring in misery at what was left of their home.

Ellie looked up at her husband, her eyes filled with tears, and asked, "Where did you bury the men?"

"There," John told her, pointing out their graves.

Quietly, Ellie and Caroline walked over to the burial site to pay their respects to the men who'd died trying to save the ranch from the raiding party that day.

Faith and Abbie watched them, sharing in their

sorrow. The sisters knew how they would be feeling right now if Mason had been killed. Wanting to comfort the women in some way, they dismounted and went to speak with the family.

"John, Ellie," Abbie began. "We know how horrible this must be for you, and we want you to know that you're more than welcome to come to the Lazy R with us and stay on for a while, if you like."

"Oh, Abbie." Ellie sighed as she gave her a teary, grateful smile. "You are so kind to offer."

"We just want to help you if we can," Faith told them.

"We appreciate your kindness, but this is our home," John said.

Ellie looked lovingly at her husband. They had discussed their future on the trip back and had decided they would not be run off their own ranch by renegades.

"It won't be easy for us to rebuild, but we'll do it," Ellie said.

Abbie gave Ellie a quick hug, completely understanding their reasoning. There was nothing she wanted more than to get back home.

"Be safe," Abbie told them.

"You, too," they replied.

John and Pete walked over to where Trent, Jake, and Hank had dismounted and were standing a short distance away.

"You're one fine tracker, Trent," John told him. "Thank you for helping me save my wife and daughter."

The two men shook hands firmly, knowing how fortunate they'd been that things had turned out so well.

Everyone said their good-byes then, for it was time to ride out. They still had a long way to go to reach the Lazy R.

"I can't wait to see Mason," Abbie said to Faith as they made camp later that night.

"I don't know who's going to be more excited—us or him," Faith said, eagerly looking forward to the joyous reunion. "You know what? I think once we get back, we should have a really big party to celebrate. What do you think?"

Abbie absolutely lit up at her suggestion. "I think it's a wonderful idea! I'll get to wear my dress again!"

They both laughed, remembering their conversation after the dance in town.

The men were tending to the horses when they heard the happy sound of laughter.

"Now, that's what I like to hear," Hank said, knowing things were finally getting back to normal.

"Me, too," Jake agreed.

Trent didn't say anything, but he was smiling.

The days and miles passed.

As they rode ever closer to home, Abbie grew quiet and her mood darkened. She found herself worrying more and more about what she was going to face when they got back. True, Mason would be glad to see her, and her other close friends, too, but she'd heard of the cruel way some freed Indian captives had been treated once they'd returned home. She feared she would be shunned, and if that happened, she worried Jake might come to feel differently about her. She loved him with all her heart. He had been loving and attentive on the trek back, but he hadn't had to face the hatred and ugliness yet. Her troubling thoughts stayed with her, and when the group stopped for the night, she wandered off by herself for a while to try to think things through.

Faith had noticed that Abbie had seemed a little distant that day, and she wasn't sure why. When Abbie wandered away, she didn't follow. Faith figured she just needed some time by herself. She waited for her sister to return, but when she didn't come back after a while, she decided to go look for her. Faith found Abbie sitting on some rocks a fair distance away from the campsite.

"What are you doing way out here?" Faith asked.

Abbie had seen her coming. "I just needed some time alone to think."

Faith sat down beside her. "Think about what?"

Abbie drew a ragged breath and looked over at her sister. It was hard for her to admit, but she knew she had to tell someone about her feelings. "Faith . . . I'm scared."

"Oh, honey." Faith put her arms around Abbie to hug her, and hastened to reassure her. "Don't be afraid. Another raiding party isn't going to get us. Not with Trent, Jake, and Hank taking care of us."

"Oh, no, that's not what I'm afraid of."

Faith frowned, drawing back and trying to read her sister's expression. "Then what is it?"

"We're going to be home soon," she said tentatively.

"Yes, I know. Trent said with hard riding we should be back home in a few more days. I can't wait."

"But, Faith, what if everyone treats me differently now? What if they think terrible things about me?" The fear she was feeling showed in her eyes. "You know what it's been like for other women who were taken captive and then rescued. You've heard the terrible stories."

"Some people can be cruel, but we won't let that happen to you. Everything is going to be fine. You'll see."

"I hope you're right," Abbie said tearfully.

Faith hugged her again. "I am. Jake loves you. You should have seen how upset he was when he heard that you'd been taken. He was determined to find you and bring you home. He rode out with me the first time, before we hired Trent, and helped me search for you. Nothing was going to stop him, and I believe nothing will ever change the way he feels about you."

Abbie struggled to pull herself together. "He is a wonderful man."

"With good taste in women," Faith said, trying to lighten her mood.

"You could say the same thing about Trent. It's obvious you two care about each other."

"I love him," Faith said simply.

"What about him?"

"He did tell me he loves me."

Abbie smiled at the news. "That's wonderful!"

"I think so, but I don't know if we'll ever have any kind of future together."

"Why?"

"Because of the way he makes his living. He's a hired gun by trade. He doesn't have a home or family. He just keeps traveling, doing his job."

"Maybe he's ready for a change. Maybe he would like to settle down, now that he's met you."

"You know, I did sense there was something special about him the first time I saw him."

"When was that? When you hired him on for the tracking?"

"No. Actually, Trent was already in town the night of the dance, and we danced together. It was the ladies'-choice dance, and I think you may have danced with him then, too."

"I don't remember. I guess I was too busy thinking about Jake," Abbie said with a smile, her mood lightening.

"No doubt," Faith said. "I had no idea who he was then. I learned only his first name while we were dancing, and then it just seemed like he vanished. I never expected to see him again, but when the sheriff found out who he was, he brought Trent out to the ranch, thinking he could help me find you."

"And he did."

"Yes, he did." She looked seriously at her sister. "I honestly don't think we would have ever have been able to track down the raiding party without him."

Abbie's gaze met Faith's. "Well, my prayers were answered. You found me."

They were quiet for a moment, just thinking about all they'd been through over the last long weeks.

"So what are you going to do about Trent?" Abbie challenged.

"There's not much I can do."

"You love him," Abbie stated simply.

"Yes."

"Then you just have to make sure he doesn't ever want to leave."

"I wish I knew how to convince him of that."

"You'll figure it out."

"I hope so. I don't want to even think about the possibility that he might move on and I'd never see him again."

It was getting late when Mason returned to the house. He had been feeling stronger and was able to work longer hours now, and he was glad. He wanted to keep busy. He couldn't stand just sitting around worrying about Abbie and Faith. It left him feeling guilty because he wasn't out there helping.

The lack of news had left Mason so frustrated that

he had been ready to just pack up and take off after the search party. Only Tom's sage advice had calmed him down and helped him to see that he wouldn't be doing anyone any good that way. They'd hired the best possible man in Trent Marshall, and they had to believe he would get the job done.

Mason knew he was needed on the Lazy R to run the ranch, but even so, that knowledge didn't ease the feeling that he could be doing more to help find Abbie. He made his way into the kitchen and found the dinner Rose had prepared waiting on the table. He sat down and ate his solitary meal. When he'd finished, he got cleaned up and went to bed. He had to be up at first light. There was work to be done on the ranch.

Mason lay in bed, staring out the window at the night sky, praying that he would hear something about Abbie soon—and that the news would be good.

"If the weather holds and we manage to keep up the same pace, we should have you home in two more days," Trent said the following morning as they broke camp.

"I still can't believe it," Abbie said. "I thought I'd never get to go home again, and now . . ."

"Now we're almost there," Jake finished. "It won't be long before everything will be back to normal."

As they saddled their horses, Abbie's darker thoughts came back, and she wondered if her life would ever be normal again. Faith's reassurance the night before had helped some, but Abbie still harbored a deep sense of unease about what the future held.

Faith had been watching her sister and noticed the slight change in her expression. She went to talk to Abbie before they had to mount up.

"Just keep in mind what we talked about last night," Faith told her. "And remember—you're a Ryan. You can handle whatever comes your way. Look at what you've been through already. There aren't many women who could live through that. You're strong, Abbie. You'll be all right."

They shared a quick hug before mounting up.

They were heading home.

CHAPTER TWENTY-FIVE

It was late afternoon, and everyone was hard at work on the Lazy R.

"Somebody go get Mason!" The unexpected shout went out from one of the hands down by the stable. "Fast!"

"Why? What's wrong?" another yelled back. They were busy working stock and didn't want to stop.

"Take a look for yourself!"

The ranch hands looked up to see what the other man was concerned about, and it was then that they spotted the riders in the distance.

"Is it . . . ?"

"I don't know. They're still too far out to tell."

Mason was up at the house when he heard all the yelling. He thought it sounded like trouble, so he hurried outside.

He stopped when he saw the riders approaching.

And he recognized Faith and Abbie.

Deeply powerful emotion filled Mason, and he stood unmoving, watching as they rode ever closer.

"Faith! Look! It's Mason!" Abbie called out to her sister when she saw her brother come out of the house.

"Thank God he's all right!" Faith's relief at seeing him up and moving was great.

Tears were streaming down Abbie's face as she spurred her weary mount to a breakneck pace. The last time she'd seen Mason, she'd thought he was dying. True, Faith had told her he'd survived the attack and was healing, but actually seeing him filled her with unbelievable joy. She raced straight toward him and then all but threw herself from her horse's back.

"Abbie!"

Mason ran to her and grabbed her up in a big hug. The moment was powerful, and they were both too filled with emotion to speak.

Mason couldn't believe Abbie was actually there, let alone that she seemed to be fine. He held her tight for a minute, then took her by the upper arms and held her away from him so he could look at her. His gaze went over her as he reassured himself that she really was there.

"You're back," he managed in an emotion-choked voice.

"And you're all right," Abbie said, crying as she smiled up at him.

Mason hugged her again just as the others all rode up. Faith quickly dismounted and went to join them.

"How are you?" Faith asked after giving him a quick hug of her own. "We've been worried about you."

"I'm fine."

"Abbie!"

They heard Rose's cry and turned to see her running out of the house.

Rose had been back in the kitchen when she'd heard some kind of a ruckus going on and had come out to check. Rose hugged Abbie just as the ranch hands came up to welcome her back. The joy of the moment was exhilarating.

Trent stood off to the side with Jake and Hank, watching the reunion. It wasn't often that he witnessed this kind of excitement or tender emotion. With his job, it was usually just a matter of money. He turned the wanted men he brought in over to whomever had hired him, then collected his pay and moved on.

Jake glanced over at Trent. "So, what are you going to do now?"

"Well, I was planning to take some time off right when this job came up, so I think I'll be looking for a little relaxation."

"That sounds real good," he agreed.

"Everybody!" Faith had to shout to be heard. When they quieted down, she went on, "We are going to have the biggest celebration ever here at the ranch tomorrow night!"

A big cheer went up. The mood on the Lazy R had been troubled since the raid, and everyone was relieved that things had turned out so well. The whole ranch was ready to celebrate Abbie's homecoming, and since tomorrow was Saturday, it was the perfect time for a party.

The men started off to go back to work. Hank went to the bunkhouse, while Rose took charge at the main house.

"Come on inside," Rose told them. "You all look like you could use a good hot meal."

"It has been a while, that's for sure," Faith agreed, looking forward to one of Rose's delicious home-cooked meals.

"I can't wait, but first I have to get cleaned up," Abbie said. Now that she was back home, she was all too conscious of how filthy she was. They'd managed to wash up a few times on the way back, but she desperately wanted to take a bath.

"You go on," Rose directed. "I'll make sure there's plenty of food left for you."

Faith knew she needed to take a bath, too, but she decided to wait until after Abbie had finished. Right then she just wanted to take it easy for a while.

Abbie slipped away to the privacy of her own bedroom. She went in and closed the door behind her. She stood there for a long moment, feeling safe and secure at last in the familiar surroundings. Her soft bed was going to be a wonderful change tonight after all those nights sleeping on the ground, and there was her wardrobe, filled with dresses. Just thinking about wearing a dress again made her smile.

She was home.

She was really home.

After gathering up the fresh clothes she needed, she went into the small room they used to bathe in and filled the tub. There was no hot water ready, but she didn't care. Cold water would work, as long as she could use strong soap. Only by scrubbing every inch of herself did she feel she could erase the haunting memory of the cruel warrior's hands upon her.

Abbie undressed and stepped into the tub. The water was chilly, but she found it refreshing. Grabbing up the soap, she began to wash.

In the kitchen, Faith, Jake, and Trent all sat down at the table while Rose busied herself preparing their meal.

"This is just a little bit different from what we've been used to," Jake remarked, getting comfortable.

"I'll say," Trent agreed.

"Rose is the best cook around," Faith declared.

"Why, thank you," Rose said as she set the dishes of food on the table before them. "Help yourselves."

"We'll do just that," Jake said. He didn't need to be told twice. He'd had the pleasure of eating Rose's cooking before, and knew how delicious everything would be.

Conversation slowed as they all dug in, and they

had just about finished eating when Abbie appeared in the doorway.

Jake gazed at Abbie, taking in the beauty of her as she crossed the room to join them. She'd washed her hair and combed the still-damp tresses into a bun at the nape of her neck. It was a simple style that became her, for it highlighted her perfect features and the slender line of her throat. Abbie looked as lovely as ever in the simple day gown she'd donned. Except for the slight bruising that still showed on her cheek, no one would ever have guessed what she'd been through. Jake knew she was as strong as she was beautiful, and his love for her grew even deeper.

"You look lovely," Jake said, getting up and going to her to give her a gentle kiss. He didn't care that there were others around. He didn't care what they thought. He was just thrilled that Abbie was back home and unharmed.

"Thank you," she said with a smile, feeling much more like her old self again.

"You come sit down at the table, young lady, and get yourself something to eat," Rose directed.

Abbie didn't need any encouragement. It had been a long time since she'd had a decent meal, and she loved Rose's cooking.

"I'll have one of the boys ride into town and let everybody know you're back. I know Larissa and her parents, Dottie, and Sheriff Fike, will all want to be here for the party," Mason told Abbie.

"I can go tell Tom to send one of the men for you, if you want," Rose offered.

"Thanks, Rose."

"What time are you going to start the celebration?" Jake asked when Rose had gone.

"Midafternoon sounds good," Faith said.

"All right, then I'm going to head home for tonight. I want to let everyone know we found Abbie and she's safe, and I want to check up on things there."

"You'll be back tomorrow, won't you?" Abbie hated the thought that Jake was leaving her, but she understood why he had to go home after having been away for so long.

"Don't worry. I'll be back," he assured her. There was more to his trip home than he was going to let on. There was something important he had to do, but he couldn't tell Abbie about it. He got up to leave.

"I'll walk you out," Abbie offered, forgetting all about food. She wanted only to be with Jake for as long as she could.

"I'll see you all tomorrow," Jake told the others as he and Abbie left the house.

When they got out onto the porch, Jake took a quick look around, glad to see that there was no one nearby. He took advantage of the moment of privacy and swept her into his arms for a hungry kiss. It was with great reluctance that he finally put her from him.

"You stay out of trouble while I'm gone," he told her, grinning down at her.

"You just hurry back," she countered.

"I will." It was a promise.

He gave her one last quick kiss and then went to mount up. As he rode away, he glanced back to see Abbie still standing there on the porch watching him go.

Deep emotion filled Jake.

Abbie was safe—at last.

When Abbie and Jake had gone outside, Faith decided it was time for her to get cleaned up, too. She went off to bathe, leaving Mason and Trent alone in the kitchen.

Mason looked at Trent across the table. "You're going to stay on for the party, aren't you?"

"I'd like that," Trent answered.

"Well, you're more than welcome here. You know that. We've got room out in the bunkhouse for you."

"That'll be fine."

Glad that Trent wasn't planning on leaving right away, Mason got up and went to a cabinet. He opened it and took out a bottle of whiskey and two glasses. Returning to the table, he poured a healthy shot into each glass, then handed one of them to Trent as he sat back down.

Mason looked at the man who'd saved his sister and knew he owed him more than money. His mood was serious as he lifted his glass in a toast to Trent. "Thank you."

Trent appreciated his gesture. He picked up his own glass to join him, taking a drink of the potent liquor. "You're welcome."

With Abbie momentarily out of the room, Mason wanted to find out the truth of what had happened during the search. Even though Jake had been acting as if nothing had changed and everything was the same as it had been, Mason needed to be ready to be able to handle whatever might come next for his sister. "How bad was it?"

Trent understood exactly what he was asking, and why. He knew then, too, what a good man and a good brother Mason was.

"It isn't often things turn out this well," he began. He told him of how the storm had slowed the search party down for a while, and how the Grays' ranch had been attacked. "The raiding party took the wife and daughter captive, too."

"So Abbie wasn't the only female captive they had with them."

"No, and John Gray told us that he had heard renegades were selling women down by the border."

"Thank God you got to them in time."

"And we did get there in time," Trent said. His gaze was intense as it met Mason's. He went on to explain, "When they sell the female captives that way, they don't touch them. The women are worth more untouched."

"But Abbie was beaten."

"She tried to escape—at least twice that I know of."

Mason was a bit surprised by the news. Abbie had always been the more ladylike of his two sisters, but, ladylike or not, she'd proven she was just as brave as Faith.

"How did you manage to catch up with them?"

Trent told him of the long miles of tracking and how they'd finally surrounded the campsite and rescued the women. "We were really lucky no one was hurt during the shoot-out."

"You weren't lucky," Mason countered, wanting to praise him. "You were good. You had to be to get in that close without the renegades knowing it. I'm just sorry I wasn't with you to help."

"Faith and Abbie have both been worried about you, but you look like you're doing well."

"I'm almost back to normal."

"Yes, you are," Abbie said, coming back inside from saying good-bye to Jake. "I was so relieved when Faith told me you were recovering." She sat down in the chair next to her brother. "It was so horrible that day."

"Yes, it was." Mason nodded, remembering the shock of seeing her horse stumble and fall, and trying to turn back to help her. "And, now, thanks to Trent, that raiding party won't be hurting anyone anymore."

"One of the warriors did get away," Trent added, "but he was wounded, so he won't be causing trouble anytime soon."

At Trent's mention of the wounded warrior, Abbie found herself wondering if he had survived. She was under no illusions about him now that she was back home. She knew he could have been the one who'd shot Mason and killed those ranch hands on the Grays' ranch, but he had protected her from the evil one's abuse, and for that she would always be grateful.

They talked for a while longer, and then Faith returned. She had donned a dress, too, weary of being in riding clothes for so long.

Trent's gaze lingered on Faith as she came back into the room. He'd known she was a beauty from that very first night when they'd danced together, and, looking at her now, he thought she was the prettiest woman he'd ever seen. The demure dress she wore looked lovely on her, and the pale length of her hair hung about her shoulders in a tumble of still-damp curls. Loving her as he did, he didn't know how he was ever going to be able to ride away from her.

"Trent's going to stay on for the party," Mason told Faith, and he noticed that her smile brightened at the news.

"Good." She was delighted that they would have more time together. "It's going to be great fun. You'll see."

"I don't doubt it for a minute," Trent said.

Rose returned just then with some news. "Some of the hands want to see you, Abbie. They're waiting outside to talk to you."

Abbie was touched by their concern and went out to see them. Trent, Mason, and Faith went along, too.

The men welcomed Abbie back warmly and were telling her how glad they were that she'd made it home safely.

Faith was enjoying watching the reunion when she noticed a slightly older man in the crowd.

"Who's that?" she asked Mason quietly, not wanting to interrupt Abbie's good time.

"His name's Tucker. We were running short on help, with me being laid up and Hank being gone, so Tom thought we should hire him on."

Satisfied by his explanation, Faith thought no more about it.

Abbie turned to Trent and introduced him to the ranch hands. Only when the men had gone back to work did they go inside again.

Sykes was excited as he went out to the bunkhouse, but he kept his emotions hidden.

The moment he'd been waiting for had finally come.

Trent Marshall had returned to the ranch.

Sykes had been hard put not to pull his gun and shoot the hired gun down right then and there, but he'd controlled the urge. He would do it, but all in good time. The opportunity was going to come to take care of Marshall, just as he had Cal Harris, but it wasn't now. He had some planning to do to make sure everything came off right. For the time being, he just had to make sure Trent Marshall didn't leave the Lazy R without his knowing it. He was going to keep Marshall in his sights in more ways than one. When the time came, he would be ready.

CHAPTER TWENTY-SIX

It was just getting dark as Jake topped the low rise that overlooked his ranch house in the valley below. He reined in and just sat there for a moment, enjoying the peace. The ranch looked fine. He'd missed being home, and he was glad his men had done a good job taking care of things while he'd been away.

When he'd ridden out to search for Abbie, there had been no telling how soon he would be back or what kind of news he'd be bringing with him when he did show up. But now he'd returned, and the news was good. His life was good, and it was only going to get better.

Putting his heels to his horse's sides, Jake headed down to the house. He noticed that some of his men had seen him and were coming out to welcome him back.

Mike Stevens had spotted Jake first and had called out to the other men working nearby to let them know the boss had returned. They liked Jake and were glad he was back. From this distance Mike couldn't read Jake's expression, and he wondered how the search had gone. He hoped the news about Abbie was good.

"You're back!" Mike welcomed him.

"And glad of it," Jake returned as he reined in and dismounted in front of the house.

"How did it go?" Mike was serious as he awaited the answer.

"Abbie's home, and she's fine," he told them all quickly.

"That's great!" The men were surprised, for they knew how deadly raiding parties could be. Most of them had been expecting the worst.

"How did you find her?" Mike asked.

"It wasn't easy, but that Trent Marshall is one good tracker. Nothing stops him when he's on a trail."

"When did you get back?"

"Just this afternoon. How have things been around here?"

"No problems at all."

"Good." He was proud of Mike and his men for being so diligent. "Come on inside. Let's have a drink and do a little celebrating."

They didn't need to be asked twice. They gladly followed him into the house, for they knew Jake kept good whiskey on the place.

The knock came at the Murrays' front door late in the day, and the physician immediately thought it was someone with a medical problem for him. He went to answer the door, ready to leave, if necessary.

"What can I do for you?" Dr. Murray asked of the cowhand standing there.

"I'm Will from out at the Lazy R," he began.

Larissa had been curious to see who was at the door and was just coming up behind her father when she heard the man say he was from Mason's ranch. She immediately grew worried and rushed to her father's side.

"What's wrong? Is there trouble? Has Mason gotten worse?"

Will recognized Larissa and smiled at her. "No, I've got good news."

"I don't understand," Dr. Murray said.

"They're back! Abbie's home! They rode in a few hours ago!"

"Are you serious?" He was amazed at the news. It wasn't often captives were saved from the Apache.

"Yes, sir," Will affirmed. "And that's why I'm here. Faith and Mason sent me into town to let you know there's going to be a big party tomorrow, starting in the afternoon. They wanted to make sure you came."

"We'll be there!" Larissa told him delightedly. "This is the best news ever! How is she?"

"She seems fine."

"That's wonderful!" Larissa was thrilled. "Do you want us to help spread the news for you?"

"Yes. Faith wants it to be a big celebration."

"We'll let folks know."

"I'd appreciate it. See you tomorrow." Will left to go find the sheriff.

"Oh, Papa! I can't believe it! She's back, and she's all right! This is so exciting!"

"It's a blessing; that's for sure. Let's go tell your mother."

"And we have to tell Dottie and the other ladies, too. I know they've been worrying about Abbie and praying for her safe return."

"We'll do just that."

Sykes had been watching and waiting, and he couldn't believe his luck when he saw Mason bringing Trent out to the bunkhouse. Apparently the hired gun was going to be around for a while, and that just made things all the easier for him.

"Trent's going to bunk down out here tonight," Mason told the men.

"You mean you don't want to camp out anymore?" Hank asked, smiling.

"I'm thinking a real bed sounds good."

"So am I," Hank agreed. "Take the bottom one over there." He showed Trent the empty bunk. "And there's a bathhouse out back."

Trent walked over and dropped his bedroll and saddlebags on the bed.

"I'll see you in the morning, Trent," Mason said as he left them.

"You any good at poker?" Hank asked, sitting down at the table in the middle of the room where a few of the men were dealing out a new hand.

"I've been known to win a few hands in my time," Trent answered, thinking a card game might be relaxing once he visited the bathhouse. After all those weeks on the trail, he was ready for a bath and a shave.

"We'd have been happier if you'd said you'd been known to lose a few hands." The men laughed.

"Well, give me a few minutes, and I'll see what I can do for you."

He went to get cleaned up, then rejoined the other men in the bunkhouse. He was ready to enjoy himself for the first time in a long time.

Sykes sat on the side of his bunk, watching the poker game. They'd asked him to join in, and he'd thought about it, but had finally decided against it. He was barely in control of his hatred for Trent Marshall, and he didn't want to do anything that might cause him to lose his temper and give himself away.

Sykes looked on as Trent made a fairly good-sized bet. He was struck by a disturbing thought—the money the hired gun was betting was blood money, money Trent had been paid for hunting down his son.

Rage suddenly filled him, and he knew he had to get out of the bunkhouse before he did something he would later regret. Getting up, he went outside. He was going to make sure Trent didn't live long enough to spend all that money he'd earned.

"You were real lucky to catch up with that raiding party," said Dennis, one of Jake's ranch hands.

They'd been sitting around drinking for a while

now. The men had told him how things had gone on the ranch while he was away, and he'd been telling them about the long days on the trail, tracking down the renegades.

"Yes, we were," Jake agreed, taking another drink of his whiskey. "Thank God we got to them when we did."

"It doesn't matter when you got to them," slurred Vic, another hand who'd worked on the ranch for less than a year. He grabbed the whiskey bottle and refilled his glass.

"What are you talking about?" Jake demanded tensely.

"I'm talking about them women—the Ryan girl and the two from that ranch. It would have been better for them if you hadn't found them. They'd all be better off dead now."

Jake grew ever more furious as he listened to the drunken man.

"Ain't nobody gonna want them women after the renegades have been all over them," he went on.

"You don't know what you're talking about," Jake ground out.

"The hell I don't," Vic stupidly argued.

"Vic, shut up," Mike commanded, not wanting any trouble.

"Why should I shut up?" Vic asked, glaring at Mike. "Everybody knows what they do to women captives. It ain't no secret that they—"

Jake had heard enough. He threw his glass violently aside, shocking everyone, and stood up. In a rage, he grabbed Vic by the front of his shirt and jerked him bodily to his feet.

"What the hell are you doing?" The drunk was caught off guard by his boss's actions. His own glass flew from his grip, and he stumbled, trying to stay on his feet as Jake dragged him toward the door.

"Get out of my house and off my ranch! You're fired!"

"What?"

Jake threw Vic out of the house and facedown into the dirt. Vic landed heavily, but got up and tried to go after Jake. Jake was more than ready for him. He hit him square on the jaw, and Vic collapsed, unconscious, on the ground.

Slowly Jake turned to face the other men who'd hurried outside to watch. His voice was deadly serious as he ordered, "Get him out of my sight!"

Mike, Dennis, and several of the other hands ran to do what he'd ordered. They knew how furious Jake was, and they wanted to get Vic out of there before any more violence erupted.

Jake watched them haul him off, then told the other men, "Don't ever let me hear any of you talking about Abbie Ryan that way. If I do, you'll end up just like Vic."

He said no more, but went back inside and closed the door behind him.

It had been a long day.

He had had enough.

When his rage finally subsided, Jake went into his bedroom and unlocked the chest where he kept his valuables. He took out the engagement ring that had been in his family for several generations. Tomorrow at the celebration, he was going to propose to Abbie. There was nothing he wanted more than to spend the rest of his life loving her and protecting her.

Jake finally managed to smile to himself at the thought of having Abbie with him always. He set the ring on the dresser so he would be sure to take it along tomorrow. Then he got ready for bed. As he stretched out on the wide comfort of his mattress for the first time in weeks, he hoped there wouldn't be too many more nights when he would be bedding down alone. He wanted Abbie beside him.

Faith, Mason, and Abbie were getting ready to call it a night. They were exhausted, but they'd waited so long for this reunion, they didn't want it to end.

"Tomorrow is going to be wonderful," Faith said, thinking of all the fun they were going to have.

"I can't wait to see everyone," Abbie said.

"They'll be excited to see you, too," Mason assured her. "Get a good night's sleep, so you'll be all rested up and ready."

"That won't be a problem," Abbie and Faith agreed, looking forward to snuggling down in their own beds.

"Good night."

They retired to their bedrooms.

Abbie curled up in her bed, tired but happy. For a long time she had believed she would never have her real life back, and now here she was at home, surrounded by the people she loved and who loved her. She offered up another prayer of thanks for all her blessings and then closed her eyes and fell asleep.

Faith changed into her nightgown, and, after washing up, she was ready to go to bed. She found it strange that she was feeling a little lost not having Trent around. Night after night while they'd been on the trail, they'd bedded down close together by the campfire, and now here she was in her room all alone.

Faith went over to her window and looked out toward the bunkhouse. Just knowing Trent was that close helped, but again she found herself wondering what the future held for them. Trent had told her he loved her, and she knew she loved him. She wondered if he would propose. She could think of nothing more wonderful than to spend the rest of her life with him. She just hoped he felt the same way about her.

Weary, Faith turned away from the window and went to bed. She sighed dreamily and closed her eyes, welcoming the sweet bliss of a good night's sleep.

The bunkhouse was dark and quiet. All the men had called it a night and bedded down.

Trent was feeling good as he lay awake in his bunk, thinking over the events of the day. Abbie was safely back home, and he'd won a big pot in the poker game. He smiled in the darkness, knowing some days really were better than others.

Trent's thoughts turned to Faith, and he realized how much he missed her just now. He had no doubt about his feelings for her. He loved her, and now that they were back at the ranch, the time had come for him to decide what he was going to do with the rest of his life. One thing was certain: Faith would have to be a part of it.

Across the bunkhouse in his own bed, Sykes pretended to be asleep, but in truth he was watching every move Trent Marshall made. He'd managed to bring his rage under control, but just barely. Soon, very soon, he would have his revenge. Soon, very soon, he was going to kill Trent Marshall.

CHAPTER TWENTY-SEVEN

Larissa was excited as she rode out to the Lazy R with her parents and Dottie.

"I can't believe everything turned out so well," she said, eagerly anticipating seeing Abbie and spending the day with Mason.

"It's a miracle, that's for sure," her mother, Eve, said.

"That Trent turned out to be a fine young man. I can't wait to see him again," Dottie added.

"It must have been so frightening for Abbie," Larissa said sympathetically.

"I'm sure it was," her father put in, "but today is a day for celebrating. I think it would be better if we were careful not to bring up anything about the time she was a captive. I'm sure Abbie wants to forget all about it as fast as she can."

"That's right," Dottie said. "We're just going to show her how much we love her today."

"You don't think anyone will say anything bad to her, do you, Papa?" Larissa asked.

"Let's hope not. Abbie's been through enough already."

Faith and Abbie had gotten up early to help Rose prepare for the party. It was close to noon when they finally returned to their rooms to change clothes and freshen up. The guests would be arriving soon, and Abbie couldn't wait to see everybody again.

Abbie donned the dress she'd chosen to wear, then went to stand before the small mirror on the wall to brush out her hair. As she stared at her mirror image, she saw the bruise on her cheek and was reminded of all the ugliness she'd just lived through. In that instant, all the frightening memories she'd been trying to put from her returned with a vengeance, threatening to overwhelm her.

"What's wrong?"

The unexpected sound of her sister's voice so close by startled Abbie, and she almost jumped. She turned quickly away from the mirror to find Faith standing in her bedroom doorway, watching her.

"Nothing," Abbie replied quickly, embarrassed.

"Something's wrong," Faith insisted. She knew Abbie too well to believe her answer. The look of sadness on her face revealed far more than her words. "What is it? What's bothering you?"

Abbie admitted nervously, "When I saw the bruise . . ."

Faith immediately understood the problem and

went to hug her sister. "No one is going to pay any attention to the bruise. You'll see."

"If you say so." Abbie was still uneasy.

"I do," Faith said with certainty. "They're just going to be real glad to see you. Come on. Let's go have some fun. You need it."

"You're right. I do need to have some fun." She drew a ragged breath and deliberately didn't glance in the mirror again. "Let's go. I'm as ready as I'll ever be."

The Murray carriage was just pulling up as they went outside.

"Abbie!" Larissa, Eve, and Dottie cried out, thrilled to see her. They hurried to climb down once the carriage stopped and then went to hug her.

"We are so glad you're home!" Larissa told her.

"So am I," Abbie said, returning their hugs. "You're the first ones here!"

"Good, that will give us more time together to visit before things get too crazy," Larissa said.

Tables had been set up outside with an area cleared off just in case anyone wanted to dance later on. They all went to sit at one of the tables so they could talk.

It wasn't long before they saw Jake riding in, and Abbie quickly got up to go greet him.

"It's about time you got here," Abbie said with a smile as she waited for him to dismount and tie up his horse. He was so tall and handsome, and she wanted to go straight to him and kiss him, but she controlled herself. It wasn't easy.

"Been missing me, have you?" he asked with a grin as he faced her. His gaze quickly went over her, and he believed she looked more beautiful than ever—if that were possible. The green day gown she was wearing fit her perfectly, and she had left her hair unbound today, so it tumbled around her shoulders in a soft cascade of golden curls.

"You know I have," she replied in a soft, enticing voice.

The temptation of her words almost overruled his sensibilities. He wanted to kiss her, but since it was broad daylight and there were other people around he held himself back.

"I've been missing you, too. You sure look pretty today."

"Why, thank you," she said, smiling up at him. "You look real handsome yourself."

They moved off together to talk for a while, just wanting to enjoy each other's company.

Dottie spotted Trent with Faith up near the main house and decided to go chat with them.

"I do have good taste in dance partners, don't I, Faith?" Dottie said with an impish grin as she joined them. Her opinion of Trent hadn't changed from that first night. He was a very handsome man.

"Yes, you do," Faith agreed. "Trent, you remember Dottie, don't you?"

"Oh, yes." Trent smiled down at her, recalling how she'd cornered him the night of the dance in town. At the time he hadn't been sure what to think, but now he was glad. If it hadn't been for Dottie's daring invitation, he might not have met Faith. "It's good to see you again."

"If we get any music going tonight, I expect a dance with you, young man," she told him in a stern tone that was betrayed by the twinkle in her eyes.

"It'd be my pleasure. I'll be more than happy to oblige."

"Good." She turned to Faith, her mood becoming more serious. "It's wonderful that Abbie's home. We were all so worried about her."

"I'm glad everything worked out the way it did."

"What are you planning to do next, Trent? Are you going to stay around Coyote Canyon?"

"I don't know. It depends on my next job."

Trent's words tore at Faith, but she quickly masked her feelings. She tried not to let on that she desperately wanted to throw her arms around him and never let him go. Somehow, some way, she had to find a way to convince him to stay.

"Do you have anything lined up yet?" Dottie asked.

"Not yet."

Dottie was always perceptive, and she'd seen the look of pain that shone in Faith's eyes for an instant. Watching the two young people together, she had a feeling there was more than just a simple friendship developing between them, and she hoped she was right. She felt Trent and Faith would make a wonderful couple.

"Well, stay around until you do. We like having you here. Isn't that right, Faith?"

"That's right, Dottie."

More people arrived from town.

Even Sheriff Fike came. He wanted to congratulate Trent on a job well-done. He sought Trent out, and they moved off away from the crowd, so they could talk privately.

"Did you hear what happened in town while you were gone?" the lawman asked Trent.

"No." Trent was surprised by his question. He hadn't heard any talk at the ranch.

"Cal Harris died."

The grim news surprised Trent, and he quickly asked, "How did it happen?"

"That's what's so strange. A call went out that there was a fire down at his office late one night, and then we found him there, dead in the ruins. I thought the fire looked suspicious, but I couldn't prove anything. There was no way to figure out exactly what happened because of all the damage."

"There were no witnesses?"

"There were a few who saw people on the streets, but as late and as dark as it was at the time, they couldn't be certain of anyone's identity."

"Did Harris have any known enemies?"

"None that I'd heard of. I've been asking around, but no one seems to have any idea why someone would have wanted him dead."

Trent was puzzled, too. It might have been a robbery gone wrong, but there was no way they could know for sure. If Harris had been murdered, the murderer had wanted to make sure he would never be caught. "If you find out anything new, let me know."

"I'll do that."

The music started up then, provided by several ranch hands who played banjos and guitars.

Trent saw a number of couples get up and start dancing, and he knew better than to wait to seek out Dottie. If he didn't go after her, she would come after him.

"I'll see you later," he told the lawman. "There's a lady waiting for me."

He headed over to the table where Dottie was sitting with her friends from town.

"I believe this is our dance," he told her.

She laughed in delight as she put her hand in his and let him draw her up to join the other couples.

"I never pass up the chance to dance with a good-looking man," she said flirtatiously.

"And I never pass up the chance to dance with a pretty lady."

Dottie was in heaven as Trent squired her around to the music. She'd always known that being a bit brazen paid off, and it sure had tonight. She was dancing with the handsomest man at the party.

Larissa and Mason were sitting at the table with her parents, just enjoying the moment.

"It's over. It's finally over," Mason said, still finding it hard to believe that everything had worked out the way it had.

Larissa reached over and took his hand. He was almost fully recovered, and she knew that was a blessing in itself. "Since we are here to celebrate, aren't you going to ask me to dance?"

His gaze met hers, and right then there was nothing he wanted more than to have her in his arms. "I think I can do that. Would you like to dance?"

"I'd love to."

He escorted her out among the other couples and took her in his arms. The moment was magical for them as they began to dance. Larissa just relaxed and enjoyed the thrill of being held so close to him. She closed her eyes and followed his lead, treasuring every moment of this special time.

Sykes finished the work he had to do and then joined the party. His plan was to stay as close to Trent Marshall as he could without being obvious. He wanted to listen in on his conversations and find out about his plans. He was more than ready to make his move, but he had to find a time when he wouldn't be implicated in the shooting. He found a place at a table near where Trent was sitting with Faith, and he settled in.

"Sheriff Fike was right when he said Trent was a great tracker," Faith was telling the others at their table. "I rode out on the first day with Jake and some of the men, and we did our best to follow the trail, but we weren't good enough. We lost it and had to give up and come back home." She looked over at Trent. "I don't know what we would have done without him."

Sykes's anger continued to grow as he listened to her singing the hired gun's praises, and he wondered how much more of this he could listen to.

Jake was dancing with Abbie. He'd been trying to figure out the best way to propose to her, and he believed he finally had it figured out. He was going to make a scene and get everyone's attention before he popped the question.

Abbie noticed that he seemed lost in thought, and she looked up at him questioningly. "Are you all right?"

"I'm fine. Why?"

"You look like you're worrying about something, that's all."

"I'm never worried when I'm dancing with you. You're all that's on my mind."

She was beaming over his answer, and Jake realized this was the perfect moment to put his plan into action. The dance had ended and they were standing in the middle of the dance area.

Wanting to get everyone's attention before the musicians decided to start up again, he called out, "Everybody! I need your attention! There's something I want to say tonight."

Not quite sure what to make of Jake's coming announcement, everyone grew quiet.

"What are you doing?" Abbie whispered, a bit embarrassed by his actions.

"You'll see," he said, giving her a warm smile.

At his smile, her heartbeat quickened.

"Abbie Ryan," Jake began, turning to her, his gaze meeting and challenging hers as he went on, "you are one special woman."

She found herself blushing as he continued to sing her praises.

"You are beautiful and smart and . . . and I love you, Abbie." Jake said it nice and loud, so everyone could hear him.

A murmur of excitement ran through those gathered there as they anticipated what was to come. They watched as he reached into his pocket and took out a ring.

"Abbie, will you marry me?"

Abbie's throat tightened with emotion, and tears filled her eyes as she stared down at the ring he was holding and then lifted her gaze to look up at him. "Oh, Jake . . ."

Oh, Jake wasn't quite the answer Jake had been hoping for. He'd hoped she would say yes. He waited for a moment longer, but when she said nothing more right away, he grew nervous. He wasn't quite sure what he should do, so he just asked again, and this time his tone was a little sharper. "Abbie—will you marry me?"

Abbie had been completely taken by surprise at his proposal. She was overwhelmed, for she'd never known she could be this happy. When he proposed the second time, she eagerly answered him, "Yes— yes, oh, yes! I'll marry you, Jake!" With that, she threw herself into his arms and kissed him, right there in front of everybody.

Jake had been close to thinking she was going to refuse his proposal, and now that she'd said yes, he was as happy as a man could be. He grabbed her up in his arms and spun her around in a circle as he continued to kiss her. Abbie soon would be his wife! When he set her back on her feet, they were a bit dizzy, but neither cared. They were in love, and they were going to get married.

"Here," he said, offering her the ring.

Abbie extended her left hand to him, and he slid the engagement ring onto her finger. Ever so gently, then, he bent down to her and sought her lips in a sweet, loving kiss.

"I love you, Jake," Abbie told him when they finally moved apart.

"I love you, too."

CHAPTER TWENTY-EIGHT

When everyone heard Abbie accept Jake's proposal, cheers of excitement went up.

Faith rushed to her sister and hugged her before turning to give Jake a hug.

Trent followed Faith to where the couple was standing and congratulated them.

"Thank you," Jake said, slipping an arm around Abbie's waist and drawing her close to his side.

Mason made his way over to join them. He was happy for Abbie. He knew she loved Jake. He reached out and shook Jake's hand. "I always wanted a brother. I've been outnumbered on the Lazy R for far too long."

"We'll have to see what we can do about that." Jake laughed.

As the other guests came up to offer their good wishes, Faith and Trent moved away. Faith was smiling as she watched her sister being overwhelmed by the pure love of their friends. If ever there had been a time in their lives when Abbie had needed this show of support, it was now.

Trent glanced down at Faith, studying her. He'd never known anyone like Faith before. She was beautiful and intelligent, not to mention strong-willed. Trent knew he'd met his match in her, and he knew he couldn't lose what they had together. He loved her, and she loved him.

Since his brother's death, Trent's work had been his whole life. Usually he finished a job, collected a paycheck, and then rode away, never looking back, but that wasn't going to happen this time. Things had changed.

Faith happened to glance up at Trent and saw that he was grinning down at her.

"You look like you're up to something," she told him.

"I was just wondering . . ." He paused, then went on, "Do you think your sister would mind a double wedding?"

Faith was stunned. "Are you . . . ?"

"I love you, Faith, and I want to spend the rest of my life with you," he told her simply.

"I love you, too," she whispered with heartfelt emotion. Without thinking twice, she went straight into his arms and kissed him.

"Hey! What's this all about?" Mason called out when he saw them kissing. He drew the attention away from Jake and Abbie for a moment as everyone turned to look at Trent and Faith, catching them in the act.

Faith was blushing when they broke apart, and she faced her brother. "I have to ask Abbie a question." Looking over at her sister, she asked, "Trent wants to know . . . would you mind having a double wedding?"

Abbie's gaze met Faith's and pure delight bubbled up within her. She was laughing as she answered, "I think a double wedding would be wonderful, but do you think Mason can handle it?"

Everyone laughed.

"I can handle it, but I don't know if Jake and Trent are up to it." Mason grinned. "Do you boys know what you're getting yourselves into?"

More laughter erupted, and more celebrating and congratulating followed.

Mason went to hug both of his sisters.

What had started off as a welcome-home party had turned into a double engagement party.

The women moved off to sit at the tables and start making wedding plans, leaving the men to their own devices.

Mason looked over at Trent. "Are you going to give up working as a hired gun? We could sure use you here on the ranch."

"I haven't made up my mind yet," he answered honestly. He knew he needed to talk it over with Faith when they had some time alone.

Sheriff Fike spoke up. "Don't be in too big a hurry to quit, Trent. There aren't many men out there who are as good at tracking as you are. Just look at how you found the raiding party. You found that outlaw Matt Sykes and brought him in, too."

"It was amazing how you were able to follow the raiding party the way you did, especially since the trail wasn't fresh," Jake said. "You saved Abbie, and I'll forever be grateful to you."

"I'm glad we found her, too," Trent replied.

"I heard some talk about Sykes a while back. Wasn't he a stage robber?" Mason asked.

"Yes. He and his partner had robbed a stage and killed the driver and the man who was riding shotgun," Trent answered. "The posse managed to bring in his partner, but Sykes got away. That's when the stage line contacted me, and I went after him."

"Sykes was nothing but a cold-blooded killer," the lawman added in disgust. He knew about the outlaw's reputation.

"Well, thanks to Trent, he won't be causing anybody else any more trouble," Jake said.

"That's right," Sheriff Fike agreed. He was always glad when a murderer was brought to justice.

Sykes was sitting nearby, listening to their conversation. Hearing the other men praise Trent had left him fuming, but he'd managed to control his anger until they began to talk about how Trent had brought Matt in.

It was then he knew the time had come.

He was going to get his revenge—tonight.

Sykes was so furious he was almost out of control. He wanted to pull out his gun and shoot Trent down right there in the middle of the crowd, but he realized that if he did, he wouldn't get off the Lazy

R alive. The sheriff was armed, and so were most of the other men at the party. He would do it later, when he could corner Trent alone. He wanted to see the expression on his face when he had the hired gun in his sights and told him he was Matt Sykes's father. Then Trent Marshall would know what it felt like to be hunted down—and killed.

Sykes smiled.

As much as he wanted to kill the hired gun right then and there, it would be worth the wait for that moment.

Sykes knew that if he was going to stay in control, he had to move away. He'd heard enough of what the men were saying. The others didn't notice when he got up and left, and he was relieved. He would be nearby watching—and waiting. When the time was right, he would make his move.

Mason had been watching Larissa while she'd talked with the women. She was a beauty—there was no doubt about that—and for a moment he thought about making it a triple wedding, but then decided against it. When his wedding day came, Larissa would be the woman waiting for him at the altar, but he wasn't quite ready to settle down just yet.

Mason noticed that Larissa looked his way briefly and then left the other women to walk toward him. He went to meet her.

"Have Faith and Abbie got the wedding plans all made yet?" he joked.

"Not yet, but they're working on it. Dottie's helping them. It's going to be so wonderful." She sighed.

Mason couldn't even begin to imagine what that day was going to be like. One wedding with the likes of Faith or Abbie would be wild, but both of his sisters on the same day . . . Pure chaos came to mind, but he'd worry about that later as the day came closer.

"Mason." Larissa frowned, glancing past him again to where one of the ranch hands had gotten up from the table and was moving away. "That man . . ."

He glanced over and saw she was looking at Tucker. "What about him?"

"Who is he?"

"He's a new hand we hired on. With Hank gone, we needed some extra help."

"I noticed him for the first time when I was looking at you just now. Something about him reminds me of the man I saw on the street the night the fire was discovered at the stage office. Do you think I should say anything to Sheriff Fike about it?" She was troubled by the thought. "It was dark, and I'm not completely sure, but—"

"It couldn't hurt. Why don't we go talk to him now?"

They moved off to where the lawman was laughing with some of the townsfolk.

"Sheriff, could we speak with you for a minute?" Mason asked.

"Sure," he answered. He excused himself from

the people he was talking to and followed Mason and Larissa off a ways. He noticed that their expressions seemed a bit troubled. "What's wrong?"

Larissa was uneasy as she answered, "I'm not one to accuse anyone lightly, but . . ." She paused, then continued, "I saw a ranch hand here tonight who looks something like the man my father and I saw in town the night of the fire."

Sheriff Fike was instantly alert. "Who is it?"

"He's over. . . ." Larissa turned to point Tucker out, only to discover he'd disappeared. "He was sitting there by Trent and Jake a minute ago."

"He must have gone off to talk to someone," Mason said, then went on to explain. "His name is Tucker. He was passing through town and needed work. We were shorthanded, with Faith and Hank gone, so we hired him on to help out until they got back. As best I can recall, Tucker did go into town that night."

"I'd be interested in talking to him. If we don't spot him again, I can ride out tomorrow and see what he's got to say for himself."

Larissa smiled in relief. "Thanks. I can't be certain he was the man, but if there's any chance . . ."

"I appreciate your help."

Mason and Larissa moved off to join some of their friends.

It was starting to get late when the celebration came to an end.

Jake was reluctant to leave Abbie, but he knew that in a very short time they would never have to part again. They managed to sneak away for a quick kiss before he started back to his own ranch.

Mason had no such luck. Larissa's parents were there when the time came for her to go. He watched her leave with them, wishing the party could have lasted longer.

Once Larissa and her parents had gone, Mason went down to the bunkhouse to see if he could find Tucker. He'd been keeping an eye out for the man, but had seen no sign of him since they'd talked to the sheriff. Mason was surprised to find Tucker wasn't in the bunkhouse with the other men. Puzzled, but not overly concerned, since the sheriff planned to return the following day to speak with him, Mason went on up to the house to get himself a drink and relax for a while.

After the guests had gone, Faith and Trent finally found a moment to get away by themselves. It was just starting to get dark as they slipped off to a tree-shrouded spot not too far from the house. It had been Faith's special place ever since she'd been a child. She'd always gone there when she'd wanted to spend time alone away from her pesky brother and sister. And right now she definitely wanted to be away from her siblings—and anyone else who might be around. By themselves at last, Faith went eagerly into Trent's arms.

"I love you," she whispered, looking up at him.

Trent gazed down at her and knew he was blessed that she had come into his life. He lifted one hand to caress her cheek as he bent to claim her lips in a passionate kiss—a kiss that told her more clearly than words ever could the depth of his love for her.

Faith responded hungrily to his embrace, clinging to him, wanting to get as close to him as she could.

The feel of her soft curves crushed against him fed the fire of his need to make love to her, and Trent was hard-pressed to keep his desire under control. When they finally did break off the kiss, Trent gave a low, sensual chuckle as he asked, "Is there a justice of the peace anywhere close? We could run off and get married tonight, you know."

Faith gave a throaty laugh, wishing the same thing. "There's one in town, but I don't think we could get away with eloping tonight, after all the excitement about the double wedding."

Trent kissed her again, and she lost herself to the ecstasy of his kiss and touch. Her eager response was such a temptation to him that he was forced to put her from him, although it was the last thing he truly wanted to do.

"You'd better go on up to the house now. I'll see you in the morning."

Faith gave him one last tender kiss, then regretfully left him.

Abbie had gone to her room, and Mason was sitting in the parlor, enjoying his whiskey. His thoughts were mellow as he savored the potent liquor.

Life was good—very good.

Larissa cared about him.

Abbie was back.

He was almost completely healed.

And both of his sisters were about to get married.

That thought in particular made him smile. Soon—very soon, if things went as he hoped and Trent stayed around—he would not be the only man of the family on the ranch. Yes, life was very good indeed.

He heard Faith come into the house then and got up to go speak with her.

"Happy?" he asked with a grin.

"Can't you tell?"

"Where's Trent?"

"When I left him he was down by the trees."

"You took him down to your secret hiding place?"

"That's right," she told him, and she was smiling as she went to her room.

Mason moved out onto the porch, hoping to have a word with Trent on his way back to the bunkhouse.

CHAPTER TWENTY-NINE

Sykes was ready.

He'd seen Trent and Faith sneak off together and had moved in close to keep watch. Trent Marshall wasn't going to get away from him—not tonight. When he saw Faith go back up to the house alone, he knew it was time. Though it was getting dark, there was still enough light to see by. He wasn't going to miss.

Sykes drew his gun and started to close in on his quarry.

Mason didn't see Trent heading back up to the bunkhouse, so he decided to go find him and see if he wanted to have a drink before calling it a night. As he was heading toward the trees, he caught sight of someone moving cautiously in the same direction. He thought it looked like Tucker, and he wondered what was going on. He remembered what

Larissa had told the sheriff about the man, and started to worry as he hurried after him.

Trent had been enjoying the peace of the moment when he heard someone coming. He thought it might be Faith returning, and he turned to welcome her. He was surprised to find it was the hired hand named Tucker, coming toward him with his gun drawn.

Trent immediately thought of renegades. Had another raiding party been spotted? "Has there been some trouble?"

Sykes's expression was cold as he answered, "There's trouble all right—and it's all because of you."

Trent tensed at his answer. He could see the gleam of hatred in the other man's eyes. "What are you talking about, Tucker?"

Sykes lifted his gun to aim it straight at Trent. "My name ain't Tucker. It's Sykes—Ward Sykes—and you killed my son." His voice was filled with fury.

Trent suddenly understood what he was facing.

Sykes went on before Trent could say anything. "You can't get away from me. I hunted you down, just like you hunted down Matt, and now you're going to die. I killed Cal Harris and now I'm going to kill you!" He cocked his gun, enjoying the sense of power he felt at having the other man helpless before him.

Trent was ready to try to dive out of the way.

Out of nowhere, Mason suddenly appeared, his gun drawn. "Hold it right there!"

Sykes was shocked that anyone else was around, but he wasn't about to stop—not now. "Like hell!"

Mason had no doubt the man meant to kill Trent, and he knew it was up to him to stop him. He fired just as Sykes got off a shot in Trent's direction. Mason's bullet found its mark, hitting Sykes in his shooting arm and knocking the gun from his grip.

Trent had gone for his own gun as he dove for cover, and he was relieved when Mason's shot took Sykes down.

Mason immediately raced forward, keeping his gun trained on the wounded would-be murderer.

"You all right?" Mason called to Trent.

"Thanks to you," Trent answered. He quickly got to his feet and, gun in hand, came to help Mason.

Mason had already picked up Sykes's gun and shoved it in his waistband, and he was now standing over him, his own gun in hand. The man he'd known until now as Tucker was clutching his bleeding arm, cursing him. "He deserves to die!"

"Shut up!" Mason ordered.

Hatred gleamed in Sykes's eyes as he glared up at the two men. He was livid, and in one last desperate effort, he went for Mason's gun. But Mason was ready. He pistol-whipped him, and Sykes fell back to the ground, unconscious.

Mason stood over the unmoving Sykes, shocked by all that had happened.

Trent turned to Mason and told him seriously, "That was one good shot. Thanks."

"Larissa told me earlier that she thought she'd recognized Sykes from the night of the fire in town, and then when I saw him sneaking over here, I wondered what he was up to, so I came after him," Mason explained.

"I'm glad you did," Trent said. "You saved my life."

They heard shouts coming from the direction of the house and weren't surprised when they spotted Faith and Abbie running their way, followed by Hank and Will and a number of the other ranch hands who'd heard the gunshots, too. They were all armed and ready for trouble.

"We're over here!" Mason called out.

They found Trent and Mason standing over the unconscious man, guns drawn. All were shocked.

"What happened?" Faith asked, going straight to Trent.

He put an arm around her as he quickly explained. "Mason just saved my life. Tucker's real name is Sykes. He's Matt Sykes's father. He came here looking for me, wanting revenge."

Faith began to tremble as she realized how close Trent had just come to being killed. She clung to him, never wanting to let him go, as she looked over thankfully at her brother. "Thank God you got here in time."

Mason quickly explained what Larissa had told him.

Abbie spoke up. "So he was the one who killed Cal and started the fire in town?"

Trent nodded. "He was the one."

"What do you want to do with him?" Will asked as he noticed Sykes starting to stir.

"Let's get him out of here. Tie him up and we'll take him into town tonight. Sheriff Fike will be glad to know we've found Cal's killer," Mason said.

"We'll let the law deal with him now," Trent said, satisfied that Sykes would get what he deserved.

Will and Hank quickly took charge. They dragged Sykes to his feet and bound his wound to stop the bleeding. That done, they tied his wrists together behind him, so he wouldn't be able to escape on the trek to town.

"You coming with us?" Will asked Trent and Mason.

"Yes."

Both men wanted to make sure Sykes was safely locked up in the jail.

Trent turned to Faith. "We'll be back."

Faith only nodded as she watched Trent walk away with her brother. She had always considered herself a strong woman, but at that moment she was having her doubts. The long weeks of worrying about Mason and Abbie had taken their toll on her—and now the shootout had left her feeling completely devastated.

If Sykes had shot Trent . . .

The thought that Trent could have been killed tore at her.

She loved him.

They were going to be married.

And tonight he could have been taken from her.

A painful shudder racked her as she drew a deep

breath and struggled to calm the fears that were tormenting her.

"Faith, What's wrong?" Abbie asked.

"Trent could have been killed."

Abbie was quick to reassure her. "But he wasn't. He's fine. Everything is going to be all right."

Faith finally voiced her concern, "But what if Trent decides not to stay here on the ranch and keeps working as a hired gun? I'll never know where he is or if he's safe. . . ."

She didn't know if she could live with the constant terror once they were married. She loved Trent and didn't want to be apart from him.

"Then you have to tell him how you feel," Abbie advised.

"I know."

Nothing more was said as they returned to the house. Abbie gave Faith a hug before going to bed.

For Faith, though, there would be no rest. She was going to wait up until Trent returned. It would be hours, but she didn't care. She had to talk to him. She had to let him know how much he meant to her and that she couldn't bear for him to keep working as a hired gun. Uneasiness racked her, for she feared he might leave and never come back.

"Faith?"

The sound of his voice close by jarred her, and her heartbeat quickened as she spun around to find Trent coming into the house.

"I thought you were going into town."

"I am. They're waiting for me down by the stable," he told her. "I just had to see you before we rode out."

Looking death in the face as he had just done had made him realize what was most important in his life. It was Faith. He closed the distance between them and took her in his arms to gaze down at her.

"I love you."

"I love you, too." All the torment she was feeling shone in her eyes as she looked up at him. "You could have been killed tonight."

"I know."

She could no longer hold back the tears that had been threatening. She began to cry.

Trent held her to his heart until, at last, she quieted; then he bent to her and claimed her lips in a gentle, cherishing kiss. They clung together, needing each other, loving each other. When they finally moved apart, he smiled tenderly down at her.

"How would you feel about being married to a rancher?" he asked, his gaze meeting and holding hers.

Her eyes widened in surprise—and heartfelt joy. "You could give up being a hired gun? You could be happy here on the ranch?"

"Yes," he answered. "As long as I'm with you."

"Oh, Trent." She threw her arms around him and kissed him again. "We are going to be so happy!"

317

"I know, love. I know." His voice was deep with emotion as he held her to his heart.

One Month Later

Trent and Jake were standing in front of the altar in church, waiting. When the music began, both men turned to look down the center aisle and saw Mason starting forward with Faith on one arm and Abbie on the other.

It was time for the double wedding everyone had been anticipating.

Faith and Abbie looking stunning in their wedding gowns, and both Trent and Jake smiled as they watched their brides coming toward them.

Those seated in the pews looked on in delight as they passed by.

Reverend Prescott came to stand with Trent and Jake. When Mason reached them, he helped Faith and Abbie to lift their veils and then handed Faith over to Trent's keeping and Abbie to Jake's. He then took a seat in the front pew with Rose and Tom as the double ceremony began.

"Dearly beloved, we are gathered here today to join this man and this woman"—the reverend addressed Faith and Trent first, before turning to speak to Jake and Abbie—"and this man and this woman, in holy matrimony."

All listened with reverence and joy as the ceremony continued. The minister spoke of unconditional love and the commitment needed to make a marriage work. Then it was time for the couples to take the vows that would bind them together as man and wife.

"Do you, Trent Marshall, take this woman, Faith Ryan, to be your lawfully wedded wife, to have and to hold, in sickness and in health, for better or worse, for richer or poorer, until death do you part?" he asked.

"I do," Trent answered solemnly.

"Do you, Faith Ryan . . ." He turned to Faith and repeated the vow.

"I do," she told him.

"Do you have a ring?"

Trent took out the gold band and slipped it on her finger.

"I now pronounce you man and wife. What God has joined together, let no man put asunder."

The minister then turned to Jake and Abbie.

It was their turn.

All remained quiet in church while they took their vows and pledged their undying love for each other. Jake slipped the wedding ring he'd bought onto Abbie's finger.

"I now pronounce you man and wife," he told them. "Congratulations, Mr. and Mrs. Marshall, and congratulations, Mr. and Mrs. McCullough. Gentlemen, you may kiss your brides."

Trent and Jake didn't need any more encouragement than that.

Trent turned to Faith and kissed her. It was a loving exchange.

Jake smiled as he bent to Abbie and gave her a soft kiss, too.

The moment all four had dreamed of had come to pass.

They were married.

The music began again, and they proceeded out of church to greet all their guests outside. A reception was held in the church hall, and everyone gathered there to celebrate the beauty and wonder of the day.

Mason claimed Faith for a dance early on. He was feeling a little sad, for he knew things would never be the same again out at the Lazy R. Over the last few weeks, with the help of the ranch hands, they'd built a small house for Faith and Trent, and he knew the main house was going to seem empty without his sisters around.

"I'm going to miss having you and Abbie with me," Mason told Faith as they danced.

"But just think of it," she teased. "You're going to have the whole place all to yourself for the first time ever. Don't you remember how many times, growing up, you told us you couldn't wait until we got married and moved out? Well, it's finally happened."

He laughed at the memories. "You're right. There were a lot of days when I wanted to be an only child."

They both were smiling.

"It's going to be good having Trent working with us."

"We're going to be more successful than ever,"

Faith assured him, knowing the future looked bright for the Lazy R.

Mason danced with Abbie next, and she realized she was going to miss him as much as he was going to miss her.

"I love you, Mason," she told her brother.

"I love you, too."

When the song ended, Mason escorted her back to Jake.

"You take good care of Abbie," he told him.

"Don't worry. I will," Jake promised, gazing down at his new bride.

When the reception ended and it was time to go, Faith and Abbie were both excited and a little nervous.

This was a beginning for them as well as an ending.

They changed out of their wedding gowns for the trip to their new homes. Once they were both ready, they gave each other a hug and bade Mason good-bye before joining their husbands outside. Mason walked out with them and stood there watching them as they drove off—Abbie and Jake to Jake's ranch to start her new life, and Faith and Trent to the new house on the Lazy R.

Trent was driving the carriage at a comfortable pace back toward the ranch. Faith was puzzled when he reined in and stopped once they were out of town, though. She looked over at him questioningly, and when she saw the look on his face, she understood completely.

Trent had been wanting a moment alone with Faith since they'd taken their vows, and he'd never gotten the chance—until now. Now that they were alone at last, he turned to her and embraced her. His was a hungry kiss, and Faith responded fully, letting him know she wanted him as much as he wanted her.

"Let's go home," Faith said breathlessly when they ended the embrace.

"That's a real good idea," he told her, slapping the reins on the horse's back to move him along.

When they finally reached the house, one of the hands who'd stayed behind came out to take the carriage from them so they could go inside right away, and Trent was grateful. He walked with Faith to the door and then lifted her up in his arms. She linked her arms around his neck and kissed him as he carried her over the threshold.

Trent didn't stop just inside the door, though. He carried her straight into the bedroom and laid her on their bed. He'd thought she would let go of him when he put her down, but Faith kept her arms around him and pulled him down on top of her.

"Kiss me, Trent," she whispered.

But instead Trent unlinked her arms from around his neck and moved away from her, leaving her puzzled and a little hurt as he started from the bedroom.

"Where are you going?" Faith asked, her feelings of rejection obvious in the tone of her voice.

He gave her a wicked grin. "I think I'd better close and lock the door, don't you?"

She blushed a bit and couldn't help laughing. She'd been so caught up in wanting to be with him, now that they were finally home and husband and wife, that she'd forgotten little things like closing doors for privacy.

"That's why I married you," she told him.

"And why is that?" he asked, stopping in the bedroom doorway.

"Because you're so smart," came her answer. "Hurry."

"I will."

And he did.

Trent returned quickly and joined her there on the wide comfort of their bed.

He didn't speak.

There was no need for words.

He didn't need to tell her how much he loved her. He wanted to show her, and he spent the rest of the night doing just that.

With infinite tenderness, he began to kiss and caress Faith, slowly introducing her to the joy of loving intimacy.

He wanted her.

He needed her.

But he also wanted her first time to be special—a gift, the gift of their love for each other.

As their passions flamed to life, they stripped away their clothes and came together in a searing embrace. Trent's body was burning with his need for Faith, but he also knew he had to be patient. He wanted to take his time and show her how beautiful their loving could be. With each kiss and caress, he stoked the fire of their need for each other, until at last they could bear being apart no longer.

"Love me, Trent—please," she begged, pulling him down to her for a heated kiss.

He obliged.

They sought the heights of ecstasy, giving and taking, pleasing and cherishing.

They loved.

They reached passion's peak together and knew the beauty and bliss that came from being husband and wife—from being as one. Afterward, they collapsed back on the bed, savoring the exquisite excitement that had just passed between them.

Faith had never known such rapture.

"You're smiling," Trent told her as his gaze went over her, visually caressing her silken curves.

"I know," she said in a sultry voice, reaching out to him again. "You make me smile."

"Good," he growled as he moved over her to make her his again.

It was much later when she finally fell asleep in Trent's arms.

Trent lay awake long into the night, holding Faith close and knowing that he had finally found the peace he'd been searching for. Here with Faith he knew true love, and he was going to do everything in his power to protect her and care for her. It was the least he could do after all the love she'd shown him.

Faith was his love. She was his life, and he was going to spend the rest of his days proving it to her.

Trent closed his eyes, at peace and in love.

Faith came awake slowly. She opened her eyes to find Trent asleep beside her. She let her gaze caress him—his broad, powerful shoulders and wide, hard-muscled chest. He was male beauty personified, and he was hers.

She smiled, oh, so glad that Dottie had stopped him that night in town and made him dance with her. For that she would always be grateful to her friend.

Unable to resist any longer, Faith shifted closer and softly pressed her lips to his. Trent awoke instantly and pulled her down to him, deepening the exchange.

The loved long into the night, celebrating the beauty of the life they had found together. They would live happily ever after—that was Mashall's new law.

DEFIANT
BOBBI SMITH

Clint knows that although he stands reading his own epitaph, the words are true. Ever since the attack that killed his entire family, he's been dead inside. Only one thing keeps him going—the burning need to bring in the outlaws who did it.

Posing undercover to infiltrate the gang, Clint can let no one know his true identity or the fact that he was once a Texas Ranger. Not even the pretty daughter of a preacher man who bursts into the Last Chance Saloon. As far as she knows, he's a gunslinger who has no right to touch a good woman. But sometimes a man's got to break all the rules, ignore common sense to follow his heart, and get downright...*Defiant.*

BOBBI SMITH

Writing as
Julie Marshall

MIRACLES

For the devout members of Lydia Chandler's prayer group, faith provides a shining light through even the darkest times. To George Taylor is given the grace to face his cancer and leave a lasting memorial. To Jim Hunt is granted the wisdom to turn away from the temptations of alcohol and peer pressure. And for lovely Lydia, who refuses to despair in the ugly side of life that her reporting often uncovers, there is an earthly love to bring laughter and joy to all of her days.
